GOOD AS
GOLD
A NOVEL

BERNARD MARIN

**HARVARD
PUBLICATIONS**

First published in 2017 by
Harvard Publications
Level 6/432 St Kilda Road
Melbourne 3004

 A catalogue record for this
book is available from the
NATIONAL LIBRARY National Library of Australia
OF AUSTRALIA

ISBN 978-0-646-97873-4

Cover image by PeopleImages/Getty images
Design by Adrian Saunders

ACKNOWLEDGMENTS

I was fortunate to have the support of many people while writing this novel, which would not have been possible without the help of Anna Purcell. I learned a tremendous amount about writing from her. She has been a source of great wisdom and guidance and I owe her a huge debt of gratitude for her incredibly generous support. I am truly grateful to her. She gave willingly of her time and I have benefited from her patience, insight and direction.

I am grateful for the help of my editors. Myfanwy Jones helped me arrange my thoughts in the preliminary drafts, and Nan McNab's considerable work in editing the manuscript has been invaluable. She has made this book immeasurably better. Not only did she iron out many inconsistencies, but she freely did additional research and I have greatly benefited from her insights, advice and assistance. She has been exceptionally patient with me, nothing was too difficult, and she was a delight to work with.

My heartfelt thanks to Bob Sessions for his support and guidance in the editorial and publication process. I have also benefited from the endless hours of typing, retyping and researching by Laura Lagalla, Noni Carr-Howard, Emma Younis and Anne Fortunato. And Sam and Diana Seoud who set aside a table at their café, Dundas and Faussett, to enable me to write.

Finally, many friends have been there for me along this journey. They are too numerous to name – you know who you are. Thank you for your support and encouragement. And last but not least, thank you to my family who have helped me keep everything in perspective.

DEDICATION

For my wife, Wendy; daughters, Amy and Rachel; daughter-in-law Deb and son-in-law Joel; granddaughter, Goldie, and grandson, Ziggy.

In memory of my parents, Anne and Stan Marin, and my friend and confidant, Ron Castan AM QC.

This book is dedicated not only to the thousands of Aboriginal children who were removed from their families before 1970, but also to those who are being removed in greater numbers today.

CHAPTER 1

IT SEEMED AS IF THE whole town gathered to send off my father – except Jim.

I watched the crowd jostling to catch one last glimpse of the town's most admired sportsman, or all that was left of him: the man who'd coached the Mooroopna Cats to three consecutive victories; the only man who'd been granted the key to the city; the man who'd trained Mooroopna's only gold medallist – my brother, Jim.

Hundreds of people craned their heads to watch as the casket was lowered onto the planks straddling the grave, which seemed to sag with the weight of him – that big, dead weight. The wind whistled and a faraway bird cried as Father McNab intoned the committal rites, then nodded to the pallbearers. They grasped the ropes and dragged the planks away, and I shuddered at the hollow creak of tightening rope and the sound of the planks scraping against the casket. Jen, my wife, squeezed my hand as the coffin sank into the grave, bumping the sides of the pit with a cold hard thud. It was impossible to believe it contained my father, those strong sinewy arms tanned until they were almost as dark as Jim's, those tree-trunk legs, that indomitable life force.

When I looked up, Jim was sitting on the corner of a distant grave, elbows on knees, legs splayed. Even from this distance I could see he was drunk. He wore a blue jumper over a creased white shirt and khaki work pants. His cheeks hollowed as he took one last drag on a cigarette then ground it into the dirt. A woman stood behind him, one hand resting on his shoulder.

Jim stared at the mourners as Mum stooped to gather a handful of soil and dropped it into the grave. I gathered my own handful of dirt and dropped it onto the coffin, hating the hollow thump and what it represented. After the long weeks of Dad's dying, when he would look up hopefully at any new step in the hall then settle back resignedly when it was not Jim, I was in no mood to forgive my brother. Here he was, finally, come to farewell the only father he could likely remember. 'He trained you to a gold medal,' I wanted to yell. 'He made you a household name! *He loved you!*'

I felt the blood beating in my temples. Instead of farewelling the man who had devoted so much of his life to a skinny Aboriginal kid, instead of sitting with the family, carrying the casket or standing here by the grave, Jim looked almost indifferent, though his lips were clamped together and his eyes were fixed on the ground at his feet.

Mourners filed up to offer their condolences to Mum and me and Jenny, then moved on to Ben and Kate. I was proud of the way the two of them were supporting their grandmother, Jen and me. Mum responded warmly through her tears to all the platitudes; Jen smiled and nodded, red-eyed from weeping. I agreed with whatever they said – now was not the time to discuss the complexities and contradictions of Jack Pickering, husband of Betty, father of two sons, one black and one white, grandfather to Ben and Kate and mentor to who knew how many other young people? Slowly they walked back along the avenue of palms to their cars, some wiping eyes with the backs of hands or dabbing at noses, and headed into town for the wake at the clubhouse.

'Hang on for just a minute,' I said to Jen. 'There's someone I have to see.'

Jim didn't look up as I approached, but when I reached him he glanced at me and flinched.

I stood there for a while, aware of the gulf between us now. Finally I asked, 'Are you okay?'

"Course,' he said, running a hand through his hair. He didn't get up.

'It's been a while,' I offered.

'Yep, a long time,' he replied, managing each syllable carefully to avoid slurring. But his eyes looked empty and he didn't think to introduce the woman behind him.

I never imagined Jim would come to this, I thought, then turned to the woman and held out my hand. 'Robert,' I said, 'I'm Jim's brother.'

She shook my hand, her grip firm and dry, and said with a quiet smile, 'Mary. Your father was a good man . . . he meant well.'

I was surprised to hear her offer an opinion, and merely said, 'The wake's at the clubhouse. I hope you can come. It'd be good for Mum . . .'

She nodded, and reached a hand down to Jim's shoulder once more.

I dropped into the car beside Mum and squeezed her hand. She was managing as she always managed, that steely inner resolve carrying her through this last hard farewell. I glanced back and saw Jim climb into a dusty ute and join the end of the procession as we turned onto the shimmering highway, headed once more for the clubhouse, but this time, without Dad.

We drove out of the gusty cemetery, the afternoon sun glittering in the treetops and casting shadows across the road. As we turned onto the Midland Highway heading towards the Goulburn River, we passed the Ardmona factory, the sweet fumes from the processed fruit wafting over the town. I recalled climbing the narrow iron ladder fixed to the side of the factory to reach the rooftop where you could see all of Mooroopna and beyond.

Jim and I loved to scale that ladder and hide out on the roof. Gazing north beyond the town, we'd see a tapestry of land scorched by heat, and closer in, people on their verandahs or an occasional dog disturbing the tranquillity as it barked at the wheels of an infrequent car. A little to the east was the Mooroopna Primary School where we spent the early years of our childhood, and to the west was Dad's beloved Cats footy oval, where Jim and I spent long hours daydreaming about our big-city life after he won gold. If we looked in the opposite direction we saw the clear water of the Goulburn River, and beyond it the forest- and scrub-covered plains.

I suddenly remembered one day when I'd been sitting on the factory roof with Jim while he gazed out at the bush. The land looked grey and dusty – the drought had well and truly settled over the country by then – and the bush looked brittle and dry. I recall Jim's pointing finger weaving across the landscape below us, and his voice in my ear, the words no longer distinct, but the timbre, the tone, so clear it was as though we had never been apart.

I pushed the sounds and images from my brain and thought about Mum's friend Mrs Peterson and her farm, which we'd been able to see clearly from the factory roof. Her story was such a familiar tale out here. The farm was deserted now – Jenny and I had driven past it on the way up from Melbourne – but Mum used to take us there on Saturday afternoons when we were little and Dad was out coaching the Cats towards their next grand final. I remember Issie, Jim and I racing about as kids in a perpetual dizzying game of chasey, coming in with our T-shirts and pants wet and streaked with grass stains. Mum and Mrs Peterson would be murmuring over their teacups in the easy companionship of old friends. In summer the paddocks became a bleached barren tract where we had to watch for snakes, and I remember seeing the long stalks of wheat being sucked into the harvester, and wondering whether any snakes were being chewed up with the straw.

Despite Mrs Peterson's determination to make the farm work, she had failed. The grey ruins were nearly the same colour as the decimated soil. She'd had to walk off the land and buy a tiny old place in town. Issie grew up and moved to the city, and Mrs Peterson, worn out from years of grinding work, went to bed one night and didn't wake up. Mum said it was a blessed release, but she could not hold back her tears at the funeral of her old friend.

'Was that Jim?' Jenny asked.

'Yes,' I said quietly, glancing over at Mum. 'He's coming to the wake.'

'Good,' Mum said.

The footy oval was on the edge of town – Dad's home away from home. He used to take us to the footy on Saturdays so Mum could have some 'peace and quiet' and, of an afternoon, the smell of beer would waft off Dad as he sat down with Harry out on the verandah while Mum was inside cooking the weekly lamb chops. Harry was our next-door neighbour – a builder and Dad's closest friend. Unlike many in town, Harry was a man interested in the world around him. He had supported Dad through everything, and was closer to him than Dad's brother Ian. I was pleased for Mum that he was there.

We pulled up outside the red-brick building, and Uncle Ian ushered Mum inside, where she sat between two surviving cousins while people came up to her with their stories of the past. I stood with my Uncle Ian and his wife Shirley, looking out over the oval where, in the mind of the town, Dad's true heroism had been displayed. Ian smiled guardedly. He was a big square man with broad shoulders, looking slightly uncomfortable in his grey suit and black tie rather than his more usual mechanic's overalls. Shirley looked like a caricature of a fifties school ma'am in a black pleated skirt, green blouse and drab grey stockings. Now she sighed heavily. 'He was a good man.' I noted sourly that her face was full of self-pity, as if she were the widow.

'Meg and the grandchildren will be here soon, they said. David was caught up at the Alfred operating,' Ian said.

'He didn't suffer,' Shirley persisted, her voice setting my nerves on edge.

I turned and saw Jim and Mary standing a few metres away, and heard Mary say, 'Go and speak to her,' in a low voice. I couldn't hear Jim, but I saw that his jaw was clenched hard and his eyes were uncertain as he walked slowly towards Mum. I was not the only one in the room watching.

Mum gazed up into Jim's face, perhaps searching for a sign of the skinny boy she'd raised, but there was little left, except for the dark sorrowful eyes. Now, the black skin was heavily lined, the long lean muscles blunted by a layer of fat. It was as though she were familiarising herself with someone from her past. The tall, athletic boy who had won Olympic gold? The sad, skinny kid who had turned up one wet night? He had been such a huge part of her life and now here he stood, a heavy, weather-beaten man. She looked small as she tilted her head to one side, then I saw a faint smile.

'Jim,' she said, her voice gentle. 'It's good to see you.'

Jim was watching Mum intently, his eyes wide and still. The years had withered her and I saw suddenly the Betty Jim had seen last – proud, strong and commanding – now a bent old woman. He seemed torn between a long and affectionate habit, and some deep bitterness that I could not begin to understand.

They regarded each other in silence for what seemed a long time.

It was Jim who finally broke the silence. 'I'm married now,' he said, his voice thin and tight. 'I think you know Mary?'

I saw Mum swallow and fight back tears as she turned towards Jim's wife. 'I'm sorry to meet in these circumstances,' she said, and held out a hand.

'Jack was much loved,' Mary offered, taking the old woman's hand in both of hers. The contours of her face made me think she must have been even more beautiful in her youth. She was still slender, with clear dark eyes, strong eyebrows and thick wavy brown hair pulled back in a loose coil, greying a little here and there.

'I'll miss him; we were together a long time,' Mum said.

'Yes.' She trailed off awkwardly, looking from Jim to Betty and then across to me.

'So,' Mum went on, 'you're married . . .' The planes of her face shifted, and she looked sad and weary. Caught in her own thoughts she looked up at Jim and I had the feeling she could not go on.

Mary began to talk about their children, and as she did so, Mum's whole body seemed to be soaking up the details of a life from which she'd been excluded. When Mary finished, Mum turned to Jim and smiled. 'You never told us, Jim.'

'No,' he said, unsmiling, and looked away.

'The family are coming home after the wake. Can you join us?' Mum asked.

'We can't,' Jim said gruffly. 'Sorry.'

Mum looked from Jim to Mary, perhaps hoping for a different answer, but the silence lengthened. After a moment she said, 'Well, I'm glad you came, and I'm so happy to meet Mary. Give my love to the children.'

Jim stepped forward and stumbled, grabbing the back of a chair for support. In that instant, conversation stopped, and in the sudden silence, Mary steadied Jim and rested a hand on Mum's arm.

'Nice to see you again, Betty,' she said firmly.

'Yes, I hope to see you again,' Mum replied, her eyes on Jim, who by now had regained his balance.

As they turned and walked to the door, I saw Mum's eyes fill with tears. I knew she hardly recognised her second son. The taut muscles had softened, and he looked battered and wrinkled. His eyes were bloodshot and his hair was turning grey. He was not yet fifty but he looked older. Mum was clearly upset by what he had become.

'I'll be back,' I told Mum, then hurried after them.

They were at the bottom of the stairs when I called out, 'Jim, wait a minute.'

They stopped and turned. Jim looked at me blankly, waiting for me to speak; Mary's eyes flicked between us. I saw the intelligence in her, the warmth, and thought suddenly, *She's good for Jim.*

'Can we meet?' I said.

Mary smiled, but Jim was frowning, and for a beat I thought he'd refuse, but he said dismissively, 'Why not,' his voice dry and flat.

I noticed the last of the clouds had blown away and the sky was clear.

'When?' I asked.

'I'll call you,' he grunted. 'Still the same number?'

'Yep. I can come to you, but I don't know . . .' I thought how sad it was having to ask my own brother for his address, and wondered if he would ever call.

'We live near the Barmah State Forest.'

I fumbled for a notebook and pen and he gave me the address.

'Thank you,' Mary said, as they turned and walked away.

I was heading back inside when my cousin Meg pushed through the door.

'I need a smoke,' she said. 'Come and keep me company.'

We strolled around the oval, and I waited for the usual condolences, but they didn't come. Meg seemed preoccupied with her cigarette. We stood together silently for a bit, gazing out at the oval, my thoughts running back to the countless training sessions I'd endured. Then my memory presented me with another event.

'I remember one Saturday morning,' I said, 'when I was about twelve, when you were staying with us,' I said. 'I heard you crying.'

She looked at me surprised.

'I got up and went to your room – your parents had gone to Melbourne for the weekend. I could see you sitting up in bed and Mum was perched beside you with her back to me.' Meg was watching me intently, her eyes a clearer green from crying.

'Go on,' she said, and prodded me with an elbow.

'I'm not even sure why I'm telling you this.'

She waited for me to keep talking.

'You were crying. I remember the sun was streaming in through the window and I could see the sky behind you. There were clouds too.' The memory was vivid, and when I looked at Meg she nodded and smiled, knowing what was to come. 'I heard Mum say, "It's normal. You'll be okay." You were pale and you looked scared. Mum put her hand really gently against your cheek.'

Meg nodded. 'I didn't know you were there for that.'

'Sorry.'

'Why didn't you say something?'

'Dad came up behind me and led me away; told me to leave you to it.'

We stood still a little longer, staring at the oval. 'I wanted to stay and watch Mum touch your cheek like that. I was so jealous of you then,' I said, rubbing my forehead. 'But it was . . .' I trailed off, shrugging, 'I don't know . . . it was beautiful.'

I felt ridiculous saying this to my cousin at my dead father's wake more than forty years on. 'God, listen to me. Getting sentimental in my old age.'

In a rare burst of courage and clarity, Meg took my hand. 'About time!' she said. And we laughed.

She ground out the cigarette and went back inside, but I stayed out there a little longer, nursing the last part of the story that I had not told. Dad and I had had an argument that morning, after I'd refused to train with the Cats. It was early on Saturday morning when I saw Dad's silhouette on the wall as he stood near the foot of my bed.

'Get up, we're running late,' he said, prodding my foot.

'I'm not coming,' I muttered.

He stepped back, took a deep breath and looked at me as if lost for words, and his face went tight. 'Why?'

Startled by his sharp response I propped myself up – I was still half asleep – and the words, 'I don't like football,' slipped out.

'What's wrong with you?' he said, as if his son had suddenly become an alien life form.

I didn't say anything, and after a few seconds he turned and slammed out of the room.

In that moment, I realised I had done something others had never dared to do: I had gone against Dad's wishes. I had never contradicted him before; I'm not sure anyone had.

That day I went fishing and got home late for tea. At first I felt scared, unsure of what Dad might say or do, but he studiously ignored me. 'Beat 'em by five goals,' he said, grinning at Jim and Mum. Nothing was ever said about what had happened between us that morning.

CHAPTER 2

I NEEDED A DRINK, BUT as I headed back into the clubhouse, my son Ben came up to me and said, 'Was that Jim?'

I nodded. 'I'm getting a drink – d'you want one?'

'Sure, and can you get one for Kate, too? It's so stuffy in there – we're going to stay out here for a bit. You don't mind do you?'

''Course not. Back in a bit.'

I didn't feel up to talking to Ben about Jim. Perhaps I should have, because later, as I approached with their drinks, I overheard him arguing with Kate.

It was obvious that they had spoken about Jim before.

'I'm surprised he came,' I heard Kate say. 'If I were him, I don't think I'd be here.'

'You're telling me that if you had a fight with Dad you wouldn't go to his funeral?'

'No, what I'm saying I guess is that I actually feel sorry for Jim. I know they had a big falling out and it must have been pretty bloody serious because they didn't talk for years.'

'Well we all know why they had a fight, don't we,' Ben's voice was tight.

'Ben, to be fair, we've never even met Uncle Jim. This is the first time either of us has set eyes on him. So saying "we all know" is a bit rich don't you think?' Kate said. 'We actually don't have any idea why they had a fight. What we do know is something seriously wrong went down.'

I felt self-conscious eavesdropping on their conversation but I was loath to interrupt them. To hear Kate defending Jim was a surprise. Why would she? Part of me felt angry, betrayed almost, but my daughter was not that sort – she didn't take sides, always giving people the benefit of the doubt – but even so, I found I was biting my lip. I stepped back slightly and wondered whether to retreat altogether, but curiosity got the better of me.

'What do you think went down?' Ben said, somewhat mollified by Kate's reprimand.

'I can tell you what I *think* went wrong but I genuinely don't know because every time I asked Grandpa I hit a brick wall and every time I asked Dad I got some banal comment about how ungrateful Jim was.'

'Of course they're not gonna say. Of course Dad is going to defend his father. They had such a stuffed-up relationship – it took him until he was nearly forty to get it back on track. So he's not going to admit to himself, or anyone else for that matter, that Grandpa did something wrong – that would ruin everything he'd achieved,' Ben said.

So the kids knew that Dad and I had struggled to understand each other. Had Jen spoken to them? *Of course I could admit my father did wrong*, I thought, but even as I considered it I had a sinking feeling. What would it mean if Dad were wrong? It would mean that my whole life was built on unstable foundations. I set the drinks down on a windowsill and steadied myself.

'Did anyone ever ask Jim?' Kate asked.

'No. But it wasn't necessary. It was money. They fought over money.'

'But Nan said Jim was never like that. He wasn't interested in money.'

'Everyone says he changed after he won his gold medal. All of a sudden, he became entitled.'

'They say he changed. They don't say he became entitled.'

Ben ignored her. 'Look at Dad – a house, a business, he was financially successful, and what's Jim got? I bet he wanted Grandpa to give him some dough – it's obvious.'

'I'm not sure about that. Dad was still a student when they fought, so I can't see how it could have been about money.'

'Well, he turned his back on the family, you can't argue with that. He didn't come to Dad's fiftieth birthday and he wasn't at Nan and Grandpa's wedding anniversary.'

Suddenly an image of Jim standing in front of a government building leapt to mind. It was the last time I'd seen him, and I hadn't expected him to be in Melbourne. I remembered the bitter line of his mouth, his eyes flat with disbelief. Before Dad's final illness, I had hardly thought about Jim for twenty years, but listening to the children speak and seeing him at the cemetery made him real to me again.

'But he didn't come because Grandpa didn't want him there. Grandpa didn't let Nan invite him,' Kate said. 'It wasn't that Grandpa was the good guy. He kicked Jim out of the family. He refused to talk to him.'

'After all the awful things he said in the fight Grandpa didn't want to see him ever again.'

'I don't know why you're defending Grandpa. We both know how controlling he was. Look at how he treated Nan. And Dad spent his whole life sucking up to him. You can't deny that.'

'I don't deny it, I just don't think it was the main cause.'

'I do. I reckon Jim was just sick of Grandpa controlling his life. Maybe he wasn't like Dad. Maybe he wouldn't put up with it.'

Suddenly, Ian came up behind me, and I hurriedly indicated the drinks and asked him to carry one for me. There was a very long and awkward pause as we approached.

'I heard what you guys said. It's no way to talk about your grandfather. I want a word with both of you.'

Ian looked puzzled, but Kate clearly thought I was angry about her slandering her grandfather at his funeral. She and Ben followed me back inside, leaving Ian to gaze out over the oval.

'Just so you know, I overheard that entire conversation, warts and all.'

Kate couldn't look at me and even Ben was blushing.

'Dad—'

I held up my hand to silence him. 'For what it's worth, I get it, I think you're right – about me and your grandfather.'

They both stared at me, shocked. Kate looked doubtful. After a long time she said, 'And Jim?'

And Jim? Jim was the unknown factor in all this.

After the wake, I was guiding Mum to the car when the caretaker – an unshaven man in his sixties – handed her a canvas bag with Dad's football jumper, training boots and a plaque celebrating his three grand-final wins. He walked with us to the car, extolling Dad's virtues as a player, a coach and an all-round good man while Mum and I listened politely. I thought he, too, might raise the subject of Jim, but instead he opened the door for Mum and shook her hand. 'Hope this isn't the last we see of you, Mrs Pickering, or you young Rob,' he said with a grin, helping her into the car. 'It's a great loss . . . he was a great man. The things he did for that Aboriginal lad . . .'

Mum smiled, nodded, then stared down at her dry, sun-spotted hands, lying in her lap. Was she thinking about Dad, or was she, as I was, ticking off the years in her mind, counting backwards to that day of the storm when Jim first came to our home?

That night, the night I first met Jim, lightning blazed and thunder cracked and rolled overhead. Wind ripped a howling percussion from the house and I remember wailing for Mum from my room. I could hear the voice of Dad's best friend Harry loud above the din.

'The water's rising,' he said. 'Grab some towels.'

Rain hammered on the roof and slammed against the windows, water gushing down the pipes and pouring out of the gutters. I lay rigid, my heart pounding, certain that at any moment the roof or walls would fly away and leave us at the mercy of the storm. Then the rain turned to hail, hammering at the house like a panicked neighbour until it was all I could hear. I was a scrawny seven-year-old caught in a nightmare of noise and ragged glimpses of thrashing trees in the weird electric blue light.

Finally, Mum came to my room, a silhouette against the doorframe until she turned and held the candle up before her. 'You're making nearly as much racket as the wind,' she said and placed a gentle hand on my forehead as she set the candle beside the bed.

'The rain has knocked the power out,' she said softly. 'Don't be scared.'

We sat like that for a while, listening to the house being beaten as though by a cosmic broom, and then she got up quietly.

'I don't want to be alone, Mummy,' I said, wiping my eyes and sniffing.

She smiled briefly and stooped to gather me up – it was a long time since she'd carried me like that, and I leaned into her, drawing that old sweet comfort from her body.

After the dark hallway the lounge seemed bright, though only the open fire and a couple of candles provided any light. Shadows flickered across the ceiling, as Harry stood by the window looking out at the storm. My Uncle Ian, a burly man of six feet, leant towards the crackling fire, rubbing his hands to warm them. I noticed his socks were wet, and that he'd taken off his boots before he'd stepped into the lounge room.

'It's bucketing down out there,' Harry said, his voice deep and rich as mud and thunder.

Outside, Elizabeth Street was in deep darkness between flares of lightning. I imagined water banking up in the gutters and overflowing onto the road, wires swinging from lampposts like stray skipping ropes.

'Haven't seen anything this bad in my lifetime. This beats '32, I swear,' Uncle Ian said.

Just then lightning bleached the room and thunder exploded overhead. I jumped as Mum's face lit up and then it was dark again.

'It's okay,' Mum said, rubbing my back. 'It's only lightning.' But her voice had changed. The patient almost humorous tone she normally used at these times had tightened into something that sounded almost like fear. Her hand on my back no longer felt steady and sure.

She walked me over to my uncle by the fire and I could feel her trembling.

'Here, you get yourself nice and warm with Uncle Ian,' she said, 'and I'll . . .' She began to pace back and forth, glancing anxiously out the window every minute or so, rubbing her forearms as if she were cold.

Harry reached out and put his arm around her. 'He'll be fine,' he said. 'How about a mug of hot chocolate for Robbie here?' he suggested. 'And I wouldn't mind one myself.'

Mum nodded absently and disappeared into the kitchen.

She was back in five minutes, setting our mugs down on the hearth, but she barely touched her own drink before she was back pacing the room again. 'He's been a long time.'

The silence in the room thickened. Nobody could think of a thing to say.

Ten minutes later we finally heard Dad's ute in the drive.

He burst in through the front door, a flashlight in one hand, an Aboriginal boy clasped to his hip with the other. Titan, the family terrier, was drenched, and Mum rushed to fetch towels while Titan shook himself vigorously before the fire, droplets spitting in the flames. She knew better than to complain about a wet smelly dog on her clean rug. She'd lost that battle long ago.

Dad's raincoat was soaked and water dripped from his hair. His cheeks were flushed and his sodden pants were tucked into his gumboots, which sloshed with trapped water.

'Jesus, Mary and Joseph!' he gasped and unceremoniously dropped the boy to the floor while he stripped off his coat and boots and shook himself like his dog.

Mum tossed an old towel at me and said, 'Give Titan a rub, Robbie. *No Titan!* Don't let him get your pyjamas wet!'

The boy stayed where he had been dropped on the floor in an awkward conglomeration of wet limbs, hair and clothes. He looked about my age. He kept his head bowed, but I could see his eyes roaming, dark and alert. I felt his glance brush across us – Harry, Uncle Ian, Mum – then when he looked at me he stopped, and his shoulders stiffened as though he were bracing himself for something. His eyes flicked restlessly on, pausing as he watched Titan roll on his back to have his belly dried, then finally stopping at our mugs of hot chocolate on the hearth. His head was up now; he must have forgotten himself.

Mum, seeing the child's wide eyes, walked to the hearth and picked up a mug.

'I'll take it,' Dad said. 'Let me give it to him.'

The boy clung to the mug, his eyes watchful.

Dad urged him to warm himself by the fire, then turned to us with a grin. 'This is Jimmy,' he said. 'He's going to be living here with us now.'

I was watching the boy and I saw the tears mingle with the rain on his cheeks and his shoulders slump as he sat cross-legged in front of the fire.

Mum bent down and wrapped Jim in a big soft towel, setting aside the mug and drawing him to her.

He stiffened instinctively but she cooed and gentled him in that way mothers seem to know so well and I watched as his body slowly relaxed against her and his eyes glazed over in the warmth.

I stared at the flickering flames and at this strange boy in my mother's arms. For a few moments nobody spoke, and the only sounds were Titan licking himself and the popping and spitting of the logs.

At last, Mum put Jim down beside me on the rug and went to the kitchen to make Dad a hot drink. Sitting side by side, we gazed into the fire, not saying a word to each other. Titan rolled against Jim and gazed up at him, clearly wanting a rub. He was damp and smelly but Jim stroked the little dog until it fell into a blissful doze. Jim seemed calmer, too.

I could hear the men discussing the storm, how Dad had seen fences washed away, trees down, and the Goulburn running a banker.

Mum came back a few minutes later with tea for Dad and Uncle Ian, her eyes locking onto my father's as she handed him his mug. Some kind of silent communication passed between them.

Once he'd drunk his tea, Dad caught my eye and smiled.

'Okay now Robbie?'

I nodded.

'You'll sleep well tonight,' he continued.

Mum picked up Jim and Dad carried me in his big warm arms. As they walked down the hall I felt my body soften. 'I'm glad you're home safe, Daddy,' I murmured.

'Me too, Robbie boy.'

They carried us to my room and I watched in alarm as Mum put Jim in my bed. I turned to Dad to protest but he said firmly, 'You sleep on the portable, Robbie, you hear? We'll sort out beds tomorrow.'

Before Dad left he kissed me and whispered in my ear, 'Be nice to Jimmy, that's a good boy. You're brothers now.'

It was my last memory of the night Jim arrived, except for Titan sneaking in and jumping onto the bed. I waited for Dad to order him off, but he didn't, and the little dog circled a few times then settled down to sleep in the curve of Jim's legs.

I glanced at Mum. 'Remember when Dad brought him home?' I said.

She smiled. 'I'll never forget it.'

'Tell me about it. I remember Dad and Jim and the storm – they were both as wet as shags – and you made us hot chocolate, and Jim got to sleep in my bed, and so did Titan . . .'

'Titan – that dreadful smelly old dog. Yes,' she said, 'we put both you boys to bed, then I asked Jack, "How was it – collecting him?" And just at that moment the lights came back on.

'Your father shrugged. "Wet," was all he said.

'I remember asking him if he was sure. It seemed such a big step.' She glanced out the window.

'"His parents are dead; we're going to foster him," Dad said. He sounded confident, almost cocky, but he could tell I was uncertain. He just didn't want to talk about it.

'"Before we do this," I said, "I want to be clear."

'He looked up at me but he didn't say anything at first, then he just shrugged and said, "The father's gone."

'"And the mother?" I asked, but he wouldn't look at me.

'I remember thinking, it's now or never. It's not too late. We could send him back. And if we were really worried about his wellbeing we could pay for his schoolbooks, or help in other ways. I felt the seriousness of it – that poor lost little boy, your confusion . . . But the idea that scared me most was, what if someone else took him? Someone who might not understand what he had lost? What was good about it, good about him . . .

'I remember your father saying over and over, "We'll give him a good life", and "Anything's better than what he had."

'I don't remember much else. I think Jack was getting annoyed with me, so I stopped trying to talk to him. You remember how stubborn he could be, how he would just pull the shutters down if anyone challenged him, or fly off the handle . . .'

I nodded, uncomfortably aware that we were speaking ill of the dead, and that something Mum had said was niggling at me. Perhaps she felt uneasy, too, because she straightened her shoulders as we pulled into the drive, and firmly changed the subject.

But I could not so easily forget those early days when Jim first came to live with us – the long nights of listening to his ragged breathing as he lay in bed trying to hide the sound of his weeping, his crushed look at breakfast and the darkness around his eyes, his bowed head at school. The other Aboriginal kids kept their distance, and Jim seemed embarrassed or ashamed somehow, although I wasn't able to recognise it then. To me he just seemed beaten. I imagined Jim getting into the car with Dad, the rain pelting down on the windscreen, a seven-year-old Aboriginal boy locked in a car with a thirty-eight-year-old stranger, hour after hour, driving from one white place to another and another. Was he thinking about his mother? His family? Whether he would ever see any of them again?

The morning after Jim came to live with us is still clear in my mind. I woke at dawn. Jim was in my bed, his face turned to the wall. I knew he was awake, but neither of us moved, each listening to the other breathe. Titan was still curled up, sound asleep. The air was fresh on my cheeks and soon I could stand it no longer. I hopped out of bed and tiptoed to the window, pretending not to notice that Jim was awake. Titan opened one eye and looked at me.

The world had been washed clean by the storm, and there was thrilling wreckage wherever I looked. A rooster, perched on a side fence, greeted the new day as if nothing was out of the ordinary, but the backyard was like a war zone, and the neighbours' chook shed must have been damaged or the rooster wouldn't have been free.

Steam rose from the muddy concrete pavers, fallen branches lay strewn around the yard, and the back door, which had been ripped from its hinges, lay like a giant mat on the lawn. A couple of sheets of tin from neighbours' roofs were propped against the clothesline, and there were puddles big enough to swim in. One thing was certain, there'd be no school today. I couldn't wait to get outside and start exploring. Who knew what else had blown in with the storm? If it could bring me a new brother, anything was possible.

I padded down to the kitchen in search of breakfast to find Mum and Dad hunched over the table talking in hushed voices. I couldn't make out what they were saying, and as soon as they saw me they stopped.

Dad's face was stiff and Mum looked solemn.

'Good morning Robbie my man,' Dad said. 'Mum and I want to talk to you. We have something to tell you.'

'Come and get yourself some breakfast first,' Mum said, giving Dad a pointed look. 'Is Jim awake?'

'Not sure,' I said, helping myself to cereal and milk. 'Titan is.'

'I'll let him out for a wee,' Mum said.

Dad was not to be distracted. As soon as I had a mouthful of cornflakes, he began to talk. 'Robbie, Jim has nowhere to go, understand? His parents are dead, so Mum and I have decided to take him in.' I remember Dad's voice sounded loud in the kitchen, and I remember he said 'dead', not 'died', not 'gone' but 'dead'. I remember the baldness of that word shocked me.

There was a long uneasy silence. Mum came back to the table and sat down, but she seemed uncomfortable. I wondered why.

'He has nobody to look after him,' Dad continued, looking me in the eye. Mum glanced at me with a hopeful smile, then went to the back door to let Titan back in before he scratched the door to bits.

'What happened?' I asked.

'His father died some time ago and his mother is also dead.'

'But, what about his other family?' I asked.

'He has none,' Dad said, his voice gruff. He got up and walked slowly to the window and stared out into the sunlit yard, Titan following at his heels. When he glanced back at me, he seemed unable to hold my gaze, and turned back to examine the yard.

'It'll be great. You'll see,' he said heartily, and stalked out the back door, letting in the sun and a sharp breeze.

Mum and I finished our breakfast in silence. I didn't have anything to say, and Mum looked preoccupied, her eyes shadowed.

When Dad came back inside, tightening his belt, he seemed happy with himself. His face was more resolved and his voice was easy.

'Be nice to Jim, okay?' Dad said, giving me a straight look.

'Okay,' I said, forcing a smile.

The two of them walked down the hall to my room and I followed, keen to hear what they had to say to this new boy, this orphan.

Jim was sitting on the side of the bed staring blankly out the window. His face looked grey. Mum stood inside the doorway and Dad sat facing him.

'Jim, we have some bad news.'

Jim's eyes shifted to Dad, but otherwise he was completely still.

'Your mother has died,' Dad said.

At first Jim didn't move. It was as though the words had snap-frozen him. Then he searched Dad's eyes to see if he was lying. After a few seconds he started to tremble. He covered his face with his hands and bent in half, as if he had a bad stomach ache. Then he turned away from them, rebelling against anyone witnessing his pain. Mum went to him and put one arm gently on his shoulder and wrapped the other tentatively around his back. Soon she began to rock with him, tiny movements, back and forth.

I don't remember thinking of the devastation Jim must have felt when he heard his mother was dead. Dad's words were not flippant, or thoughtless or superficial, but I would come to understand that they were calculated. I saw the pain in Jim's eyes as he lurched forward, anguish shooting through him as he tried desperately to hide his tears. Maybe Dad thought he would never be called upon to explain.

'Don't worry,' Mum said softly. 'We'll take care of you.'

Dad's face was calm. 'You'll live with us,' he said.

Jim glanced up at Dad in shock.

As I sat there looking at his forlorn face I felt my first brief moment of selflessness. I felt older, somehow, and safer. My parents were alive and well, not dead and buried, lost to me forever.

I do not know how long it was that we were all suspended like that. I was squatting, but only later did my legs cramp. Jim began to sob, violent jags of sound as if he were choking. It was awful. Mum held him tighter but he was pulling away from her, his pain turning to rage. Eventually, she let him go, and he crawled to the edge of the bed, his back curled against us. Mum sighed and looked at Dad imploringly. He shrugged. She got up and straightened her slacks. 'Come with me,' Mum said, taking my hand. 'I'll make Jim some breakfast.'

I looked down and Titan was standing at the foot of the bed, his head cocked. Dad patted the bed and said, 'Come on, boy. Up you get.' The little dog sniffed at Jim then curled up once more against his legs and tucked his nose under his tail to sleep.

Back at the kitchen table, I thought about Jim, but this time the thoughts had a different tone. Having a brother didn't seem so bad, especially one rendered powerless by grief. I could not imagine what he was thinking. It seemed, though, that my room was like a prison to him rather than a haven. I played with my cornflakes, stirring them in the bowl, drowning them in milk, then idly spooned some into my mouth. Mum's voice reached me through my daydreaming: 'Robert, you will look after him, won't you?'

I put down the spoon, annoyed. Why did they keep saying that? Why was Jim my responsibility? Mum and Dad had brought him into our house – he was their concern. Resentment curdled in me. Had I asked for a brother? No.

The present leaked into my awareness, and I began to understand that my childhood, and Jim's, were far more complex than I had ever considered. I realised that my self-absorption had shielded me from understanding much of what was going on, and yet the people I had loved were still firmly present in my head, in those memories left unexamined for so long. Rather than feeling daunted by the prospect of revisiting this shifting and uncertain past, I yearned for it. The loss of my father had snapped an anchor chain, and now I felt cast adrift. Maybe in finding Jim I might finally find some clues to the self I had buried in my quest to please my father all those years ago.

CHAPTER 3

MUM SEEMED TO HAVE SHRUNK since the morning. I helped her out of the car and into the echoing house, noticing the smell – all the odours of home overlaid with the smells of sickness and old age. The kids had headed straight back to Melbourne to jobs and friends and the vigorous life of the young, and Ian, Shirley and my cousins had left too, with repeated apologies from Shirley and assurances that she would be in touch.

'I'LL PUT THE KETTLE ON,' Jen said. 'When all else fails, there's always tea.' She smiled ruefully.

Mum slumped in her favourite chair, and gazed absently about her, her eyes unseeing, but when Jen came in with a tray, she rallied.

'A good service,' she said, as Jen poured the tea and passed the cups.

I thought of the open casket on the trolley at the front of the church.

I'd looked for Jim as we walked towards it, my eyes panning the crowd, but I couldn't see him. Mum was sitting in front of the coffin, her face concealed by a black veil. She was still a believer, having sought guidance from God every Sunday of her adult life, trusting in his compassion and power. Jenny and I took our places in the front row beside her and I turned to scan the mourners a second time. There was not a single black face. My Aunt Shirley sat to Mum's left, looking puffy beneath her makeup, as if she hadn't slept. Dad's brother Ian sat next to her, clearly distressed, rubbing the pocket of his black suit jacket with one hand.

'Harry did a good job with the eulogy,' Mum said, sipping her tea and drawing me back to the present.

'Hmm.' I wasn't so sure, but how could anyone do justice to my father, even his oldest friend? Harry had started conventionally enough in his faded scratchy voice, about what a privilege it was, and how Dad had accomplished twice as much as any one of us was likely to achieve in our lifetime – he'd captain-coached the Cats to three consecutive finals in the fifties, he'd been given the key to the city, and the team had been honoured with a ticker-tape parade. Then Harry had paused to adjust his glasses.

'Jack was a man of great conviction. Many of us here today, myself included, did not always see eye to eye with him. It matters little whether or not we agreed with his sometimes controversial views on the way we should deal with the blacks or other groups. What is important is that Jack was a man we respected. We respected his courage in standing up for what he believed to be right; we respected his determination to make changes for the better; we respected his drive; we respected his good intentions; and more than anything else we respected his down-to-earth decency.'

I could hear people beginning to shift nervously, wondering what Harry might say next. Would he start on Jim? It was supposed to be a eulogy, so why had Harry decided to dredge up all the divisive stuff about Dad's life rather than detailing, as anyone else would have done, his sporting triumphs?

Harry trudged on, describing the way Dad had worked tirelessly to have the humpies cleared away from the Flats beside the Goulburn River and replaced by decent housing. 'Jack and the premier agreed,' Harry said with a wry smile. 'They agreed that the people should be housed in the town, but they lost that fight, and the new houses were built at Rumbalara, a couple of miles out of town down the Toolamba Road. I remember Jack was furious.'

Harry had been right about one thing: Dad did provoke strong feelings. Harry went on to tell the story of the All Blacks, another battle Dad had lost. The All Blacks, a team of Aboriginal players from the Flats, had been formed in 1946, and quickly defeated all the local teams in the league, winning their first ten games and taking out the premiership that year. Dad had been filled with admiration for the way they played, and spent time with the team and their coach, Shady James, who'd played for Fitzroy. But the citizens, and they were all white back then, were not happy. The officials voted to exclude the All Blacks from the league, 'despite the best efforts of their would-be white saviour'.

I realised as I sat in the church listening to Harry that I was angry. His words made me want to grind my teeth. I felt my father's distance, his desolate, displaced love turning to anger, all of it percolating deep within me. Why had he never mentioned the All Blacks? What had their shoddy treatment meant to him? Had his obsession with the team of young black footballers simply moved on to a very young black runner?

Harry was winding up now. He turned to Mum and smiled sympathetically. 'In short, Jack was one of a kind: caring, considerate, inspiring, influential – in many ways remarkable. And yes, sometimes divisive. But he was truly a great man. Sadly, many great men are not always fully appreciated during their lifetime, but once they are no longer present to illuminate our lives they are sorely missed.'

Harry's eulogy was surprising in its honesty. We had all been expecting something trite and sad but celebratory, certainly nothing that mentioned Dad's fight to improve the lot of 'the blacks' and assimilate them into white society. But it needed to be said; it was true – Dad was really like that. Perhaps refusing to accept the status quo had been one of his greatest strengths and greatest weaknesses. Harry didn't understand even now that assimilation was the greatest insult of all, and I wasn't sure Dad did either.

As we drank our tea, Mum and Jen discussed the rest of the funeral – Father McNab's effusive sermon, the high school brass band leading the funeral procession past the footy club where the players in their Cats footy gear formed a guard of honour, their heads bowed, silent and sombre. It was the kind of traditional gesture that many in Mooroopna would have thought touching or respectful, perhaps even my own mother thought of it as a fitting homage.

I understood that my feeling sour and critical might be easier than feeling sad, but my grief seemed to be locked away somewhere deep inside me. I recalled the moment when we'd entered the cemetery and come to a stop at a waist-high mound of dirt and clay beside a six-foot hole. I'd felt a chill down my spine. The image of that body, a long bulky shape covered by a white sheet, flooded into my mind. This was where it would remain. This was where Dad would be for all time.

It was a mark of my mother's exhaustion that she allowed Jen and me to prepare the evening meal. None of us was particularly hungry, and neighbours had been generous with casseroles and quiches, so there wasn't much to do.

I thought back to our family dinners, and their old-fashioned formality. Mum made us wash our hands before we ate, and set the table. We had to sit up straight and keep our elbows off the table while Dad said grace. We were animated but polite, talking one at a time – there was to be no arguing during dinner. And you could be sure that while Mum served the dinner Dad would ask her about her day and Mum would regale us with stories about the town, her work with the parish, the voluntary work at the hospital or the library. While we all ate, we'd listen to her voice, animated at times and hushed with delighted secrecy at others. Then Mum would always ask Jim and me, 'How was school today?' and we would have our time for storytelling.

Now, I stood at the kitchen window and looked out at Dad's prized camellias. Behind them was the fence that I'd helped Dad build all those years ago, separating the order of Dad's carefully tended garden from the chaos of the ever-encroaching bush on the banks of the Goulburn.

Dad seemed to hate the bush, the confusion of dense scrub and pale trees, the giant red gums along the river, the wetlands buzzing with mosquitoes, the unkempt grass and wild dogs. The lack of order upset him. To Dad, bush tracks meant litter, dung and blowflies. He saw no beauty in the landscape, in the river carving out a course between boulders and trees – the natural order of things looked like bedlam to him. It needed to be dealt with, and he was just the man for the job.

Jenny switched on the radio to catch the news and I turned my back on the window. A reporter was speaking with an Aboriginal man.

'Who's that?' Jen said.

'Don't know. An elder I guess,' I replied.

'"More black children are taken from their parents today than at any time during the period of the stolen generation," he said.' Jen glanced at me across the table.

I felt somehow complicit in all this, which was ridiculous. Jim was an orphan; Dad didn't 'steal' him. But still, the feeling persisted. 'That's ridiculous,' I said. 'It was more than thirty years ago.'

'We've come a long way since then, surely?' Mum said.

'I'm surprised, but not that surprised,' Jen said. 'Don't you remember the *Bringing Them Home Report* – all those stories of Indigenous people who were stolen?'

'I remember the hearings. They were all over the newspapers.'

'Really horrible.'

'We have stopped taking children from their parents when their backs are turned,' the elder continued. 'Now, we take them because they are living in squalor – we spend more money on surveillance and the removal of Aboriginal children than supporting those same families in need.'

'How many children have been taken?' the reporter asked.

'Nobody knows. But they say somewhere between one in three and one in ten black kids were removed from their homes.'

'That's huge,' I said. 'Is it possible? I think there are only about three hundred thousand Indigenous people in Australia.'

Mum concentrated on her food. Outside, the sky flushed a rich orange-pink as the day ended. Despite myself, my thoughts returned to Jim.

'I wonder whether Jim was affected?' Jen asked, as if she'd read my mind.

'What do you mean? His parents died.'

'No, I'm talking about his family – uncles, aunties, cousins . . .'

'How would I know? It was never discussed.' I heard the sharp note in my voice and decided the funeral had taken more of a toll than I'd realised.

After that we sat at the table in silence, and perhaps because the past was so alive in me, I noticed the differences: Jim was not here; Mum was mute; Dad was not at the head of the table, perched on the edge of his chair with both forearms resting on the cloth. Memories of my father's voice, his expressions, his gestures, flashed before my eyes. When he spoke to me of Jim's triumphs, his hands were like a conductor's, drawing out feeling from those around him. 'Seeing him running that record, the crowd hanging on every step, I'll never forget. They loved it!' His arms rose, we had reached the climax now. 'They bloody loved it!' His eyes were dark, the irises glittering discs as he basked in Jim's achievements.

Mum glanced up and smiled briefly in acknowledgement of the meal. She seemed pale and withdrawn, and her eyes were stoic.

Jenny said, 'I spoke to Bill Chambers at the wake. He said he'd never seen a coach like Jack.'

'He was one of a kind,' I said, dragging my eyes away from Mum. 'Remember his first grand-final win?'

Suddenly, I saw Mum's eyes grow wide and agitated. 'What I remember is waking to the alarm every morning at 5.30, listening to him rummaging through the cupboard in the dark and hearing the door slam behind him,' Mum said. 'Dad was obsessed. It didn't matter whether he was swimming in the middle of winter or lifting weights at night. He was relentless.'

'And he expected the same from his players,' I said. 'He had them running up hills dragging a truck tyre tied to their waists. They were fitter and stronger than any other team, more aggressive, tackled harder and never gave up.'

Mum looked at me as if considering my comments. 'He was certainly a man of conviction.'

'There was no bullshit about him, and he built a great team spirit,' I said, awkwardly aware that our conversation sounded like his eulogy and that I appeared to be channelling some member of the Cats football club. 'The players respected him; I think they liked that he socialised with them, even though he wasn't a great drinker.'

'Remember when he was working for the council and tried to persuade them to bring the Aborigines into the town and house them decently?' Mum said. 'There were a lot of wooden faces at the council meeting that first night, apparently. They didn't want the blacks in town, and Ernie Woodhead was ropeable. Dad thought he could persuade enough of the council to support him – the premier agreed with him, so for a while he had hope – but in the end they chose an old fruit packing place way out of town.'

'Not in my backyard, eh?' Jen said, glancing from me to Mum.

'Exactly. The town should have thanked him after all the problems caused by those horrible little concrete boxes out at Rumbalara. They were boiling in summer and freezing in winter, and they didn't even have sewerage, or hot water. It was a disgrace.' Mum sighed. 'He didn't win that fight, or the fight for the All Blacks, but Jack never gave up – once he made up his mind there was no changing it.' There was something hard in her voice that surprised me.

'That was Jack,' Jen said, reaching across to pat Mum's hand.

Then, all of a sudden, it seemed as if an enormous burden had settled on Mum's shoulders. She sat at the table no longer noticing us, her eyes dull. She looked exhausted.

'He was a determined old bugger,' I said, hoping to lift the mood.

Mum said, 'I feel tired,' and another silence settled over the table. The clink and scrape of cutlery on plates was so ordinary it was painful. When Mum finally spoke, her voice sounded as if it came from a long way off. 'Do you remember the day Jim got his Gold Boomerang at Scouts?' She glanced at the mahogany coffee table Dad and Jim had made years ago.

Jen reached over and put her hand on Mum's.

'He must have been ten at the time. There he was on stage in his shorts, socks pulled up to his knees and the sun streaming down on his shoulders. I remember the smile on his little face; his eyes panned the room looking for me and Dad. He seemed so proud and innocent.'

'What did he get it for?' Jen asked.

'Community involvement – shopping, gardening, helping those in need.'

'He was a good kid, wasn't he,' Jen said.

'Yes,' Mum replied softly. She exhaled, her body folding into itself.

Mum didn't seem to accept that Jim had turned his back on our family, and it occurred to me that she might never be reconciled to his absence. I suppressed a sigh and glanced at Jen, who gave me a sad smile.

I knew Mum was thinking about Jim, about the fight. But how could I not have taken Dad's side? What other option was there? Finally I felt I had won his love and respect, and I wasn't about to throw that away on . . . on what? Why all this reminiscing about Jim? He hadn't come to see Dad when he had the chance. After all Mum and Dad had done for him – bringing him into the family, loving him better in a way than they loved their own flesh and blood.

But it wasn't that. I knew Jim hadn't replaced me. Jim was a relief to Dad, who found me and my reading and my acting and all of those 'namby-pamby' pursuits frankly baffling. It was clear now – now for god's sake – that Dad had been threatened by a world he couldn't understand. I was incomprehensible to him, but Jim's running made sense.

My father was one of the most respected men in Mooroopna. He was the sort of bloke for whom small country towns build monuments. I remembered years ago I had said to Jen, 'I reckon our kids will see a bronze statue of their grandfather kicking a footy out the front of the Mooroopna Football Club one day.' Jim's ability gave Dad the chance to prove something. To himself, to the town, and perhaps even to me.

That first time Jenny came to meet my family we sat down for a formal dinner just as we had always done. Titan sat under the table at Dad's feet, deaf and half blind now. Dad had never gone anywhere without that dog. Every Saturday as he headed out to the ute to drive to the footy, he'd whistle and Titan would leap onto the tray. Titan never missed a game. At night when Dad got home from work Titan's ritual began: he'd wag his tail excitedly, then fling himself over on his back with his paws in the air waiting to be tickled. It was, I thought unkindly, exactly what Dad wanted in a dog, a friend, or a son.

That night, Mum had ladled out her vegetable soup and when we were all served Dad had said grace. 'For what we are about to receive may the Lord make us truly thankful.'

'Where's the game on Saturday?' Jim asked as he raised his head.

'Shepparton. Beat them by six goals last time,' Dad said, 'and we'll do it again.'

Jim looked at Jenny and smiled. 'Dad captained the Cats to three flags – best full forward they ever had,' he said, glancing at Dad with a grin.

'Typical,' I reflected. Jim never missed a chance to put Dad on a pedestal. I looked at Dad's clean-shaven face.

'I guess I was lucky,' he said uncharacteristically. 'A full forward needs bulk.'

In the centre of the table was a cane basket of bread rolls. Mum picked up a roll, buttered it and looked up at Jenny. 'Robert says you love debating.'

'Yes,' she beamed.

'Captain of the team,' I butted in. 'They won the final.'

'What was the topic?' Dad asked.

'Vietnam – the war,' Jenny said, tearing off a piece of roll.

'Are any of your family involved in the war?' Dad looked inquiringly at Jenny.

'No, not Vietnam, but Pa was a soldier in the Second World War.'

'I served with the Australian forces in New Guinea.'

'Not Milne Bay by any chance?' Jenny said.

'Yep, I was part of that blood bath when they attacked the airfield.'

'Pa told me about it. They lost seven hundred men—'

'And we lost three hundred and seventy of our finest, but we got rid of the bastards.'

'It must have been terrible,' Jenny said. 'When you know a soldier, you can never dismiss what they do. It's why I feel so torn about Vietnam,' Jenny said.

'Terrible climate,' Dad said. 'I got malaria and was laid up in Townsville for a long time.'

'Little wonder, with no mosquito nets, quinine in short supply, and all the men in shorts with their sleeves rolled up,' Jenny said.

'As soon as I got better I was shipped off to Borneo! I hate the tropics.'

Jenny smiled, and I wondered how she knew so much about the war, and why Dad had never mentioned any of this to us.

'When I went to fight in '42 my brother was too young so he stayed and looked after the shop with my father,' Dad said.

'But I thought your father sold the shop?' I interrupted.

'That wasn't until '46 – after the war,' Dad said. 'Ian was strong and able to cart boxes so he looked after the place while Dad did the ordering. When Dad sold the shop I got the job as council overseer,' he continued. 'Best thing that ever happened – apart from marrying your mother, of course,' Dad said, sounding a bit sappy.

'That's where you met Harry,' Mum interrupted, adding to the well-worn story.

I remembered those long summer evenings when Dad and Harry sat on the front porch drinking and talking about Menzies' determination to maintain a strong defence alliance with the United States, or mocking his 'British to his bootstraps' comment. Harry would park himself on the cane chair, the black birthmark on his right temple as dark as the night sky, and I recall both of them applauding the government decision to give Aboriginal people full citizenship rights.

I watched as Jenny cast her eye over the members of my family, finally coming to rest on me. She smiled warmly then turned back to Dad.

I think it was at that moment that I truly fell in love with her. No one had ever dealt with my father so easily before, certainly not a woman, and no one in my family could have done it with such grace.

Dad felt a special affection for Jenny. He was a man's man and had little experience of women, but it pleased him to find things he could talk to her about. And in later years they'd sit in the lounge, Dad in his favourite chair, Jenny on the couch next to him, watching *Pick-A-Box* and challenging each other to see who could answer the most questions.

That night I saw a side of Dad I hadn't seen before. He was different from the man who came home every Tuesday night from his Masonic meeting with the smell of whisky on his breath. And he was different from the man who puffed out his chest and talked about captain-coaching the Cats to three consecutive finals. That night when he spoke to Jenny his voice was gentle, he listened to every word, careful not to interrupt, and waiting patiently to speak. He didn't agree with everything she said but he didn't raise his voice and he took the time to explain his thoughts. After thrashing out the pros and cons of Australia's involvement in Vietnam, they were able to agree on the toll it was taking on young Australian men – boys really – who were still too young to vote. Neither of them supported conscription, although Dad didn't necessarily agree with Jenny's passionate accusations of government injustice.

The special bond Dad and Jenny shared was forged during that conversation. It was not just because she was my fiancée, nor was it what she said that impressed him. I sensed he saw much of himself in her, and to me, the similarities were clear. Like Dad, Jenny was fearless and forthright, and stood up for what she believed to be right; she was also determined to make the world a better place. If anyone else had looked at him with that open gaze he would have felt threatened and talked over them. But with each word he spoke to Jen he seemed to lower his guard. Strangely, he seemed more at ease with her even when he must have felt more exposed. Jenny never let him get away with a thing, but her affection for him was always obvious.

Jenny went off to her single bed early, tired after the long drive, but I sat up with Dad, relishing his openness. We talked far into the night in a way we'd never managed to do before. He was deeply concerned about Meredith Langdon, a local Aboriginal girl, still making slow progress in the Mooroopna Hospital, and the apparent lack of concern by locals.

Thinking of that breakthrough now, I was overwhelmed by sadness and regret. Jenny had given me a chance to know my father in a way I'd never thought possible, to be drawn into that inner sanctum, and to finally have the love and respect I'd dreamt about since I was a small boy. But it wasn't all easy after that. We were still fundamentally different.

Still, from that night on, my relationship with Dad improved, and I started to see him in a different light. He'd really listened to Jenny, and for once he hadn't pretended to know better. Perhaps there was a chance he and I could understand each other one day. I went off to bed feeling lighter and happier, and from the look on Dad's face, I think he felt much the same.

CHAPTER 4

NEXT MORNING MUM SAID SHE wanted to get out of the house, so I suggested we go for a walk through town. Clouds cruised across the sky, moderating the heat, and trees swayed in the breeze. We walked down our street past the war memorial, following the highway.

I started to tell her about a big money-laundering case involving bank fraud that had landed on my desk, but I noticed her attention drifting away from me. She pointed to a vacant block on the other side of the street. 'Did I tell you Nancy Wong's ancestors came from China in the 1850s to pan for gold? Nice people,' she said. 'That's where they used to live, but a builder bought it and pulled it down. She told me her husband's ancestors bought the house with a nugget of gold he found, which was stolen and later recovered.'

Her face brightened, and for a moment she seemed less withdrawn, less preoccupied with her own sad thoughts.

'On school holidays Maggie, Nancy and I rode our bikes down McLennan Street to the park. We'd catch yabbies, raid mulberry trees and eat until our mouths were purple, while we planned the term's social events. There were always barbecues, picnics, and dance parties in the school hall, even the occasional jaunt to Melbourne. It was wonderful. I remember one time, the head prefect, Johnny Carter, had a dust-up with Jamie Thomas for Brenda Taylor, the prettiest girl in school. Maggie and I would pick out the dance partners we fancied, and arrange times to meet them on the school oval.'

I looked at Mum. Her face was flushed with schoolgirl colour and she looked far more animated.

'Years later, each Saturday afternoon Maggie and I sat with Nancy on that sagging verandah, ivy winding its way up the rusted pipes to the gutters, drinking tea, eating shortbread and chatting about our children. Nancy told us there were times when she was out shopping and she'd see people looking at her and whispering. Even after all those years – she was born here – she felt she didn't belong.'

Why am I not surprised? I thought to myself.

'She and Mr Wong began their married life in that house and three years later Mr Wong took over the management of the saw mill from his father. They say he squandered much of his father's wealth at the race track but he managed to save the house and the mill after his father died suddenly.'

As Mum spoke I recalled standing in the kitchen many years ago when she had told the same story. It seemed so long ago. I wondered whether she had begun to reflect on her years of marriage.

We continued on our walk, a breeze cooling our cheeks. We passed all the familiar landmarks, the squat red-brick tower near the Watt Road bridge, the silos and the water tower that Jim and I wanted to climb as children, the Agriproducts factory near the corner of Mill Street. In the time I'd been away things seemed to have changed a lot. I felt as if I knew no one in this town, but perversely wanted someone to know I was back.

'Remember when we were saving for Jim's trip to Sydney to compete in the Australian Championships?' Mum volunteered.

'That's ancient history,' I said.

Mum had often told us stories of her family and her past, as she taught us to mix scones in the kitchen in a bowl that seemed bigger than me, as she made a game of cleaning our room, as she put on her red lipstick when she got ready to go out with Dad for an evening. I remember Jim and I sitting transfixed as we watched her transform herself from our mum into someone else, a starlet we might have seen on the silver screen, the red lips still dropping stories as we kicked our feet against the side of the bath. It was so private, so intimate to be in there with her, as if we were sharing some secret women's world from which we would very soon be expelled.

I stopped, surprised at the intensity of my memories. Had that really been inside me all these years? How much influence had this woman had on me I wondered?

Mum continued her stories about the town, and I retraced her life in my mind as she did.

She'd gone to Mooroopna Primary School with her best friend Maggie, and so the long friendship between Maggie and Betty had begun. When I knew Maggie she was Mrs Peterson; she used to wear men's blue overalls and her hands were calloused and worn, the oily strands of her hair always hanging in her face until she flipped them away. She had a good heart, Mum always said.

Maggie and Mum were 'two peas in a pod', Dad used to say. They were both determined and stoic. Like Mrs Peterson, Mum had been brought up on a farm. She was the eldest of five and the only girl. Her father and brothers worked long hours on their thirty-acre dairy property on the outskirts of Shepparton. The boys were in the sheds milking cows before sunrise, often returning home in the dark at the end of a long day, dipping their heads in the bathroom basin, soaping their arms and faces and drying themselves. They'd sit down to dinner in their filthy overalls and talk of bloat, or mastitis or scours. As they joked and laughed it was Mum's job to clear the table, wash the dishes, and do any darning or mending before she went to bed. Mum had once described herself as a small freckle-faced kid with holes in her shoes who might stand forever at her mother's table, pounding a lump of dough as if it were a piece of her own soul.

When her family lost everything in the Depression, her brothers had taken labouring jobs on neighbouring properties and she'd found work cleaning for the Beauford family. Not a day went by that 'Sir John' didn't lecture her on how to clean the toilets, scrub the floors or polish the silver. Mum had spent her whole life taking directions from others; that's how she was brought up. Before Dad came along she did what her parents, her teachers, her employer told her to do, and, like Mrs Peterson, she was happy to yield to her husband and follow his lead, even if, at times, it was against her better judgment.

Mum ended up hating farm life and decided that, when she found a man of her own, he would not be a farmer. She had watched her brothers grow from keen and loving little boys into men who were hardened and unhappy. On Saturday nights, fuelled with alcohol, they got into brawls and came home beaten. When her youngest brother, Alec, turned up one Saturday night with his young football coach, Jack Pickering, Mum was pleased.

Mrs Peterson had no such ambitions. My mother always said that life had taught Maggie to be a practical, capable woman. When she was fourteen, her father fell off a roof and killed himself. She, as the eldest of three girls, had to care for her sisters while her mother managed the farm. She learnt to keep house for them – cooking, cleaning, washing clothes, darning jumpers and listening to their complaints. At night she taught herself to cook vegetables from the patch she tended at the bottom of the garden. When she married Mr Peterson she kept working, but this time she also worked alongside him on the farm. She kept house, worked in the paddocks herding stock or mending fences, and when Mr Peterson came in from a long day, she had dinner waiting for him on the table.

They had cleared scrub and grubbed out stumps together, to run livestock and sow wheat on the property they'd bought. But as the years passed, the summers got drier without the trees, and the earth without the native grasses loosened and blew away. But even when the Petersons had to buy in water and their debt grew, they persisted.

Now the house was all but gone. When we'd passed it on the drive up, I'd seen tractor tyres and rusty machinery strewn in the front yard and a Hills hoist tilted in the steady north wind. Tyre tracks reached from the highway to the drooping carport, which seemed to be held up only by the tangle of vines wrapped around the brick pillars supporting it.

It didn't seem that long ago that Dad and I had driven past and he had bemoaned the disrepair all around him. 'What a waste,' he'd said. I'd agreed with him, thinking about the sheep they'd had to slaughter in the drought, the thousands and thousands they'd sunk into the farm, which just got harder to run every year. Now the land stood barren and useless, overrun with straggling weeds, and home to foxes and feral cats.

Maggie Peterson had been a broad, tough woman, tougher than her husband as it turned out. Like many others, in a drought years ago, he had taken his rifle and killed a bunch of starving sheep in a grey stubbled paddock. The next day his tractor flipped and killed him. As a child I didn't see the connection.

Not long after her dad's funeral, Issie Peterson stayed with us for a few weeks while Mrs Peterson 'got her husband's affairs in order'. Mum used to go out to visit her and would come back looking wan and shaken. Dinner was a quiet affair during those weeks. At the table Issie methodically cut her sausages into small pieces and put them into her mouth, her eyes always looking beyond us to the cupboards or windows, seeing something none of us could quite see.

One night about a week after 'the accident', Mrs Peterson came to our house to see Issie. Her eyes were hollow and dark and she looked tired and drawn. Instead of her usual gruff voice she spoke softly as if she were afraid of causing ripples in the air around her.

She arrived in Mr Peterson's old ute and when Isabelle heard the splutter of the engine she ran outside and jumped on her mother.

'When can I come home, Mum?'

'Soon, love.'

Mrs Peterson stayed for dinner, her dry red eyelids veiling her gaze. Mum had always spoken of Maggie with a sort of reverence and I knew she would do anything for her. When Mrs Peterson finally spoke, she said she was determined to keep the farm going. Now she had her husband's life insurance, she could pay off the debt and start afresh. She spoke about repairing fences, improving pasture and replenishing the flock.

'But it didn't work with Mr Peterson,' I blurted, having listened to Mum and Dad fretting about the Petersons for years. 'Why will it work without him?'

My mother was horrified that I would interfere in their conversation at all but Mrs Peterson just looked at me, surprised. Then she laughed. 'Out of the mouths of babes!' she said. She slipped back into her reverie but my mother gave me a withering look.

I watched Mrs Peterson. Her eyes were bloodshot and unfocussed. She looked calm in a way that I could not understand. Her daughter hung off her, desperate to be close to her mother in any way she could. There was a flickering desperation to her that seemed somehow more real than her mother's serenity. But I dared not speak another word. My mother's face was all support and, I realised, awe at her friend's resolve.

We walked on, and Mum pointed out the street where Dad had worked with his father in the grocery shop. She had admired his rugged good looks when she went into the store. I remember sitting at the kitchen table after school with Jim as the sun poured through the window and we ate chocolate meringue while Mum reminisced about Dad's tall frame and straight black hair. How she had smiled when she said that. How she had winked at us kids and deliberately turned her back to Dad so he could not see her blush even then, years after their courtship had ended. She would go into the store on any pretext to see him and when he served her she saw the smile on his face and knew he'd noticed her.

Alec teased her. 'You hang on every word,' he mocked, and, 'You can't get enough of him.' Dad was a town boy and the bush held no appeal to him. When Alec said, 'You love him,' Mum blushed scarlet but said nothing. Deep down she saw an opportunity to escape the drudgery of farm life and knew Dad was the man for her.

Thinking back, when Mum used to tell us about her courtship with Dad, she always spoke with dignity and self-assurance, and there was a look of pride in her clear eyes. My father always seemed to dominate the house when he was there, and even on the days when he was not. But now I understood that Mum's pursuit of Dad had been calculating and pragmatic as well as romantic.

On Saturdays, they went to the movie matinee in Shepparton and sat in the back row holding hands; on Sundays they picnicked in the park. How many of these stories had I heard? When they sat next to each other on the blanket laughing and talking about Dad's plans to take over his father's shop and to one day coach the Cats to a grand final, Mum saw his determination, ambition and strong will. Had she said that openly, or had I just understood it? She liked that he knew what he wanted, was self-assured and had no doubt he would succeed. She looked up to him, felt close to him and sensed he was easy to get along with – as long as she gave in to him. That part she had never said, but it was a truth universally acknowledged in our town.

Until she met Dad, Mum said she'd seen her future laid out for her in terms of what her mother had given her: a pride in her ability to keep house, a belief in telling the truth, and the importance of being quiet and unassuming. She thought highly of her mother, but recognised that the life she'd lived was dismal.

During the week Mum said she was miserable. She longed to see Jack and told her mother they needed bread, apples or tea as an excuse to ride into town to shop. Her mother was not duped. She'd seen Mum lost in her books, searching for a larger and more passionate world than the one she was brought up in. She understood her daughter's needs and said to her husband, 'I hope that Jack of hers recognises what he's getting. She has dreams, that girl, and I hope he understands that.'

'Was it so bad on the farm?' I asked her.

She looked at me and I could see her weighing the question in her mind as she might have weighed a pear in her hand. After a long minute she smiled. 'The farm wasn't all bad,' she said.

'Tell me,' I said, happy to distract her from her grief.

'There were lots of workers on the farm. My favourite was Ted. He was a big man – broad shoulders, big belly. His face bristled with whiskers and he had deep lines running down his cheeks. I remember his hands – all calloused and cracked. Ted spent his days fixing barbwire fences. Mum would send me down with his lunch every day. It used to baffle me to hear the way the townsfolk talked about him.'

I looked at her quizzically. 'Why did they talk about him?'

Mum stared at me like I was daft. 'Because he was black. You know how they go on about "black fellas" around here – even now! Didn't matter that he was the best station manager this town has ever seen or that he had a wicked sense of humour.'

'Hang on. What? Ted was Aboriginal? You've talked about Ted for as long as I can remember, but I don't recall you ever saying he was black.'

'I'm sure I did.'

'Don't think so.'

'Anyway, who cares? He was a wily old bugger, but I was very fond of Ted. On summer holidays he'd tell me Dreamtime stories of creation – about the river, where certain birds came from.

'Sometimes Dad would see us and tell me to leave Ted alone because he had work to do.'

'Didn't he mind that his only daughter—' I stopped short, stiffening in anticipation of Mum's criticism, but it didn't come.

'You are your father's son,' she said, shaking her head. She stopped and rested her hand on a fence.

'Are you tired, Mum? Will we head back?'

'Maybe,' she said.

We turned, crossed the road and headed back the way we'd come. Mum was silent until we reached the road leading down to the river.

'Let's walk to Chinamen's Gardens,' she said suddenly. 'If I'm too tired we can always just go home.'

A waterbird cawed as we approached the river and walked into the shade of the gums along the riverbank.

'You can't imagine the hue and cry when your father wanted to bring the Aborigines into town,' Mum said. She pointed ahead along the track. 'Just up there is the Flats. The people walked out of Cummeragunja in 1939 because they were being treated like slaves. They built themselves little houses and humpies out of whatever they could find, all around here. Simple places. I think they were happy there, but the town was ashamed. When the Queen visited, they put up hessian screens so she couldn't see the settlement, but the kids squeezed through and waved like anything apparently.' She smiled sadly. 'I felt bad because it was my fault he fought so hard. I insisted the segregation had to end, it was wrong keeping people apart like that . . . But then he copped all the flack.'

'You were behind all that?' I was surprised. 'Why? What was so important about it?'

'I thought that if the whites kept separating themselves from the blacks, things would never improve. Why shouldn't they live in the town like everyone else? Why should they be forced to live in concrete humpies on the outskirts of town?' She looked suddenly weary.

Overhead, the clouds had thickened and were beginning to form tracts of grey across the sky. The day was cooling.

Mum stared out over the river. She seemed to drift between sadness and exasperation. Then she turned and continued steadily back towards home. I followed, silently. I sensed she had wanted to tell me something more but had decided against it.

At the end of our street Mum turned to me abruptly and asked, 'When are you going to start on Dad's papers?'

'Soon,' I said, surprised that she didn't want to do it herself. 'Do you need a rest?' I said, thinking that perhaps these last weeks had been too much for her after all.

'No,' she said, 'but let's go home.'

CHAPTER 5

MUM WENT TO BED EARLY that night, and Jenny had a program she wanted to watch on TV, so I headed into Dad's office to tackle his papers, as Mum had suggested. It was eerie walking into Dad's room; I felt a guilty sense of trespass and had to fight the urge to glance over my shoulder as I emptied drawers and cupboards and sorted papers into piles. Those I didn't trash I packed in a box, which I planned to take with me to Melbourne to sort through later.

I felt strangely distant going through Dad's things: his Freemason sash and medal, the pennies at the bottom of the drawer from another time, a box I could already tell was a sewer of memories, and Dad's dusty crumpled hat from when he was a Scout master. Every second Thursday at 5.00 pm he would drag Jim and me to Scouts where we stood to attention for roll call, sang 'God Save the Queen' and learned how to tie reef knots when we would much rather have been fishing in the Goulburn.

I kept on: the Cats cap and scarf; the stopwatch, now motionless; the council papers; a chisel and a couple of very tattered copies of the *Bulletin*. These possessions summed up my father, a conservative, a man determined to take the Cats to another grand final, a man who was passionate about his woodwork, and a man driven to train his adopted son to shave another tenth of a second off his time trials.

The messy bottom drawer of the sideboard was devoted solely to sketches and plans for his woodwork, his protractors, pencils and other tools and implements. Another drawer contained training manuals, newspaper cuttings of Jim's achievements and his time trials compared to other gold medallists. Yet a third drawer had Dad's football memorabilia packed into it haphazardly – a plaque given to him when he captained-coached the Cats to their first grand-final win, a picture of John Cain Senior, the then Premier, handing him a now tarnished trophy for the Best and Fairest in 1947, and a yellowing photo of him and the team after their 1948 grand-final win. I realised now that he would have had very mixed feelings about that Best and Fairest trophy, awarded the year after the All Blacks were excluded from the league.

Faded clippings from the *Shepparton Advertiser* filled out the story Harry had told about the all-Aboriginal team. In April 1946 there'd been a couple of working bees at Daish's paddock, with nearly a hundred helpers, including the women who provided lunch and afternoon tea. The secretary, Mr Shadrach James – 'Shady' to the journalists – saw the club's participation in local football as 'an important step forward for people of his race in this district, as part of a general move for their betterment'. Players wore gold jumpers with a blue sash.

By July, games were being played on the new ground at Daish's paddock and the All Blacks were head of the league on premiership points, 40 points ahead of their nearest rival with 32. I checked Mooroopna – 8 points – and understood a little more of Dad's reputation.

A brittle clipping was headed 'ALL BLACKS PREMIERS'. I scanned the article:

> In brilliant football weather except for a slight cross breeze, a crowd of over 1500 saw All Blacks win the premiership of the Central Goulburn Valley League Seconds from Toolamba on Saturday by a wide margin of four goals. Displaying

magnificent judgment in kicking, the All Blacks captain, Shady James, netted nine goals from 11 scoring shots. Gate takings exceeded £113.

An article from 1947 headed ENIGMA OF ALL BLACKS questioned why the All Blacks had not attended the presentation of the premiership pennant and 'Considerable informal conversation took place as to whether it was desirable that All Blacks should remain in the competition.' My heart sank as I smoothed out the final two clippings: one mentioned the defunct All Blacks team and the other explained that the premiership pennant had still not been collected. Dad had printed 'EXPELLED FROM LEAGUE' over the clipping.

Dad would have been furious, and I wondered if the story of the All Blacks' brilliance and the mystery of their expulsion had made him more determined than ever to support Jim in his athletic career.

Yet, as I trawled deeper, the drawers revealed another side to him. In a shoebox beneath the desk I found a neatly tied packet of letters marked 'Return to Sender – Occupant Unknown'. They were dated between February and November 1934 and addressed to a girl called Jane. I could see as I flicked through that they were from his high-school days, when he would have been in form three or four. His spelling was uneven, but Dad's loopy handwriting disclosed a thoughtful boy with strong feelings. Beneath the hyperbole and the clichés – *our love will never die, we were meant for each other* – I sensed real emotion. At the bottom of each page, he had drawn a heart around their initials. How distant this boy seemed from the authoritarian footy coach who had raised me.

His letters to Mum showed a similar soft sentimentality, but he had refined his abilities since his earlier attempt at wooing, although there were still ardent declarations, and I sensed that the man was just as vulnerable as the boy. There was also a candour that he had learnt to mask, or had lost entirely, by the time I came along.

In one drawer I found our teeth, each painstakingly labelled with our name and the year it fell out, the lot carefully stored in a tin box, the lid marked simply, 'The kids'.

I picked up a family photo, studying his inscription on the back. It was taken at my graduation, and the inscription stated only our names and the date and place.

It was almost midnight when Jenny interrupted me, opening the door into what had become my private world. I was staring at a photo of Dad holding a timer, Jim bent over at the starting blocks and me standing next to Dad holding Jim's tracksuit. 'I've brought you some tea,' Jenny said. Startled, colour rushed to my cheeks.

'I'm sorry,' she said, hesitating at my surprise. 'I didn't mean to disturb you.'

'Don't worry,' I said as she passed me the cup. 'I could do with a break – in fact I might finish up here and tackle the rest tomorrow.' I struggled to my feet, shaking the pins and needles from my legs. Her eyes settled on the open drawers and paper-strewn floor.

'How's it going?'

'It's taking much longer than I'd hoped, but I'm nearly done,' I said, exhaling. 'I haven't found a copy of his will, but his solicitor is bound to have it. Let's go out into the lounge. I need a change of scenery.'

I had grown up in this house and knew it intimately. Now, I walked around it, my cup in one hand, the other hand tracing all of the old surfaces – the mahogany coffee table with a deep scratch on the top, since covered with a doily; the L-shaped lounge room, where the Edwardian chest of drawers still held the last of Dad's papers; the linen press Mum used as a cupboard because one of the bedrooms didn't have a wardrobe. I knew it all like the back of my hand: the wide verandah overlooking the neat backyard with its vegetable patch, which Jim and I occasionally flattened with a football, and the window of Dad's tin shed we broke with the cricket ball.

'I can't believe—' I said, turning to Jenny, but she was already somewhere else. I don't know how long I had been there, floating in the musty fog of my memories.

Next morning I tackled the back room, which Dad had used as a storeroom. A chunky old couch with one broken leg was tilted against the wall, a chest of drawers stuffed with more papers squatted beside folded outdoor chairs waiting for the next Sunday barbecue. Suddenly I saw Dad, sitting with Harry, beer in hand, on our front verandah on a Saturday afternoon, or lounging in his favourite armchair shouting wrong answers at a game-show after dinner.

My old desk, which had been moved from my bedroom when I'd left to go to Melbourne, was stacked with cartons of books. The bottom drawer was strewn with pens, pencils, rubbers and newspaper clippings of Dad. Beneath it all was a manila folder with a glossy photo of Jim and me in it. We'd been training at the park: Jim was in shorts and spikes, a massive grin lighting up his face; I was holding a stopwatch. I stared at the photo and recalled Jim, puffing, his arms pumping like pistons as he sprinted down the track. I remember it being a hot, blustery day, dust billowing across the oval.

I pried open a grey tin that looked like a long, thin, safety-deposit box. In it was the title to our family home, birth certificates, the death certificates of my grandparents, and some other official-looking papers, including Dad's will, which I put carefully to one side, relieved that at last I had found it. A quick glance showed me that he had left a life interest in everything to Mum, and then in equal parts to me and Jim. So, he'd never given up on Jim, never given up hope.

One sheaf of documents had Jim's name written on the folded front cover, and at the bottom I saw *Aborigines Welfare Board*. I stared at the page and felt my hands begin to tremble. Someone had written, in small officious script, *'Because of the mother's neglect,* the County Court of Victoria has dispensed with the mother's consent to adoption and hereby places James Albert Clarke in the foster care of Jack and Betty Pickering.' It was dated 13 September 1957.

I felt my face grow hot, my heart start to pound, and there was a choking heaviness in my throat and chest. I was shaking with rage. A memory surfaced, sharp and sudden. I came home from school one day to see two men, who I later discovered were welfare officers, sitting at the kitchen table with Mum and Dad. Confused, I asked what they wanted. 'Go outside, Robert,' Dad said and closed the door in my face.

Sitting at my broken desk, I wanted to grab my father by the lapels, nail him to the wall and tell him just what I thought of him. But it was too late, he was dead. And what of my mother? What would she say? I wondered if her shoulders would suddenly stiffen with resolve or whether her face would fill with dread. But now, just after the funeral, was not the time to find out. What did I want her to say? What could she say? Maybe nothing she said would be sufficient.

I put down the papers and walked to the window, gazing across the lawn to the back fence. I could imagine little Jim, just seven years old, crying, barefoot, being dragged away from his mother and bundled into a car.

I turned and walked outside into the sunshine, but the garden seemed to lack colour. I climbed the back fence we'd built together, and walked down along the embankment to the river. In a stupor I went all the way to the jetty and sat there for a long time staring into the muddy water. Light reflected off the ripples lapping against the piles. Images and thoughts collided in my brain, but I kept returning to the simplicity, the sheer rawness of the fact that Jim had been taken from his parents without their permission, while they were still living!

It was late when I returned, the shadow on the lawn stretching out behind the house. Mum was on the couch watching telly and she looked up, alarmed, when I came in. I did not have the will to stop and explain myself, just looked at her and said, 'Sorry I missed tea,' and dragged myself to the verandah where Jen was sitting drinking coffee.

'You look shocking, what's the matter?' she asked, but I realised I wasn't ready to talk about it. I grunted and shrugged and took myself to the bedroom and flung myself onto the bed.

The sound of an early possum, like a choking motor, started up somewhere near the clothesline and I got up after a minute and walked to the window. The possum was nowhere to be seen but the coughing and choking sound continued. A magpie perched on the fence under the darkening sky, illuminated by light from the kitchen. It looked as though it had only one leg. I thought about the document I had read earlier – Jim's so-called adoption papers. If only I could burn them or tear them up and erase forever the knowledge that was now lodged in my brain. A wave of fatigue swept over me.

Staring out at the night sky I tried to remember the last time I had seen Jim happy. When he'd won his gold medal at the Commonwealth Games in Edinburgh in 1970 he'd stood at the podium with a broad smile, his honed body glistening. It seemed not long afterwards that he stopped laughing. And when he won his gold medal at the Olympics two years later, something was definitely wrong: his eyes were dull and blank. Perhaps being on top of the world only means you have further to fall, or maybe it was that he had fulfilled everyone else's dreams and had no idea what his own might be.

In the heavy silence, other memories tumbled through my mind, but all of them now were off key – they no longer fitted together as they should, now that I knew Jim was stolen. I felt sullied, betrayed and deceived by my parents; worst of all, I felt complicit. In all those years, to have never spoken of what they had done – what did that say about my father, about my mother, about the laws that allowed this to happen?

The bedroom door opened quietly and Jen edged into the room. 'What's happened?'

I felt blood pounding in my head, and anger building inside me.

'Come on,' she coaxed.

I stared at the ceiling with its delta of fine cracks and tried to collect myself.

'Jim was stolen.'

I could hear Jen breathing, but she didn't speak. When I looked up, she held my gaze.

'How do you know?'

'I found the documents amongst Dad's papers.'

She seemed to be struggling with her thoughts. Finally she said quietly, 'And you never guessed?'

'I don't know – no, I didn't. I believed them. Why wouldn't I?'

She rubbed the side of her face. 'I don't know.'

'Look at everything that Dad did for Jim,' I said, still wanting to exonerate him somehow. 'Who'd have thought . . .?'

I watched her change into my blue rugby top. Her movements were swift and easy. She pulled her pyjama pants on and sat cross-legged on the bed opposite me.

'Now you know why,' she said.

'What do you mean?'

'Maybe your father thought athletics was the key to a better life for Jim or maybe he just felt guilty.'

'Guilty?'

'About taking Jim from his real parents.'

'Who knows? Maybe he was ashamed of what he'd done. But can you believe that I went through almost my whole life till now without my parents saying a word? To be kept in the dark all these years. And why didn't Jim say anything?'

Her eyes grew wide with exasperation.

'Listen to yourself, it's not about you. And what was Jim supposed to say? He was a small child. And didn't you say your father told him his mother was dead?'

I baulked at her bluntness but she did not back down. 'Yes. We were both told his parents were dead,' I said. 'All those years . . . he could have been with his birth parents, not feeling constantly ashamed of being black in a white community, being bullied and driven to prove that he was—'

I stopped. Jen had raised an eyebrow.

'Well, he must have been taken for a reason,' I said.

'But maybe no good reason.'

'He couldn't have had a better life than living with my parents. Look how some of those people live.'

'You sound just like him, like your dad. I think he probably did believe that Jim needed rescuing, that "those people" needed to be rescued from themselves.'

I wondered if Jim would have been so different from the man I'd just met if he had lived over there on the other side of the river. If he'd lived in squalor. And how would I have felt about him then? I realised with a shock that I was asking myself whether I could have loved him if he was black, truly Aboriginal, one of 'them'. Suddenly I was overwhelmed with disgust at myself.

I was already regretting my words. 'I didn't mean it like that, I – I didn't—'

'You didn't even know you thought like that?'

I shook my head. 'You think that's why they took him? Because of stuff like that?'

She shrugged. 'Who knows? Was there anything in the papers about his parents?'

'Yes – they mention neglect.'

'If that was true, then they didn't need to lie.'

'No, you're right. They didn't need to take him for life if it was neglect. He could have gone to grandparents or other family, or he could have visited his people sometimes.'

'Are you going to talk to your mother?'

I sighed. 'Not yet.'

I sat on the bed beside her and pulled off my shoes, feeling wearier than I had ever felt.

CHAPTER 6

DESPITE MY MENTAL AND EMOTIONAL exhaustion, or perhaps because of it, I found I couldn't sleep. I lay in bed, my mind racing, while Jenny slept beside me, her dreams apparently untroubled. I thought of my childhood, which came back to me now in a series of snapshots of school plays, race meets and the occasional fracas with a hard kid called Craig and his mates: the sort of problems that had been washed with the soap of time so that they were comfortable and clean, not the bitter, brutal experiences they had been. Jim was there, of course, but he was somehow out of focus, his features and expressions obscured by my solipsism. Did I feel any sympathy for him, believing that his parents were dead? Sure. But life can move on quickly for kids and I soon forgot about Jim's sorrow and grief. Now I regarded every memory through a new lens, which sharpened and redefined every experience we had shared.

For a long time after Jim arrived, I had the sense that he didn't really live with us so much as squat in our house. He kept to himself and seldom spoke. His silence was the self-imposed silence of a stranger, of a young boy for whom everything was unfamiliar. He wandered around the house as though he were in a museum. He was shy, and whenever Mum and Dad tried talking to him, he responded with only a yes or no. He watched people, cautious and uncertain, as if he had no idea what to expect from them, as if home life was confusing for him, and school and the town were downright bizarre. It was not that he was unfamiliar with the life of white people, it was the sudden shift in his role within it that undid him: now he was one of us, but not really, not truly, and that threw him off course.

This was plain from the outset at school. A few days after the storm that had blown Jim out of his own home and into ours, debris had been cleared from the grounds of Mooroopna Primary and the school reopened. Thinking back on that day, I am not sure Jim really understood what was happening, but he covered up any lack of understanding with his silences and his powers of observation. On the first morning Mrs Axen called Jim to the front of the class and said rather formally, 'This is Jim. He's new.'

My eyes roved around the room. There was a humming under-current in the class. Most of the Aboriginal kids glanced at Jim, then lowered their eyes to their desks. Other students stared at him, or whispered behind their hands. Jim's eyes roamed over the Aboriginal kids, then stopped on me, his face confused, stoic and frightened all at the same time. As he sat down, the class bully, Craig, turned to his friend Ken and, tilting his head towards Jim, in a slow gesture that no one in the room could miss, turned his thumb down. There was a sudden hush as all eyes flicked from Craig to Mrs Axen, who pivoted sharply as she caught the last of Craig's gesture.

'Craig! That's enough. Go and report to Mr Paterson at once and tell him why I've sent you!' she snapped, but we all knew Craig had merely made public what most of the white kids were thinking. The damage was done.

Walking home from school that afternoon, Jim didn't say a word. It was his first day of school and already the abuse had started. It would be relentless, and for Jim there was no safety in numbers. From what I could see, the other Aboriginal kids kept their distance. He seemed to exist in a kind of no-man's land.

'What's wrong?'

'Nothing,' he said, kicking the ground.

'Is it Craig?'

'No,' he said.

When we got home, Mum took one look at Jim, his head hanging, and asked, 'What's wrong?'

I butted in. 'It's school.'

'What do you mean?'

'It's Craig – he's picking on Jim.'

'Craig picks on everyone.'

'He called Jim a black bastard.'

'We'll have none of that language here, Robert.'

'He called him a coon.'

'Robert, stop it! Go outside and have a run around,' Mum said. 'That will make you feel a bit better, and I'll get you both something to eat.'

Jim didn't say anything but his face turned slightly towards mine, his forehead wrinkled with confusion as if to say, 'Why doesn't she believe you?'.

'Have you ever panned for gold?' Mum asked Jim, then turning to me said, 'Why don't you take Jim down to the creek? The tools are in Dad's shed.'

I shrugged and headed for the shed. 'Grab those pans,' I told him as I lifted the shovels so he could reach them. 'We'll need some rakes too,' I said, seeing if he'd bite. I motioned towards a collection of tools standing by the door, which were taller than we were, and smirked to myself at the idea of him lugging the useless implements down to the creek. Jim looked at me passively but didn't move. He was onto my game. *The kid's not stupid*, I thought to myself. 'Okay, don't worry,' I said, embarrassed.

We squelched through the mud and slush left after the rain, slapping at mosquitoes and listening for the chuckle of running water until the creek revealed itself. Jim watched as I shovelled gravel and mud from the creek bed into the pans, dipped mine into the water and shook the pan vigorously from side to side. He mimicked me, swirling the lighter grit away and leaving the heavier granules. We didn't talk. I peered into the pan and noticed a speck of gold. Excited, I looked up and, without thinking, turned to Jim. With a small tug, as if the pinkie of a puppeteer had lifted, he smiled. This kid would be my brother.

But at school I held back, not wanting to jeopardise my popularity by being tarred with the same brush as Jim. I was no saint, and although I never actively tormented Jim, I did nothing to defend him. Being the target of deliberate malice from Craig and his friends made Jim's life a misery, I knew. He was the butt of their endless jokes, with no one to defend him, not even the teachers, who often watched, indifferent if not amused. The boys gloated over their victim without shame, picked on him every chance they got, taunting him in any way they could. What was I doing? I was watching, saying nothing, allowing the torment to continue: scared, torn, wanting to defend him but fearful that if I did, they would pick on me, too. He would mutter, 'Leave me alone,' but there was no conviction in it. I did not know then how much fight he had in him. I assumed that, like me, it was fear that made him weak, but there was much more to it than I understood.

At home, around the dining-room table, Jim pretended the bullies didn't affect him, but his eyes were hollow and his skin had grown ever more dull and dry and he looked as if he were fighting hard to smile.

I did not really comprehend what Jim was experiencing. We spent a lot of time together but Jim went off by himself sometimes, simply disappeared, and I had no idea where he went or what he did. Perhaps he went walkabout, I told myself, knowing nothing about Aboriginal people or their way of life, despite living beside them and going to the same school. I had only the clichés I'd absorbed from books and films, and they were few enough. My life was essentially happy and I assumed Jim's was too. Yes there were bullies, and I knew Jim's parents were dead, but it was easy for me to forget. I was gaining a brother, and the details of how or why, or what he was feeling about it, were lost in the whirl of being seven, almost eight. It was a fantasy Jim seemed happy to endorse, for he never called me out, even when the bullies were at their meanest, even when we left school.

In those early weeks, we wandered home from school together, not via the most direct route, but along any road that looked relatively empty, down to the Goulburn, stopping to piss in the river.

'Look Jim,' I boasted, holding my dick out to try to piss as far into the water as possible. I saw a faint smile on his lips.

'I can do better,' he said, undoing his fly.

At other times, we sat beside the river, filled anthills with sand and waited for the insects to swarm out through another hole.

He'd turn to me, the smile still hovering, and say, 'Let's go fishing, eh.' As I wandered along behind him, guilt would begin to build in me. I made no effort to support Jim at school but he was always good to me. His enthusiasm and innocence scratched at my conscience.

On the way home we tracked through the dry scrub and pretended we were a posse on the trail of Ned Kelly and his gang – at least I did. Who knows what games Jim was playing in his imagination – he seemed content to let me tell the stories.

'Stop here,' I said, hiding behind a tree holding a stick for a gun.

Jim nodded, his fingers already solemnly raised like a gun.

We often played on the banks of the Goulburn River. I'd chase Jim as he wove through tall trees, disappeared behind boulders or dropped into the shrubs and grasses. He always left me flat-footed, not knowing where to look. He was fast and I could never keep up with him – he was always a step ahead.

In a short time we had become good friends. I was an only child and my cousins were too small to be much use as playmates, so Jim was my first real companion.

Inside the house, around Mum and Dad, we were quiet, good

kids – we made our beds, did our homework and cleaned up after dinner without complaining. Each school night Mum stood on the verandah and called us in from playing backyard cricket to do our chores: 'Robert, sweep the back verandah, Jim, peel the potatoes,' she'd say, although the tasks changed each day.

At the tea table, when Mum asked us about school, Jim often looked down and pretended not to hear the question. He was having a hard time, copping a lot of abuse and bullying from the other children for being black. All the Aboriginal kids were bullied, but they weren't isolated like Jim. He was a good kid, volunteering to be ink monitor or to clean the blackboard – nothing was too much trouble – but Craig and the others made fun of him relentlessly. Craig was well known for being a 'troublesome little shit' as I had overheard Mr Frank, the sports teacher, say to Mr Paterson. For an eight-year-old he had a mouth like a sewer, but because he was the star of the junior cricket team, he usually got away with his bullying unscathed. On top of that, his father, Ernie Woodhead, had been appointed to the Mooroopna Shire Council, so they thought they were next in line to royalty.

One Saturday night, soon after Jim had moved in with us, we were sitting around the dinner table. Jim was quiet, as usual. He found the formality of our mealtimes baffling. The rules about which way to tip your plate and what to do with your bread wearied him, and no matter how often I showed him how to eat without scraping the plate, he just couldn't manage it. The truth was, he couldn't see the point, and I had to agree with him. Jim asked Mum for the bread but Mum didn't hear him above Dad's chatter and the music she had put on in the background 'for a touch of festivity' she said every Saturday. Ours was a house of ritual.

'Aunty!'

Mum and Dad stopped speaking abruptly; Jim had finally made himself heard. He hung his head, embarrassed. 'Could you please pass the bread?' Mum passed him the bread and whispered to him, 'Jim, dear, we don't shout at the dinner table.' Her voice was stern but patient.

Mum resumed talking but Dad did not respond. He chewed noisily. It was an ominous sign. We all knew that when Dad didn't speak there was something brewing.

Mum's conversation trailed off and the music engulfed us.

'I'm going to try out for the school play,' I said, hoping to dispel the sudden gloom. 'They're letting all the classes try this year, not just the big kids.'

'Well done,' said Mum. 'How exciting!' I saw her glance at Dad, a visual prod, but Dad said nothing. 'When is it?' Mum asked. 'What is it?'

'It's Robin Hood, and it'll be on next term,' I said, aware that no one was really thinking about the play, but rather about why Dad was angry. Was Jim raising his voice to get attention that bad? Mum had told him off already.

We lapsed into silence.

At meal's end, Jim and I began to collect the plates, even though they were heavy; Mum said we had to contribute. As usual, we both thanked Mum and that was when Dad exploded, slamming his glass down on the table.

We all jumped and stopped dead. I closed my eyes, frozen, dreading what was to come. Dad's fury was unpredictable, and it was usually safest to stand still.

'She's not your aunty!' Dad yelled. I am ashamed to say relief flooded through me when I realised that it was Jim, not me, who had upset him. It was the first time that Jim had been the recipient of Dad's wrath; until now, he had been treated almost like a guest.

'She's your mother, for Christ's sake. You're not on the bloody reserve now.'

Silence. I tentatively glanced over at Jim. He was staring at Dad. He did not look afraid so much as astonished. Dad barked at him, 'Well? What do you have to say for yourself?'

I heard Jim mutter something in language beneath his breath and glance at Mum.

'You will speak English in this house, do you understand? Don't you ever let me hear you speaking that gibberish.'

Jim looked from Dad to Mum, and I could see something shift inside him. Then he bowed his head solemnly. 'Sorry Dad,' he said, at exactly the right pitch. I realised he was mimicking me. Dad didn't seem to notice.

'Don't do it again,' he said, 'and if I hear you've been hanging around with any of those kids from the Flats, there'll be trouble, hear?'

'Yes Dad.'

My body relaxed and I turned to Jim. He had a look I would recognise more and more: a blank slate, or a stage suddenly emptied of actors. It was a look he was to refine over the years, bottling everything up, particularly around Dad, until the last vestiges of grief and rage could no longer be discerned.

At night I'd look up from my homework to see him staring at me. If I caught his eye, he would look away, embarrassed. Then he would walk gingerly into the kitchen as though he were afraid to make a sound. But most of the time he stayed in our room.

Initially, I found Jim's shyness around others frustrating, but it wasn't long before I realised he was also unsure of himself, having been thrust into an unfamiliar world that was quick to criticise. We began to spend more time with each other, enjoying the same boisterous pranks. I was the talkative one; Jim seemed hesitant to share his thoughts with me or anyone else. So we amused ourselves playing cricket and kicking the footy in the yard. He was always quicker and more fluid than I was, but his natural ability at sport was no cause for concern when we were so little; it was a fact about him, like his colour and his name and his smile. I didn't even realise I was beginning to love him.

After dinner that night, I went out onto the verandah. I could hear Dad talking to Mum quietly in the lounge room, and when I heard Jim's name, I crept along the wall until I was under the window.

'That wretched Mrs Shields bailed me up outside the hardware,' Dad said.

'Really? What for?'

'These people are appalling.'

'Why, Jack? What happened?'

'She tackled me about Jim. People were staring. We had quite a crowd by the end. Mr Chapple – I'd always thought he was a good bloke – said he felt sorry for me!'

Mum laughed shortly.

'I'm not sure if that made it better or worse,' he said.

'Jim Halloran said, "He should be with his own people. No matter what you do, you can't make him white."

'Then Mrs Shields stuck her oar in again. "It's not too late to send him back,"' Dad mimicked her sanctimonious tone. '"If God wanted us to live together, he would have made us all the same." Genius!' said Dad. 'She ought to run for parliament.' I thought it was meant to be a joke, but Dad sounded agitated and angry.

'Then she got started on the whole Aboriginal housing mess. "Those people don't know how to live decently. It's a good thing they're out of town. That's where they belong." Stupid old biddy. What kind of future are we going to have if we can't live side by side? What chance do they have to learn our ways if they're stuck out of town in a concrete camp that's hardly better than the humpies on the Flats? At least it was their choice to live there, but they had no choice about Rumbalara.'

I crept back to the verandah and rolled into the hammock that we'd strung between two of the posts. I gazed up at the stars and thought about the changes Jim had brought. Not a week passed when I didn't overhear people comment about us and Jim, and it was never positive. Even Carl, who played with Aboriginal kids like I did, said, 'Dad says your father doesn't know what he's doing.'

One day, in the year after Jim had moved in, I was buying mixed lollies at Benny's shop and overheard a conversation between two women who couldn't see me over the shelves.

'You know that boy Jim,' one woman said.

'The black one?'

I heard a smug, overdone sigh. 'What is wrong with those people?'

At that point Benny coughed loudly and said in a carrying voice, 'Will that be all, Robert?' I nodded. He looked down at me, his big round belly swathed in a slightly grubby white apron. I did not know whether to be scared or grateful. He gave me the lollies and waved away my money. 'Get outta here,' he said with a sigh. I sprinted home and shared the lollies with Jim. It seemed wrong to eat them on my own.

When I'd told Dad about what had happened at Benny's, he'd just said, 'Horrible people,' but hadn't said a word about how I felt, or about how Jim was coping. Things were tense around the house. Dad didn't speak, but I could tell he was fuming. He sat in his chair in the lounge watching *Pick-a-Box* on the telly and I could see angry red spots on his cheeks.

The next night Dad's friend, Harry, came over after tea for his usual nightcap. Mum ushered Harry onto the verandah and offered him a beer. I was in the hammock, hoping they wouldn't notice me. Finally the conversation turned to Mrs Shields, and Dad's voice got louder and louder as he told the story. I could tell Harry was trying to find the right words to calm down his mate.

'You've seen the boys, Jack, chattering away, completely at home with each other,' Harry said warmly. 'His skin may be black, but so what? Children imitate those around them. He'll soon become like you and forget he knew any different.'

Dad mulled over what Harry had said. 'Maybe,' he replied thoughtfully. 'I know it's early days but he seems even more like them than he did before. I thought . . .'

'What?'

'Well, they say his face will change, you know. From talking like us and eating our food.'

There was a pause.

'Ya know they always say that couples who live together begin to look like each other. They even say people start to look like their dogs! But I'm not sure it's always the best outcome,' Harry said, trying for a lighter note.

'I'm gonna educate this kid, put a roof over his head, then get him a good job. By the time I'm through, he'll be one of us,' Dad said in a firm voice, 'and no one can take that away from him.'

Looking back now, I think that Harry felt for Dad and trusted his good intentions, but disliked what he had done.

'It worries me that he's got no confidence,' Mum said, catching the tail end of the conversation as she came out onto the verandah.

'But in time he'll feel more secure,' Harry said gently.

Dad sighed, 'So d'ya think maybe Mrs Shields is right?'

No one said anything. Harry rubbed his forehead with a rough hand.

Finally Dad broke the silence. 'We give him a home, food, clothes . . . with us he has a future.'

During the night I woke to the sound of Dad's footsteps. After a few moments I got out of bed and followed him down the long hallway, standing quietly at the door of the lounge room. Dad was gazing out the window. He turned around, saw me looking at him and rubbed the side of his cheek. His eyes seemed too small for his big face.

'Go back to bed,' he said, distracted. After a few seconds, I went back along the quiet hallway without saying a word. The walls seemed close around me, the dim light cast my small shadow on the floor ahead of me and silence rang in my ears. My eyes felt tired. I knew Dad was worried about Jim. I remembered Harry's reassuring words: 'In time he'll feel more secure.' I flopped into bed and soon fell asleep.

The following morning Mum tried talking to Dad but he sat at the table with his head down, eating his cornflakes.

'Are you all right?' Mum finally asked.

Dad didn't respond, just kept on spooning cereal into his mouth.

'Jack?' she continued.

Dad raised his head to look at her. 'Yeah?' he said, staring at her blankly. Neither of them spoke. Finally, she gave up and we ate our breakfast in silence. I tried to ease the tension. 'Who are the Cats playing on Saturday, Dad?' I asked, my voice sounding very light in the kitchen.

Dad looked at me and Jim startled, as if we'd woken him from a deep sleep. Dad was about to say something but Mum interrupted. 'Why don't you take the boys with you on Saturday? They'd like to see the Cats play,' she said.

Dad let out a deep breath. 'Yeah, good idea. Why don't you boys come with me on Saturday.'

'Great!' I blurted with relief. Jim looked at me, smiled, and turned to Mum who nodded encouragingly. Then his eyes moved to Dad who, with an effort, gave him a wink.

On Saturday, Dad sat Jim on one side of him and me on the other, on the fold-up coach's bench inside the fence. Each time the Cats kicked a goal Dad leapt to his feet and thumped the air. At the half-time siren, with the Cats in front, he put Jim on his shoulders and marched him towards the change rooms. I realise now that it was an unmistakeable gesture to the town. I trotted along behind.

Dad took his place at the front of the players and started his usual half-time speech. The players sat in front of the metal lockers around the walls, the smell of liniment making my nose itch and my eyes water. Dad's voice bounced off the brick walls and reverberated in my ears. 'Fred needs to be at centre half-forward and Bob needs to be on the back flank,' Dad said. 'And Jones you need to be right out front and centre, don't hide back in the wings. Show 'em your glory. That's what we need to win.' Amongst all those men, Jim looked small and skinny and uncertain, and yet he would outshine every one of them in the years to come – he would show them his glory.

Thinking back, it must have been then that Dad decided to take a stand. Repulsed by the Mrs Shields of the world, he dared to confront the beliefs and prejudices of many in the community. He clearly believed he had done nothing wrong and had the courage to defend what he thought to be right. Looking back now, it seems a simpler time, but even so, I wonder if Dad could have known what Jim had lost. And yet still he felt vindicated.

CHAPTER 7

JEN HAD TO GO BACK to Melbourne to work, but I'd cleared my calendar so I could spend time with Mum and get Dad's affairs sorted out once and for all.

But even the death of a husband wasn't going to change Mum's routine. It was the day to 'do her messages' as she called the shopping, and so we had to go to the supermarket, despite the fact that the fridge was still groaning with food from the wake and from thoughtful neighbours. After a painful hour of fetching and crossing things off the list, we piled everything into the car and drove home. We pulled up in the driveway of Mum's house, and the roar of cicadas battered my eardrums as we hauled the shopping to the front door and through into the kitchen. Mum shooed me out so she could put everything away in peace. I went straight to the study to ring my secretary, Georgia. I wanted to clear my mind of the burden of work before I spoke with my mother. I knew this next conversation was not going to be easy. But as I issued instructions and discussed plans, for the first time in days I felt that life was manageable rather than chaotic and suffocating.

After the call, I returned to the kitchen, but Mum met me at the door and handed me a plate of lamingtons, ushering me into the lounge like a child. *Why weren't we going to sit in the kitchen as we always did,* I wondered – the lounge was for visitors and formal occasions.

Mum pulled back the lace curtains and the sun streamed in, warming the room.

'Did you make your calls?' she asked.

'All done,' I said, my voice too sharp.

She nodded, taking her cue. She looked calm and composed.

The formality of the lounge suddenly seemed appropriate and I knew why we were here. 'I've been through most of Dad's papers,' I said as I sat down. 'I guess you know what's in the will.'

Mum nodded. There was a short silence while she sipped her tea, sitting more erect than usual, which unsettled me. She looked as though she had been waiting for this conversation for a very long time.

I took a deep breath, but when I didn't speak she nodded, as if to say, 'Go on.'

'There were birth certificates and other papers,' I continued, then stopped. There was no delicate way of phrasing this, no words I could hide behind. I listened to the racket of the cicadas.

'Why did you tell us Jim's parents were dead?' I asked.

She didn't speak for a moment, and I saw how thin she'd become since Dad's illness and death. She looked gaunt now, her face pale, her eyes sad and distant. But I saw the strength in her stillness and sensed that the wall of secrecy had crumbled with Dad's death and she no longer saw this conversation as a threat.

'Harry said we should tell you both the truth, but Dad thought you were too young. It was better you didn't know.'

Her words seemed rehearsed, or at the very least carefully chosen. I wondered how often she had repeated them, trying to convince herself of their merit.

'Dad was wrong.' How could any reasonable person tell a child his mother is dead, knowing it is not the case? They robbed Jim of everything important to a child. They took his family, home and security from him – deprived him of his roots. Didn't they realise they would be found out, that Jim would eventually discover the deception?

'When you were older Jim was focussed on his training, you on your studies, and it didn't seem to be relevant any more. The moment had passed. It was Dad's idea. He thought we could improve his situation.'

'Improve his situation?!'

'Dad said we could give him a good future.'

Why was she blaming Dad? Why make Dad the scapegoat? Was she unable to admit her part in it? Was she trying to absolve herself of guilt? Why not take responsibility for her part in Jim's forced adoption?

'Was Jim being mistreated, malnourished?'

'I believe so.'

'Why did you go along with the lie?'

She hesitated. 'Everyone thought it was for the best. Robert, you have to remember it was government policy back then.'

I had the feeling even she didn't believe what she was saying.

'It is not easy to go against what everyone believes,' she muttered. She examined the back of her hand, stretching her fingers out wide as one might to better admire a ring. I realised then that the excuses had run out. She had thought she was prepared, but it was not as easy as she had imagined. She fiddled with her wedding ring, moving it back and forth, back and forth. Finally, she sighed and looked up, her eyes sunken with grief.

'We got it wrong.' She hesitated. 'I've never said this before.' She sounded surprised. 'We should never have done it. We should never have taken Jim.' Her voice strengthened.

'The papers said that Jim's parents were neglectful. So were both his parents alive when he was taken?'

'They were alive. I don't know if they still are.'

'Then why did you lie to us? Why did you need to say they were dead? If the parents were neglectful, all you had to say was that Jim was better off with us.'

Mum was watching me with something akin to dismay, as though I really hadn't grasped what she was saying at all.

'Tell me you wanted to protect Jim, shelter him from suffering at the hands of neglectful parents. Tell me you thought he was being abused. Tell me anything, but not this, Mum.'

Something like anger flashed across her face.

'This is not about you!' she shouted. Then in a lower voice she went on, 'You're not listening. I am asking to be forgiven. I held that boy in my arms, knowing that somewhere there was a woman who knew that smell as intimately as her own, who knew every inch of that boy and whose arms were empty. This had nothing to do with Jack's grand ideals, or assimilation or the promise of a better life. I knew better than most how they lived – the bonds, the stories, the knowledge of the land. He had a home and a place in the world, and we tore him away from it. Every time I held him in my arms I remembered what we'd done.

'I am not talking about the lying or what you or anyone else knew or didn't know, Robert. I am talking about what we did to Jim. About what we took from him. About having stolen him. It's not about you.'

I did not miss the echo of Jenny's words in Mum's. Was I not allowed to be hurt and angry and upset? Did I not live that life too?

'All these years and now you say you regret having taken Jim?'

'We made excuses – we told ourselves he – all black kids for that matter – were being abused and mistreated. That's what gave us permission to take them. Everyone thought the same back then.'

'And he won a gold medal to prove it.'

'That bloody gold medal,' she spat. 'I've come to hate it.' She looked at her hands to calm herself and focus. 'Dad told Jim that the gold would prove something, show everyone. I guess he meant it would rescue him from the squalor of being Aboriginal.' Her tone was biting.

'Well, it did for a while.' I spoke without thinking, and just for a moment, I thought Mum might punch me.

'Robert! Clearly you understand nothing. Telling Jim he had to win a gold medal was the same as saying he wasn't any good without it, that he had to prove himself.'

'But that's not what Dad meant,' I said.

'Wasn't it? It's what Jim heard.'

'You don't know that.'

'Did you see Jim bow his head when he won that gold medal? Kids get their values from their parents, whether they accept or reject them. Those values are the foundation upon which they build their identity. We robbed Jim of that.'

'No, surely you gave Jim as much as he lost. You gave him an identity. You became his parents.'

'We gave him a white identity, not his own identity. We imposed an identity on him.'

'Well, is that so wrong?'

'It told him that what he knew and believed before he came to us was worthless. In truth, we didn't – and we still don't – trust Aboriginal people. We looked down on them. That's why we took Jim. We didn't think his parents or his family had anything valuable to give him. And we thought – we think – we are better, more advanced than them. And then we wonder why they drink.'

'But that's crap. He won a gold medal. He won respect. If you hadn't taken him, he might never have got an education, never even had a decent roof over his head, let alone won that medal.'

'It's true, he may have had a different education.'

'But not an education that would have led to a job.' I could hardly believe what I was saying, but I felt a rising panic, as if I had to hold something at bay. I felt the underpinnings of my life starting to shift.

'Dad wanted him to become white. Don't you remember he used to joke around and tell Jim he'd be "good as gold"? The poor kid already was, but Dad wanted him to excel, to live in a white world and be respected as a white man.'

'Well, what's wrong with wanting your kids to be successful?'

'There's nothing wrong with wanting children to be successful but it is not the same thing. Anyway, it was not about Jim at all. It was about your father proving himself to the world, proving that he was right – about all kinds of things. But towards the end of his life, he seemed to lose a lot of confidence. Something in him crumpled and he started to withdraw into himself. Little things started to preoccupy him. He wouldn't even let me in. In his last months we drifted further and further apart and I could see he questioned more and more our decision to take Jim.'

I recalled my last visit before Dad died. His ailing heart was still beating, but he was nothing more than a hump under the blankets. I lowered myself onto the edge of his bed in that musty room. The curtains were closed, keeping out the light and warmth. I listened to his breath, and watched his thin chest raise and fall. 'Jim?' he croaked. His eyelids rose slowly.

'It's me, Dad.'

I am not sure if he saw me so much as felt me there. With an effort he lifted his hand onto mine – it weighed almost nothing, a collection of twigs held together with dry skin. But there was still warmth in it. I left my hand beneath his and let a tear run unchecked down my face, for Dad, for the boys who had been Jim and me. Once again I was a child and my father was now my stick-thin comforter. His breathing slipped back to its unconscious rhythm beneath my hand, and I wished that Jim was here now, to share this.

'Don't blame Jim for any of this, Robert. Blame me, blame Dad. We got it wrong. He was doomed from the start. We stripped him of any chance he had of any sense of himself, any sense of hope.'

'That's rubbish. You raised him. You did a good job. You gave him everything a kid could dream of. He won an Olympic gold medal!' It was starting to sound thin even to me.

'No. We got it wrong. Deep down I know that we did it because we believed we knew what was better for Jim than his own parents. It is a guilt I will take to my grave.'

The knowledge that Jim had been taken from his parents changed everything. I could hardly bear to think that Dad had so callously crushed Jim's spirit by telling him his mother was dead, and that Mum had condoned it. Nothing was as I'd once thought; my entire past had been blown apart and was settling into new patterns. I found myself recalling events with new and painful insight.

I remembered one night, probably in Jim's first year with us, when we were in our room and I was helping him with his arithmetic.

'I don't understand,' Jim said.

'I'll show you.'

'I've never done it before.'

'What, no sums?'

'Not like this.'

'So before you came to live with us, what did you learn?'

'It was different.'

'What do you mean?'

'At night, we didn't do homework. We listened to stories. The old people talked to us, showed us how to do stuff.'

Even at that tender age I could feel that Jim was being deliberately vague; I could see he was unsure, worried that I might think less of him and his people, might even, like so many in the town, think they were uneducated, inferior or primitive.

I looked at him earnestly, not wanting to lose one of the rare opportunities to hear him speak about himself and his past.

'What sort of stuff did they teach you?' I asked.

Jim paused a moment to gauge my sincerity. Satisfied, he finally said, 'They showed me the land, and how to know it.'

I didn't understand what he meant; it sounded weird to me, but also powerful and intense. There was warmth in his voice as he described his people, and for the first time I became aware of his longing. I swallowed my pride and listened to him. It was one of the first times I heard the tension leave his voice. He spoke quietly, but his world appeared before me effortlessly – faces, smells, sounds, sights, stories.

I was too young to really understand the profound differences between our cultures. I didn't realise then that, to him, the land was much more than a possession, but I sensed it, and felt obscurely ashamed of our way of dealing with the country. We went back to the sums, he attentive and me distracted, feeling awkwardly burdened by this new knowledge. Strangely, I never noticed that he did not speak directly about his parents.

The next day, I walked past our room and saw him sitting quietly at the end of his bed, staring out the open window. He looked calm, as though he was in a trance.

'What's up?'

He glanced at me absently and shook his head.

In public Jim was guarded and nervous. In the street he began to walk one step behind me. The boys our age pretended not to notice him outside the school, watching the adults' reactions to measure what they were allowed to say. If Mum or Dad were not with us, everyone ignored him at first. It was as if Jim wasn't there. But it wasn't long before they began with their taunts – calling him 'that coon' while the adults turned their backs or watched with raised eyebrows to see what would happen. I'd see Jim's shoulders slump and his face drop.

Baiting Jim became a sport. 'You ain't even got parents,' Craig would jeer, or one of his mates, or even some of the other kids, goading each other to see who could upset him more. I didn't join in their jibes. I longed to be one of the gang, even though deep down I knew they were wrong. I also knew that defending Jim against them would mark me as an outsider, like him.

At dinner one night, a few years after Jim came to us, I had a brief glimmer of hope that Craig and his mates might get what was coming to them and be forced to leave Jim alone.

'Did you see Craig and Ken and Bob sitting outside Mr Paterson's office today?' Jim said. His face was carefully neutral.

'No, why?' I asked.

'They say they're the firebugs.'

Mum turned towards Dad, her eyes saying something I couldn't understand. 'I don't think that can be true,' she said, frowning. Even though she knew Jim was being bullied she always wanted to see the good in people.

'I wouldn't put anything past Craig Woodhead,' Dad said, 'if he's anything like his old man.'

'So which fires?' I said, thrilled at the idea Craig and his mates might be in serious trouble.

'The fires outside Shep last summer,' Jim said.

I imagined Craig's eager face as he flicked matches into dry grass, his mates egging him on. I could believe it. Jim's face was expressionless but I knew he must have been thinking similar thoughts to mine: that they'd be punished and locked up or kept under observation for the rest of our childhoods. But if they were punished, we never heard about it, and their behaviour towards Jim didn't change in the slightest.

To be honest, part of me resented Jim for putting me in this position, and there were times when I would have given almost anything to be part of the group, but I never really gave up on Jim completely. Sometimes I used to sneak out of the house just so I could be rid of him and play with the boys like I used to, on my own terms.

One afternoon after school, I was hanging around at the park with some boys from my class when Jim approached. I moved away to give the impression of hostility between us. As I did, I saw the shock and hurt on his face, then he turned and walked slowly back the way he'd come. I felt bad, but also relieved that he'd gone.

That night at dinner he asked me sadly, 'Why did you ignore me today, Robert?'

Dad stopped eating and looked up at both of us.

I drove my knife into my steak and kidney pie, looked Jim in the eye and said defiantly, 'I don't know what you're talking about.'

After dinner, Dad came into my room. 'Put your book down,' he ordered. 'And do it now.' I felt his eyes boring into me.

'Jim told me what happened today and I am ashamed of you,' he said. 'Put yourself in his shoes!'

'But what about me?' I said. 'The boys won't play with me if I always bring Jim along. I don't have any friends because of him. I'm not part of the group. And it's all Jim's fault.'

'Don't follow the pack; remember whose son you are,' he said, slamming the door.

I knew Dad was right but it didn't make me feel any better. I wanted to resent Jim for dobbing on me and for an hour after dinner I ignored him when he came into the room, but when I looked up eventually and saw him sitting on the side of his bed, resting his elbows on the window sill, I felt, for the briefest moment, a flush of empathy.

Where was he right then? He certainly wasn't in the room with me. I knew he had forgotten my existence, and in a rare moment of awareness that faded as quickly as it had come, my anger dissolved. How many times had I ignored him, watched while he was harassed and scorned? And he had said nothing. It was amazing he had not spoken sooner.

But what was important was that he didn't want to be here. He was staring at the sky, looking at that other life he had left behind, and I wondered how much he had already forgotten. Could he still see his mother's face? Could he still hear his father's voice? I wondered for the first time whether he had brothers or sisters that I didn't know about, or friends, favourite haunts and pastimes. I didn't say anything, just left him gazing out the window and returned to my book, but I could no longer be angry with him for getting me into trouble. Perhaps it was the first time I realised that his problems were bigger than mine.

CHAPTER 7

CHAPTER 8

THROUGHOUT OUR YEARS IN PRIMARY school, Dad's efforts to have Jim accepted into the community met with opposition. People didn't say what they felt, but in the street and on Sundays, when we'd picnic at the park, they would watch us, and when we caught them looking, they'd give us a polite smile. I remember Kelly Lanson's mum's mouth tightening up like a wrung cloth whenever Jim came near. Every day there was some little thing – a sidelong look, a chin held slightly too high – to remind our family of people's disdain. At school, black children were tolerated at primary level, considered capable of playing word games, learning to read and paint, but many thought high school was beyond them. Craig had given Jim hell with his taunts of 'black bastard', and now Mrs Shields was refusing to talk to Mum. Our lives seemed so much more complicated.

In the year Jim and I turned eleven, Dad decided to enrol us at Shepparton High School. Most kids would be going on to Shepparton Tech, or one of the two Catholic schools, but Shep High was the best secondary school in the area and Dad thought Jim should have the same opportunities in life as I did. He knew the school board might cause problems for an Aboriginal boy, so he was ready to fight.

One winter's day I'd failed a maths test and had stayed back after school to do revision with Mr Rag. As I traipsed home it was overcast; raindrops clung to leaves and dripped from eaves, splashing into shallow puddles on the footpath. I came inside and sat sodden at the table where Mum was serving tea.

Dad was at the head of the table, as usual, but his expression was ablaze. I looked over at Jim who shrugged almost imperceptibly.

Dinner was a silent affair. After we had eaten, Mum reached over and gently pressed Dad's arm. Dad rubbed at his chin with the back of his hand.

'There's no way blokes like Ernie Woodhead and Steve Chapple are going to let a black kid into their school. And they practically control the school board. I just don't . . .' He trailed off and sat back in his chair, pushing his near empty plate away irritably. *So*, I thought, *Craig is exactly like his father, Ernie.*

By now it was dark outside and I could hear the sound of a lone car driving along Morrell Street. Dad gazed off into the distance. He was staring at the still life painting on the mustard wall opposite, but he wasn't seeing it.

Jim was looking at his fingernails.

Mum stood up and took some plates to the kitchen. Dad pushed back his chair, collecting a couple of glasses from the table and followed her. When he got to the doorway, he turned to us and said, 'Grab your books – homework.' Then he shut the door.

I went to the bedroom for our schoolbooks. As I came back to the dining room Jim glanced up at me. He looked exhausted. I sat down, waiting for him to speak, but he didn't say anything, just grabbed his exercise book and we worked silently for several minutes.

'Have you looked at number three?' I asked.

I could hear Mum and Dad's hushed voices behind the closed kitchen door.

'Yes,' I heard Dad say.

Jim sat quietly, his head tilted towards the voices, his pen poised.

'Jim?'

He lifted his hand to his mouth, running his thumb along his top lip.

'Nuh,' he said.

'Don't worry,' I heard Mum say through the closed door.

'It won't be easy,' Dad said. From past experience I knew Dad was prepared to weather social isolation for what he believed. Three years ago, he had copped a lot of flak from the club and its supporters when he sacked Bill Murray, the captain of the Cats. They had failed to make the finals in the previous three years, but the following year, with Mick Dodds as captain, they had taken the premiership.

'What time's your meeting?' I heard Mum ask.

'Eight-thirty. I'd better go,' Dad said, after a long pause.

Water swished in the sink.

'Leave it. I'll do the rest.'

We waited until we heard the sound of the engine then walked into the kitchen and saw Mum standing at the sink wearing her yellow rubber gloves. She seemed deep in thought.

'Will everything be okay?' Jim asked.

'Oh!' she snapped upright, jerking back from the sink as she dropped the plate into the water. 'You gave me a fright,' she said. She turned her back on us again. 'Dad will sort it out.'

Jim and I looked at each other.

A couple of hours later, I heard the ute door slam and Dad's footsteps in the hallway. Mum's door creaked as she came out of their bedroom. I glanced over at Jim, we hopped out of bed, and crept to the end of the hall.

'What happened?' Mum asked carefully, tying the cord of her pink dressing gown. Dad stood with both hands gripping the back of his favourite chair, facing her.

'Well?' Mum prodded.

'It's not good,' Dad said.

'Go on.'

'They won't accept Jim's enrolment,' Dad said, his voice crackling with anger. I swallowed.

'What did they say?'

Dad couldn't speak. He just shook his head.

'Mrs Shields?'

Dad nodded.

Mum sighed. 'What about the others?'

'Ernie agreed with her of course and bloody Steven joined in the chorus, babbling on about how they've got their own way of learning on the other side of the river.'

'And Jim Halloran?' Mum asked, hopefully.

'Just sat there; didn't say a word.'

'This town . . .' Mum said.

The silence lengthened between them. Finally, Mum said, 'What about the tech school?'

'You've got to be joking!' The veins on Dad's temples bulged. 'No, he has to go to a good school.'

'Well, maybe he could meet some other Aboriginal kids and learn something about—'

'He's got nothing to learn there!' Dad yelled, smacking his hand onto the dining-room table. 'It's a good white school or nothing.'

At the time I wondered if Dad believed that he could make Jim white. Now I think that the idea of Jim going to a school where he might meet other Aboriginal kids threatened Dad. He worried it might jeopardise his authority and undermine his relationship with Jim. That's what Dad was afraid of: that if Jim spent time with black kids, he would become like them, he would share their language and culture and all Dad's 'good work' would be undone. It might prove Mrs Shields and his detractors right.

'Then maybe you should go and talk to Mr Ryan,' I heard Mum say.

'What for?'

'He's the principal!'

'What good will that do?'

Mum looked at Dad for a long moment. 'It's not like you to give up without a fight, Jack.'

If Dad replied, I didn't hear it.

I looked across at Jim, and jerked my head towards our room. There was a large graze on the side of his face where he'd fallen off his bike the week before when we'd raced down the rocky track by the river. He had got up after that, blood beading his skin, and laughed. We had kept riding for hours. Now the wound had formed a series of small scabs along his face from his cheekbone to his chin. His eyes seemed like twin wells in his face. I realised as I looked at him that he had been my brother for four years but I had no idea what he really felt about anything.

It never occurred to me to think what this conversation meant to Jim. I assumed he would be angry at the town for not letting him into the school, or perhaps he'd be angry at Mum for suggesting he go to a tech school, when I was going to the high school. It took me thirty years of absence from Jim, my father's death and a handwritten piece of paper to see what was there to be seen: Jim must have been reeling from Dad's refusal to allow him to be black. But to me he appeared eternally stoic, always pushing on and accepting more and more of what the world dished out to him. I sensed that one day he might break, hard, and I wondered when that would be.

We crept back to the bedroom, closed the door and jumped into bed.

Jim's voice, when he spoke, was soft. 'He shouldn't have said that.' He paused, as though it were self-evident what he was referring to, and I racked my brain, searching through what Dad had said. Was it the 'white school or nothing' comment?

Jim looked at me and could see I had no idea. He put me out of my misery. 'He said, I've got nothing to learn there. He doesn't know anything.' He spat the last word like a curse and I felt momentarily afraid.

'My uncle,' Jim said bitterly, 'he wasn't like Jack.' I was a little shocked to hear him say 'Jack' and not 'Dad'. 'He didn't say much but when he spoke it made you stand up and listen. He was big, but never bad, you know?'

I waited for him to go on, unsure of what was to come.

'He was a good man. He'd sit with me at night and tell me the stories of creation, the stories about our ancestors. He spoke, but he listened too.'

I was intrigued. I had never heard Jim speak so much about his family. Sometimes he spoke of the land, or of missing things, but he had never spoken so freely of people. I seized the opportunity.

'But what about your dad? What was he like?'

Jim shrugged. 'I didn't see him much. He was away in the army a lot. I didn't know him very well. I remember he was tall and strong. He was half white, but he understood me.'

Startled, I asked, 'Your dad was half white?'

He looked at me in surprise, aware of how little I really understood our world. He didn't bother pursuing it. I sensed he was scrabbling through his memories, hunting for his parents, his cousins, the life he had led before, on the land.

I felt suddenly exhausted with all of this. I just wanted to be able to go to high school, to not have to worry about this kid, my brother. I wanted things to be normal and easy and I wondered if maybe Mrs Shields wasn't right.

The following morning at breakfast, Mum suggested Dad drive us to school. She said he had a meeting with the headmaster of the high school, and I realised he must have decided to take Mum's advice. Dad didn't speak, just downed his coffee, slammed the kitchen door and sat in the car tooting the horn. It was clear that having to beg Mr Ryan to allow Jim to attend high school made Dad fume.

Mum took us out to the car, adjusting our collars and checking our lunches as she did every morning.

'Good luck,' she said to Dad through the car window, as we were about to leave. Then she kissed Jim and me goodbye.

The morning sun was bright as we turned into O'Brien Street, bleaching the already faded bitumen to grey. We drove past weather-beaten houses with cracked tiles, separated by worn wooden fences. Dad didn't speak.

Jim and I sighed with relief when he pulled up at our school, thanked him and shot out of the car. Before class Jim and I kicked the football end to end. Craig, Ken and their mates refused to join in but some of the other kids did. Jim pretended he was a rover and would duck and weave in and around the other players, handballing the footy to one of them who would then pass the ball back to Jim when he emerged from the pack. He was quick and none of us could keep up with him. The teachers knew he was good and at parent–teacher nights they'd told Mum and Dad.

At lunchtime Jim and I were eating our Vegemite sandwiches in the school quadrangle when we saw Craig and his mates sauntering towards us. Jim stiffened beside me then turned his head in the direction of the oval and pretended to ignore them. Craig, Ken and a few of the other boys formed a circle around us. Jim, his view of the oval now obscured by bodies, looked at the ground instead. Behind the wall of boys, I could see the firm, blue shoes of Mrs Axen striding across the quadrangle towards us.

I motioned to Craig with my head. 'Look behind you,' I said, as casually as I could.

He turned to see Mrs Axen bearing down on him, stole a quick glance at me and then jerked his chin at the others. As he walked off he raised his middle finger.

'You'll keep,' he said.

'Yeah,' Ken said and turned to follow Craig.

After school, we walked home along the river then doubled back to our place. Jim was silent. He kicked the ground and whipped the long grass with a stick.

'Forget about Craig,' I said, trying to reassure him.

'It's not Craig,' he mumbled.

'What is it then?'

Jim didn't say anything, he just scuffed his feet as he walked. I looked out across the water, which was grey and brown with the reflected light.

'Dad'll fix it,' I said. 'You'll see.'

I didn't know how Dad would protect us, even if he did get us into Shepparton High.

Later that afternoon, Jim and I were playing cricket in the garden when Dad came home. We heard the car door slam, and Jim stopped for a moment, ball in hand, looking towards the drive. I knew what was swirling around in his head. I stood there in front of the garbage bin that we used as a wicket, holding the bat and waiting for him to say something, but he didn't say a word.

'Let's go inside,' I said, breaking the silence.

We went in together.

'What did he say?' I heard Mum ask as we opened the kitchen door.

Jim and I stopped just inside the door. I felt the soft vibration of the fridge through my shoes. At Dad's feet, Titan was dancing on his hind legs, delirious with joy.

'He said Jim is welcome.'

'And . . .?'

'And if bigots like Mrs Shields don't like it, they can enrol their kids elsewhere.'

Mum's shoulders fell as she breathed a sigh of relief; she looked at Dad and smiled. I watched Jim's face and saw it change like lightning – fear, resolve, anxiety, sadness – and then, just as quickly, the torment dropped from his face as he looked at Dad.

He knew Dad was bloody-minded and I could see him decide that it was futile arguing with him.

Despite the good news, Dad's body was rigid, and his eyes were settled firmly on the three ceramic birds on the kitchen wall.

He rubbed his face with his hand.

'What's wrong?' Mum asked. 'You should be happy.'

'Nothing.'

'Jack?'

Dad's forehead was lined, his eyes seemed flooded in the light and I thought of the dark pools along the path by the river when it rained. He looked up at Mum and raised an eyebrow as if to say, 'You know why.'

'Nothing's changed at the Club,' Mum said, with more hope than relief.

'That's only because I've coached them to three finals.'

I walked from the kitchen, their voices loud in my ears, and stood in front of the window in the lounge. Outside, leaves scattered like brown paper and I stood there looking as the breeze blew them into the gutter.

'One battle at a time, Jack, one at a time,' I heard Mum say.

I couldn't help thinking sadly of Jim's love for that uncle whom he trusted and knew so intimately and wondering if he wished he could return to people who loved him for himself.

CHAPTER 9

AFTER THE DRAMA OF GETTING Jim into Shepparton High, first term there passed without much incident, well, for me. Jim was still picked on every day, but Craig was less sure of himself in the new school, and that seemed to give Jim and me a reprieve.

One quiet Sunday morning during the last weeks of term two we rose early for a sports meet. I had slept badly, and would have given a lot to roll over and sleep for another couple of hours. There was no traffic on the road, and only the occasional crow from the neighbour's chook pen or a carolling magpie disturbed the silence.

As was her Sunday habit, Mum was in bed with her tea and marmalade toast beside her before going to church; it was her own 'day of rest', as she liked to say, and she was reading Patrick White's *Voss*. I stumbled past her room in my tracksuit and runners and sat in the hammock on the verandah, the fresh morning air raising goose bumps. Waiting for Dad and Jim, I thought about my lack of preparation – if only I had spent more time on my run-throughs and sprints. My mouth went dry as I rehearsed the race. Since we had started high school, Jim had begun to take his running more seriously. He had won almost every running event there was at our school sports carnival. Our sports coach, Mr Sandilands, had decided to enter us into the interschool competition, 'Just to see what you can do.' I knew that my role was a supporting one, but no one said that. I was to run alongside Jim and had trained with him in the few weeks leading up to the meet.

We marched along the highway towards the oval and Dad put his arm around Jim while I followed behind. A single car passed.

Dad turned. 'Come on, slow-coach,' he called.

'I'm coming,' I said, wondering how I could get my legs to work at all.

We came to the footy oval, which had been painted with white lines to mark out the track. Coloured flags fluttered in the wind and school kids huddled together in groups surrounded by parents, listening to teachers giving instructions.

'Over here,' Mr Sandilands called to us. 'Jim, Rob, you're in red,' he said pointing in the direction of the weather-beaten wooden stand with a huge red banner slung across its front.

As we walked around the edge of the oval towards our group we passed the green team. Four thin strips of shade from the goal posts streaked the grass behind them. The fresh air bit at my cheeks and I had to squint in the bright morning sun. Craig, Ken and some of the other boys watched as we walked past, tipping their heads derisively.

When we reached the stand, we dropped our things on the ground and I took off my tracksuit.

'Pass my runners,' Jim said, as he sat on the large tarpaulin beside Peter, a runner from St Colman's College, who was busy stretching. Chris Callahan, the captain of the St Colman's team and winner of four medals last year, sat next to the two of them, his legs out straight, gripping his toes and lowering his forehead to his knees. I could see Craig on the other side of the track jumping high and wrapping his hands around his knees to loosen up, with Ken beside him, copying.

Mr Sandilands came over with a clipboard.

'You two guys are in the 200 yard sprint.'

Jim looked at me and smiled.

'Good luck,' Mr Sandilands said, walking off.

As we headed towards the starting line, I felt the nervous grinding in my guts begin. 'Stay calm,' I told myself, 'it's just a race.' I watched as Jim did a few short sharp sprints to warm up. He was taller than me and loved athletics, football, and cricket. He had always met with opposition, groups of boys or their fathers, throwing insults like you throw stones across a pond, because you can. Once, when Jim and I tried out for the school football team, a group of girls taunted him from the sidelines, shouting, 'Coons can't play.' I think it hurt him more when the girls did it, but he was determined to prove them wrong. Darting in and out of the pack, he scooped up the ball and kicked towards goal. He tried to look nonchalant when he walked back to the centre but his eyes were seeking them on the sidelines. The girls didn't say anything else, just melted away, mouthing their disgust as they left.

Jim's training regime was much more stringent than mine, but I thought I had done enough to get a place. Chris Callahan was my only other threat. My strategy was to go hard out of the blocks, work the bend and accelerate to the finish line.

When the race was called, Dad walked us to the starting line. Jim started shaking his arms and bouncing from one foot to the other to limber up, Chris jumped up and down on the spot with his knees hitting his chest and Craig jogged on the spot. The whistle sounded and we took our places at the starting line amongst the other competitors. Jim was in the inside lane, Chris was next to him, then me, Ken and Peter with Craig on the outside.

'I will count to three, wait for one second then fire my gun,' the starter said, looking at us.

Jim bent down with one knee touching the ground, the other outstretched behind him, his hands evenly spaced on the ground before him. Craig glanced at Jim and copied him. I got into position, looked down the track and waited for the sound of the gun. Chris was the last to settle.

'One, two—' he said.

Craig lurched forward.

'False start,' the starter shouted.

'Relax, Rob, relax,' I kept telling myself. 'Stay calm, it's only a race.'

Dad was on the edge of the track, not twenty yards away. His line of sight went straight beyond me to Jim. He had his fists clenched three inches from his body in that way he had when everything hinged on this moment. I had seen him like that in the coach's box more times than I could count. I glanced around and saw people lined up beside him along the track, parents, teachers, kids, all of whom had heard about that black kid living with the Pickering family who could run like greased lightning. More than anything then I wanted Jim to win.

I stood at the starting line, my head light with adrenaline.

'Let's try again,' the starter said.

'One, two, three—'

On the shot, Jim leapt from the blocks, his stride long and graceful. Within seconds, he was four yards in front of Chris. 'Just keep moving,' I told myself. Chris was coming second but slipping behind with each step, and Peter and I were close on his tail. The others followed. At the eighty-yard mark, I noticed Jim start to pick up his pace. Fifty yards before the finish line, he released the throttle. With each stride, he moved further and further ahead.

My legs felt heavy and tight, I had lost my rhythm and there was a twinge in my left hamstring. I realised there was no catching Jim, but I was determined to get a place.

Ten yards before Jim got to the finish line he slowed down. I felt my chest begin to rattle, a torrent of adrenaline engulfed me and I lunged forward to come third behind Jim and Chris. Peter, Craig and Ken, who had fallen further behind, followed.

Despite Jim finishing slowly, he still won in record time, breaking the record by nearly two seconds. A crowd of about a dozen or so enthusiastic teammates and three or four teachers from school ran towards him. I watched them jumping up and down, shouting with excitement and slapping him on the back. Mr Sandilands beamed with approval.

'Brilliant,' Dad yelled, grinning at Jim, who stood in the middle of the circle aware that something special had happened. He was smiling but he seemed unsure of himself. Suddenly, Jim had become the golden boy. Even though he looked bewildered by the unexpected attention, I could see he was thrilled. Dad bent down to pick up Jim's tracksuit and handed it to him.

'Put this on,' he said with a big smile. 'Keep yourself warm.'

The wind bit at my skin as I stood at the finish line to catch my breath. Dad put his arm around Jim and walked him to the tarpaulin.

'Take the weight off your feet,' I heard Dad say. Jim lay down, trying to catch his breath, and Dad stood over him proudly.

'Good finish,' Chris said to me as I walked from the finish line towards Jim. I nodded, my breath still coming raggedly.

'Great race, Jim,' I said, collapsing on the ground.

I felt the cold against my cheeks as I spoke. Jim, lying on his back, propped himself up on his elbows and gave me a brilliant grin. He said nothing and I had the feeling the magnitude of what had just happened had not yet sunk in.

'Stand back, give him room,' Dad said, looking at me and Chris.

I felt my legs stiffening in the cold air as I lay there looking up, listening to Dad. The coloured flags flickered irritably.

At the end of the day I wandered back to where Mr Sandilands was talking to Dad and Jim. 'I'll give you a lift,' he said to Dad, pointing to a blue Holden sedan parked behind the stand.

As we drove out of the grounds, shadows had started to creep over the oval.

'How often do you train?' he said, looking at Jim in his rear-vision mirror.

'As often as I can.'

Mr Sandilands glanced sideways at Dad. 'He's the best I've seen.'
We pulled up out the front of our place.

'He needs a coach,' Mr Sandilands said to Dad, as he opened the car door. Dad glanced back at him and nodded, but nothing more was said.

I followed Dad and Jim up the path and into the kitchen.

'How did you go?' Mum said, looking at Jim.

'He was fantastic!' Dad said. 'Killed 'em.'

'And what about you?' she said, turning to me.

'Third.'

'I'm proud of both of you,' Mum said with a broad smile. 'Tea won't be long – jump in the bath Robbie, then you, Jim.'

When I got out of the bath, I could hear Mum and Dad in the lounge talking. I wrapped the towel around my waist and went to the kitchen to grab a biscuit. Dad was sitting in his favourite chair and Mum was sitting opposite.

'Mr Sandilands said Jim's the best he's seen. He could go places, but he needs a trainer.'

'What do you think?' Mum said, looking at Dad.

'I think the kid could be a champion,' Dad said emphatically.

'He's blessed,' Mum said with a broad smile. 'What do you think we should do?'

'We need to find a proper trainer.'

'Can we afford it?'

'We'll have to.'

I looked to Mum when he said that, aware that something was passing between them that I didn't understand. She nodded slightly, and seemed for a moment filled with awkward love. When I looked back to Dad, his face was impassive once more.

CHAPTER 10

THE FIRST MONDAY OF THE June holidays, Jim and I were clambering over the riverbank at the back of our house when Dad called to us. 'Come up quickly,' he said. 'Mr Sandilands is here.'

Jim and I looked at each other.

'What does he want?' Jim said.

'Hurry up,' Dad yelled.

As we scrambled up the rough uneven bank, I looked up and saw Dad, Mr Sandilands and another person peering down at us. When we reached the top Dad and Mr Sandilands were talking quietly and only the intermittent call of a bird sounded in the afternoon air. The other man was not listening to the conversation, he was staring at Jim intently. Jim hunched his shoulders slightly and looked at his feet.

'Hi Jim,' Mr Sandilands said with a smile. 'This is Mr Douglas Lawrence. He's done a lot of work with athletes in Victoria.'

'Hello,' Jim said, turning to face him. Mr Lawrence was about six foot three and looked like he spent hours training every day. His body was wiry and strong, without an ounce of fat, and his face was weather-beaten.

'I rang Mr Lawrence the other day after your run at the sports carnival. He was pretty impressed. As we all were,' Mr Sandilands said, laughing a little as though he'd made a joke.

Mr Lawrence stepped forward and shook Jim's hand firmly. 'My job is to train athletes. You seem to have quite a talent,' he said.

My eye drifted to our bedroom window where I knew Jim's trophies from various school sports competitions were lined up on his dresser. They had been hard won: not physically but socially. I hadn't thought much about them until now. My sideboard was stacked with Superman comics. I knew Jim was fast, that he could beat me hands down in a race from the shops or around the oval, but now I caught a glimpse of just how good they all thought Jim really was.

Mr Lawrence was still talking. 'I can help you train, improve your times, maybe even aim for a few championships. If you want.' This last part was meant in jest but no one laughed.

Dad, standing opposite us, was nodding at Jim. He looked like a kid himself, his eyes bright, barely able to contain his excitement. I could see that he was desperate to speak, to crash headlong into the conversation, but he held himself back.

I looked at Jim, at his body. I had always taken him for granted before, not caring about the shape or height of him, not noticing the differences between us, although I knew he could always reach the taller branches in the trees, always swim faster and run faster and kick straighter, the way his arm seemed to become part of the bat when we played cricket or the fluidity of his throw when we skimmed rocks across the river. But now I really saw him. The tendons and muscles of his forearm were unobtrusive but perfectly formed. His quads and calves looked sinewy and strong. He was, simply, a born athlete. Jim smiled at Dad and turned towards Mr Sandilands, nodding his assent.

'Let's start now,' Dad said. He had a broad smile on his face.

Jim deserved it; I knew that. All those hours he'd spent running. I wondered suddenly where he ran to when he took off after school, because he never said. A part of me wanted to hug him, even tell him how happy I was for him. But at the same time, I couldn't bear it. I didn't know why. I knew how much he and Dad wanted this. I knew it would achieve exactly what they hoped – prove to everyone how great Jim was. But I felt an uncertain grief, something like premature mourning for someone I had lost. Jim had a destiny. I had a stack of comic books the size of my head. Suddenly those comic books reminded me of loneliness. I didn't want to be without him.

I turned abruptly and went up to the house, feeling suddenly bereft. I shoved the comics onto the floor, leaving them bent and disarrayed, even though it pained me. I lay back on my bed, taking the pillow out from under my head and flinging it to the other side of the room. I could hear Dad's voice across the yard. He wasn't saying much but when he spoke it made you stand up and listen. I had a sudden image of him right here at my side, tucking me up tight in bed, my feet yards away from the end of the bed, even though I was laid out flat. And his voice, woody and fresh, recounting triumphs of sporting heroes, Phar Lap, last season's footy premiership. I don't know why but I suddenly remembered a camping trip: the roar of wind and the bitterly cold bite of night air forcing itself through the tent flaps. My father, his thick solid frame towering over me, clutched the tent pole and ropes, hanging on for dear life, strong and silent in the wind; then my father's hand gripping mine as I quaked in my sleeping bag. Maybe I was four at the time. I felt utter trust, despite the tempest howling around us.

Then the memory was gone, leaving a great gaping hole in my stomach while the sound of laughter echoed through the open window from the yard.

That man, my father, was not the father I would soon know. He would no longer be relaxed and easy. He would lose interest in slow meandering conversations with Harry on our verandah over a beer about the Cold War or the merits of free trade. He would no longer discuss the few successes of the Carlton Football Club, their need for a new coach, the failure of their full forward to kick goals. There would be no more talk of the next fishing trip, let alone planning and taking one. He would become obsessed with making something of Jim, as if he had to prove something to someone, or perhaps to himself.

The September school holidays rolled in. I did not know it, but this would be one of the last holidays that Jim and I would truly be able to spend together freely. Tom, a kid who lived nearby, tagged along after us as we climbed a small rise near the river, wind rushing through the long grass and lifting the worn hessian sacks we'd taken from Dad's shed. The sun had gone, and a late afternoon downpour had thickened the mud underfoot.

Tom went first, throwing the sack onto the wet grass in front of him and, with a running jump, launching himself feet first down the wet slope. Jim and I watched as he rocketed over the slippery grass, legs out in front of him and one hand lassoing the air. We laughed as we watched him, the sound echoing giddily across the paddocks around us.

When Tom was halfway down Jim took off. He too took a running start, his hands gripping the front of the sack, and launched himself head first after Tom. He hurtled down the slope along the path Tom had flattened moments before. The wind was battering me as I waited my turn. In the distance I saw figures moving with purpose beneath the trees. There were three of them, heading our way.

In the last six months Craig had made a point of picking on Jim while we ate our lunch in the schoolyard. Bullying Jim after school outside Benny's shop was routine, and on weekends when Dad wasn't there, Craig and his thugs would interrupt Jim's training. As Jim's chief tormentor, Craig became increasingly popular with the other kids, and this notoriety only sharpened his malice and made him bolder in his attacks.

The air at the top of the rise felt suddenly cold on my skin as I looked down at Craig and his mates walking towards us. They were probably about fifty yards away by the time I had figured out for sure who they were, though the flutter in my guts recognised them well before. Every muscle in my body clenched. Jim and Tom were at the bottom of the slope, waiting for me. I rocketed down, slipping and sliding, straining my neck to see what was happening.

At the bottom, I skidded to an abrupt halt in a puddle of water and struggled to my feet. Craig, Ken and Bob stood about ten feet from Jim. 'Well, look who we have here,' Craig said in a slow purposeful drawl, eyeing Jim up and down. I felt myself step away from them.

Jim moved towards me and Tom, hovering nervously. We stood there eyeing each other off, until Craig slowly reached down, delved his stubby fingers into the sludge at his feet, and gradually rolled it into a ball. I don't know why none of us moved. We had plenty of time to reach for our own balls of mud, but we were spellbound, caught in the moment like a rabbit in a spotlight. He looked first at Ken and then at Bob, weighing the mud in his hands as he did so. And then he turned like lightning and flung the ball as hard as he could at Jim. Suddenly Ken was scrabbling at the ground, then Bob. I was shouting, Jim had a handful of mud and was hurling it at his tormentors. It splattered on Ken's forehead. I must have laughed because Ken snatched some mud from the ground and threw it, hitting me on the shoulder and shocking me out of my passivity. Without thinking, I scooped up a handful of mud and pelted Bob. Jim did the same with Craig. Before I knew it, the mud fight was in full swing, gravelly mud balls being flung about madly. Everyone was filthy, especially pipsqueak Bob, whose windcheater was thick with sludge, and the others seemed to be flagging as we moved apart instinctively. Then Craig grabbed a fistful of mud and rolled it into a slimy ball, juggling it from hand to hand. For a long moment he looked at Jim and I could see his mind ticking over. Instead of throwing it, he smeared the mud over his own already filthy face.

'Guess who I am?' he said with a sneer.

None of us said a word. I felt like someone had tightened a rope around my guts.

Jim looked back boldly at Craig. His arms were hanging at his sides but his hands were balled into fists.

'Let's go,' I said, worried that if this went on any further we might get our teeth knocked out.

But Jim just stood there looking at Craig. He seemed nailed to the ground. It hadn't occurred to him that we could get hurt.

'Come on, we'll be late for dinner,' I said, pulling at his sleeve.

Finally, after almost a minute of solid staring, Jim turned. We walked away silently but I could see he was burning inside. When we reached the fence, more than forty yards away, Craig yelled, 'Nigger!'

Every muscle in me tightened, but Jim didn't look back. Tom and I kept pace with him as we headed for home. I looked at Jim, his face now set.

'Let it go,' I said.

'I'll get him,' Jim snarled.

'Forget it,' Tom replied. 'He's a stupid prick.'

'No way,' Jim said. 'I'll teach them. I'll do something they could never do. You wait.'

It was a cool Tuesday night in spring. Jim had come home late yet again from training with Mr Lawrence. Dad had interrogated him at the table about their drills and he had come to our room determined and agitated, intent on writing out his times and exercises, his arm action and all kinds of other details. He had not been spending much time with Dad, but the two of them seemed to be growing more and more alike as time passed. I barely recognised this new Jim anymore. I wondered if he still thought about his family, his uncle or the life he'd had before coming to live with us. I had thought a lot about his uncle and his half-white father in the time since our conversation. The world was far more complex and puzzling than I had understood it to be.

I cleared my throat to get Jim's attention but he didn't notice. I said his name. Nothing. I got up and stood next to him. 'Jim!' I said loudly.

He jumped. 'No need to shout.'

'I wanted to ask you something. About your uncle.'

Jim looked confused for a moment, then he looked away. 'I don't want to talk about my uncle,' he said. He gathered his notes together roughly and went out into the lounge where Dad was listening to the radio.

The next morning when I got up Dad was planting seedlings in the back garden. I walked out onto the verandah, sat on the hammock and watched.

'Grab that trowel and give me a hand,' he called, pointing to the wheelbarrow and a pile of garden tools next to him. 'But put your old boots on first.'

I pulled on my boots and walked slowly towards him, head down, dragging my feet.

'You okay? Why so sluggish?' he said, looking at me carefully.

'I'm fine,' I said, although I felt listless

'Dig a row of small holes, six inches apart,' he said, lifting his head to smile at me.

I squatted down next to Dad on the damp grass and began to dig.

'Perfect,' he said. 'Don't listen to what anyone says – great time of year to plant seedlings.'

It was a cold overcast morning. Dad lifted the seedlings from the tray, gently teasing out the roots with his fingers as I had watched him do so many times before. He dropped the seedlings in the small holes I'd dug, his hands moving efficiently along each row and firming the soil around their fragile stems.

'Your grandpa loved nature,' Dad said.

'The bush do you mean?'

'Nah, real nature. Flowers, vegetables, fruit trees . . . When I was a boy he encouraged me to take an interest – it was the best thing I ever did. It's a shame you don't remember him.'

As Dad spoke my mind had drifted to Mrs Shields and Jim's enrolment at Shep High. Was it a good thing or not?

'Do you reckon this is the best place for Jim?' I said, without thinking.

'What?' he looked at me sharply, dropping one of the seedlings on the tray.

'I was just wondering if you've ever had second thoughts about adopting Jim,' I murmured. Was it jealousy that prompted me? Was I betraying my father by siding with Mrs Shields? My voice trembled.

'No.'

I continued to dig.

'Jim's family,' he said. He lifted the tray, turned it upside down and tapped it a few times on the wheelbarrow to dislodge the seedlings and plonked them into the holes. 'This is his home.'

'Sorry, Dad,' I said.

'Don't *ever* mention that again.'

We planted the rest of the seedlings in silence.

For the rest of the holidays I felt as if Dad couldn't stand the sight of me. He was civil in front of Jim and Mum, but if I came into the room when he was alone he made no effort to speak to me. I avoided him and was grateful when the school holidays finally came to an end – the first time I'd ever been happy to go back to school.

On the first day back Jim and I had stopped at Benny's shop on the way home from school. Craig and his friends suddenly appeared and I wondered if they had been following us.

Craig stepped closer and rubbed his hands over his cheeks. 'Guess who?' he snickered.

I forced myself to stay calm. Deep breath, Robert. Count to ten.

'I got an idea,' Craig said. 'Do ya wanna know what it is?'

I looked at him but didn't reply.

Craig leaned against the verandah post near Jim, and though Jim tensed, he stayed exactly where he was.

Craig gazed at Jim calmly. 'Australia is for white people,' he said, as he took a step closer to Jim. 'So why don't you get the fuck out of my sight?'

My throat tightened, and my muscles felt suddenly weak.

'Leave us alone, Craig,' I said, looking straight at him, trying to hide my fear. 'We're not hurting anyone.'

Craig wheeled about to face me, thrusting his face into mine, his breath stale and his voice low and bitter.

'Yes, you are,' he said, '*You* are hurting me a lot. Fuckin' hell, when I see you with him, it hurts me,' he said, poking me in the chest. 'It hurts all decent white people.'

Suddenly I was shoved from behind. I turned. Jim had been pushed into me and the three boys were jeering and heckling. I steadied Jim, who had clenched his fists and raised them defensively. Someone started clapping and the jeering grew louder as hands shoved us back and forth. All of a sudden Jim spun round and with lightning speed kicked Craig hard in the balls. 'Fuck you!' he roared. Craig's eyes popped, he clutched his crotch and tumbled to the ground screaming, tears of pain leaking from his eyes as he curled into the foetal position. Ken and Bob were too stunned to move. Jim stood over Craig, then caught my eye. I think we were both shocked.

Craig was crying now in a high-pitched wail. A thread of saliva dribbled from the corner of his mouth leaving a small, dark, wet patch on the ground.

I looked at the other boys. Bob had taken a step back and was shifting uncertainly from side to side. Ken seemed paralysed.

The fear I had felt earlier suddenly evaporated. Jim had stood up to the bastard. I looked at him with astonishment. He was angry – his jaw moved as he ground his teeth, his eyes were wild and his hands were balled into fists. I felt a rush of respect for him.

'Who's next?' I said.

Ken bent down and helped Craig to his feet, still clutching his battered balls. Bob grabbed his other arm and the three skulked off, muttering. Without saying a word, Jim and I turned and walked home.

When we got inside Jim and I were buoyant, and not even Dad's fury about us fighting could dampen my spirits. I looked at Dad and smiled, a move that seemed to shock him rather than annoy him. Maybe Dad was right – maybe Jim did belong here. He had stood up to the biggest bully in town, which somehow made me feel invincible. He could stay: he belonged here. His uncle, the town, his changing personality, nothing mattered. He was one of us. Family.

Jim turned fourteen when we were three-quarters of the way through third form. That morning Mum and Dad came into our room while we were still in bed and cried, 'Happy birthday!' Titan pushed past them and jumped onto the bed, intent on licking Jim's face while Mum, still in her dressing gown, wrapped Jim in a big bear hug. 'Titan, get out of it,' she laughed, and handed Jim his present. 'Get down you silly dog. Let Jim open his presents.' She seemed barely able to contain herself. Dad thrust his present forward, wrapped in red, white and blue paper.

It was the eighth of September; the anniversary of the day the Cats had won their third consecutive premiership. It was not really Jim's birthday, but it was the date my father had chosen for him because, like many Aboriginal people, Jim's date of birth had not been recorded.

A broad smile spread across Jim's face.

'Happy birthday Jim,' Dad said, ruffling his hair. 'Make good use of them.'

'Thank you,' Jim said, looking up at the two of them.

He tore the wrapping paper off and lifted the lid from a box. As he did so, the Adidas logo appeared beneath a tear in the paper. Reverently, he pulled out a white shoe with red trim and steel spikes.

'Running spikes,' he whispered.

'You deserve it,' Dad said. 'Make good use of them.'

'Thank you, I—'

'Open the other present,' Mum said, interrupting him.

Jim tugged off the green ribbon and paper and pulled out a book with a picture on the front of Jesse Owens running in the 1936 Olympics. Jim's eyes seemed to grow bigger.

'Jesse Owens, fantastic—'

'You'll enjoy the read.' Dad grinned, happy to see Jim's ecstatic expression.

I looked at Jim's prized black and white poster of Jesse Owens, breasting the tape to win gold at the 1936 Olympics. Jim loved Owens because he was a black American track and field athlete who had taken the world by storm by being a four-time gold medallist at the 1936 Olympic games in Berlin, in a politically and racially charged atmosphere that I imagine Jim felt he could understand. Jim had told me how Owens had won numerous track and field events at high school and university, breaking world records, how at the 1935 Big Ten Championships he competed in forty-two events, winning them all. When he looked at that poster, I know Jim saw himself one day.

Mr Lawrence officially trained Jim twice a week every week of the year without fail, but it was more like four or five times and his presence in our house seemed almost constant. I would not have been surprised if he had a key.

While I was wrapped up in school life, Jim was even more intently focussed on his training. Each school morning Mr Lawrence came to our house at five-thirty to pick up Jim. 'No pain, no gain,' I'd hear him shout. 'That's it, keep it up,' he'd continue as Jim did sprints up and down the path at the back of the house leading down to the river or along our quiet street. Then they would leave in Mr Lawrence's green Holden to work out at the park. 'We start with a six-lap warm-up, followed by exercises, stretches, sprints and a two-lap warm down,' he told Dad one night at dinner.

'Good on ya, Doug,' Dad said. 'And you, too, Jim.'

On Saturdays Jim and Dad went with Mr Lawrence to competitions, most of them in Shepparton – the council had installed a running track at Central Park a decade or so earlier. Mr Lawrence liked Jim to train on grass. 'When you dig your spikes into the turf, it builds power in your legs,' he claimed. The park was edged with trees, and nearby irrigation channels kept the grass alive over summer.

Mr Lawrence soon started to race Jim against older boys. 'It's the only way your times will improve,' I heard him say. His approach worked. Within a month Jim did a personal best at the Victorian zone titles. Sometimes he seemed to glide to the finish line, his body lean and supple, every fibre stretching elegantly towards the ribbon.

Since he had been training with Mr Lawrence, Jim had become more distant, not wanting to fish in the river on weekends or talk about the latest goings on with Craig and his idiot mates at school. Each night after school I saw him running around the park with a tyre tied to his waist or doing short intense track sessions to improve his aerobic fitness. It seemed that everything he did, everything he ate, even how long he slept was part of his program, and he followed it to the letter. Jim seemed content in his private world of ambition and personal bests. His tunnel vision was focussed on winning gold at the 1972 Olympics, and he seemed to see very little else. He passed all his subjects at school, but he never had enough time to really excel.

Races came and went and Jim seemed to win everything effortlessly. He began to miss school and I sometimes read about him in the paper before I saw him at home again with his collection of medals from regional championships.

When he came home he was exhausted and the gulf between us widened. We were part-time room mates who were friendly but distant; conversation and brotherhood were things of the past. I began to feel that our time as brothers was already over.

As it became clear that Jim was a remarkable athlete, the girls at school started taking notice of him. Vivian, a girl in our class, was infatuated with him. One lunchtime, Jim and I were sitting outside eating our sandwiches. Vivian and one of her girlfriends came and sat near us, eating their lunch, giggling, and every now and then looking over at Jim. I watched their mouths as they talked, and the way Vivian's blue eyes would slide towards Jim and settle on him when she thought he wasn't looking. Sunlight dazzled her face and I noticed the curve of her small breasts under her jumper. Her fringe reminded me of Mum's favourite actress, Audrey Hepburn, in *My Fair Lady*. Jim seemed as oblivious of Vivian as Vivian was of me, but I couldn't help feeling that Jim's life was somehow more real than my own. None of the girls seemed to notice me.

CHAPTER 11

IF JIM'S SIGHTS WERE SET on the Olympics, I had my own more modest goals. In form four I had been selected to play Puck in the school play, *A Midsummer Night's Dream*. I had four months to prepare for the part, which meant I spent weekends rehearsing in the school hall with Miss Bristol, the drama teacher, and the other cast members. Shakespeare was difficult but I enjoyed the challenge and often stayed back after school in the corner of the library, hunched over my lines. I loved the part; Puck was so mischievous and carefree, so different from my own character and the character of anyone in my family. It was a relief to be playful, even if I was only acting. English literature, history and drama interested me far more than sport, and I moved into other friendships, absorbed in a passionate – if one-sided – affair with one of my best friends, Lin, a pretty dark-haired girl with freckles, a wide grin and a wicked sense of humour.

In early March 1967, Jim had started training for the Victorian State Championships and when race day came around in April I asked if I could tag along. Jim looked at me in surprise and then, abruptly, gave me a rough hug. His arms felt hard and strong around me. In the car on the drive there Dad and Jim ignored me, as usual, but at one stage Jim turned back to check on me, giving me a big smile.

It was about eleven in the morning and I was sitting in a huge stadium, purpose built to train Olympic athletes a decade or so before. I knew how much running in this stadium would mean to Jim. I watched the other competitors warm up before Jim's main race, the two hundred and twenty yards. Mr Lawrence led Jim through exercise drills, timed his short, sharp sprints and supervised his stretches.

When the race was called, Jim walked onto the track and jumped on the spot to limber up. At the sound of the whistle he took his place at the starting line, one knee almost touching the ground, the tips of his fingers braced in front of him. Dad and I were on the boundary, not thirty yards away. Dad didn't take his eyes off Jim.

The starter's pistol cracked, and Jim was the first out of the blocks. He strode forward, his movements smooth and graceful. Within seconds, he was a yard in front and led the field going into the straight. At about the halfway mark, Jim started to pick up pace and within seconds he was in full flight. With each stride he seemed to move further and further ahead of the pack. Dad began jumping up and down, shouting with excitement, 'You've got 'em. Go Jim!' Eight yards before the finish line Jim pulled away from his nearest rival and won in record time.

'Bloody fantastic,' Dad yelled, his face nearly purple. He picked up Jim's tracksuit top, jumped the fence and ran over to him. 'Keep warm,' he said with a huge grin, handing him the top. He put his arm around Jim and walked him to the canvas mat, and I watched as Jim collapsed on the mat trying to catch his breath and Dad kneeled down to rub Jim's calves.

I stood at the fence, gripping the wooden railing, splinters jabbing my palms. Others jumped the fence and ran to Jim too, milling around him, slapping him on the back. Looking at them then I wondered why Dad was so attentive, why he went with Jim some mornings when he trained with Mr Lawrence, why he took him to his sports meets each weekend and why he trained Jim each night after school. When Dad was on the bench with the Cats he was unwavering in his determination to take them to a flag. But with Jim I sensed it was more than merely winning.

I stooped under the rail and walked towards them. 'Well done,' I said to Jim. 'Great run – you ran a fantastic race.'

Mr Lawrence decided to rest Jim before his gruelling training regime for the Australian Track and Field. Jim had trained hard for the Victorian State Championships and Mr Lawrence said his body needed time to recover. Jim, although buoyed by his win and anxious to continue training, agreed to stop running for a few weeks, spend less time training and more time on the campaign for Aboriginal people to be counted in the census.

I'd been surprised when Jim met me in the hallway at school and asked if I wanted to have lunch with him. I was embarrassed because I'd agreed to meet Lin, but I hadn't mentioned her to anyone at home, not even Jim, so I stood Lin up and ate lunch with Jim. I noticed suddenly how much older he seemed than me.

'Rob, you know about this referendum.'

'Well, sort of . . .'

Jim began to explain to me, with furious passion, why the upcoming referendum was so important. It would mean Aboriginal people were counted in the census, instead of being ignored and treated like non-citizens, and it would allow the federal government to make laws for Aboriginal people, so that states like Western Australia and Queensland, or the Northern Territory, couldn't cheat Aboriginal people out of their rights and wages.

'Are you sure?' I said. 'What kind of rights?'

'Where d'you want me to start? There are laws that stop us marrying freely, or managing our own kids, or owning property, or being paid award wages, or even moving around freely. And none of the states let us drink alcohol.' I'd never heard him speak so passionately before. He had clearly been reading a lot about it, and talking with Jack about it any chance he got. I could hear my father's words as he spoke. 'People who don't know Aboriginal people have ideas about justice and what's right and wrong. They'll most likely vote yes. But others, like those in Mooroopna, who live near Aboriginal people, have ingrained prejudices – it's much harder to get them to change.'

I was impressed by Jim's knowledge and determination and baffled once more by the injustice that seemed to be so deeply rooted in our communities.

'I want to do something around town to support the referendum,' he said tentatively, 'and I wondered if you'd help.'

'Of course I will,' I said, as the lunch bell rang.

He stood up and clapped me on the back, as though he too saw himself as the older man, and said, 'Good on you, Rob. Knew I could count on you.'

I stayed back late for rehearsals and he was asleep when I got home. Then when I awoke he had already left for training. Once again, I felt a sharp, brief pang of loss. But we had to meet to plan our referendum campaign, so that week, and many days in the weeks thereafter, I spent time with Jim every day. Lin and I sat with him discussing what we could do to mobilise support in Mooroopna – that seemed hard enough, without tackling anything beyond the town.

The day of the referendum – 27 May 1967 – came around soon enough and ninety-one per cent of Australians voted in favour. Jim was right. The vote in rural communities was less than the national average. Jim, Lin and I had spent much of our time walking around town dropping leaflets in letter boxes, helping to organise meetings, talking up the merits and explaining to anybody and everybody why Aboriginal people should be treated the same way non-Aboriginal people were. After all, if black people were willing to fight and die for their country, it was only fair they were treated the same as everyone else. It was difficult for those people who had always treated blacks as inferior to change their attitudes, behaviour and sense of superiority and see them as equal. 'We Australians like to see ourselves as fair and equal,' we'd say, 'and if we really are, then we need to vote yes.'

We all thought things would change, that Mrs Shields would relent, and maybe even talk with Mum and Dad, that Mr Chapple's campaign of passive resistance to get Jim out of the school would end, and that kids at school would no longer call Jim a 'coon' or make 'Abo' jokes.

Despite the resounding yes vote, all our high hopes and Jim's jubilation, regrettably, not much changed. 'It's a start,' Jim said, but I could see his disappointment when he realised that things had altered very little. Somehow he seemed to take this, too, in his stride; perhaps the knowledge that Aboriginal peoples would, literally, be counted empowered him. He used these competing feelings, of empowerment and disappointment, to motivate himself further and I watched him return to his training with renewed energy, as though somehow he could make equality happen all on his own. Jim's sights turned back to winning gold.

Six months after Jim won the Victorian State Championships, I was in my room reading *Catcher in the Rye* one Saturday afternoon. I heard Dad's voice echoing along the corridor from the lounge. I got up from the bed and stood for a moment in front of the window, watching rain wash down the glass like the front of Mr Tippet's fish and chip shop, then I quietly opened our bedroom door.

Dad and Mr Lawrence were talking, and with the door open their voices were clear.

'How good is he?' I heard Dad ask.

'For a sixteen-year-old, there's none better,' Mr Lawrence said. 'He demolished them at the Victorian State Championships.'

I listened to the two men talk, watching the winter rain hitting the roof of Dad's shed.

'What's next?' Dad asked.

'Jim, how about the Australian Track and Field Championships?' Mr Lawrence said. 'And, if things go well, the 1970 Commonwealth Games?'

'I want to run in the Olympics,' Jim said.

It was not the first time I had heard him say that. The Olympics loomed for him like an inevitable final challenge.

'One hurdle at a time,' Mr Lawrence said. 'Let's see how you go in the Track and Field next year.'

I stood at the window in my room for a long time. The cloudy sky seemed to give off a grey light. After a while I lay on the bed.

'When are the Australian Championships?' Mum asked.

'Sydney, next year,' Mr Lawrence said.

'And the Commonwealth Games?' Mum asked.

'July 1970.'

'Jim, how does that sound?' I heard Dad ask.

I did not hear Jim respond but instead I heard Mr Lawrence say, 'Great, we start Monday.'

During our final year of high school I was utterly consumed with my studies and Lin, who I could now happily call my girlfriend. We spent our time learning mathematical formulas, reciting dates of historic events and comparing the merits of Orwell's *1984* with Huxley's *Brave New World*, and kissing each other as we listened to the Goons. Lin could imitate Bluebottle and Eccles to perfection, and I envied her talent for mimicry, which would have been a gift for any actor.

Mum had been saving for the trip to Sydney so all of us could go when Jim competed in the Australian Track and Field Championships. It meant that any treats were cancelled until the big trip.

There was nothing in Jim's life besides training for gold, and sometimes it seemed we all had to make sacrifices for his running career. I no longer recognised my brother, and when I tried to speak to him about it once he lashed out at me. 'It's all right for you! You don't have to prove a thing. It doesn't matter if you've got ambitions or not.'

I was taken aback. It was not so much what he said – I knew about his driving ambition – it was more the way he said it: the fire in his eyes and the fierce determination in his voice made me realise that it was more than gold he was after. There was a bitter edge to his words that I wanted to forget. Running for Jim wasn't just a sport; it was becoming his identity. When he ran, his anger propelled him forward and each time he stood on the podium with a medal around his neck, his face was fixed in a look of steely determination, until he smiled.

Four months before the Australian Track and Field Championships, Jim caught a virus, which developed into pneumonia. He had a temperature of a hundred and two, and lay tossing with fever, beginning to lose what little weight he had. He said his body felt like lead. Doctor Fischer ordered him to stay in bed, but within ten days he was back on the track. That Saturday I went with him and Dad to Olympic Park. Even though Jim was not one hundred per cent and the day was hot and humid, he qualified, running second to a competitor he had easily beaten in previous time trials.

Driving home from Melbourne in the late afternoon Jim said, 'I should have won.'

'Keep at it, your form will come back,' Dad said over the drone of the engine.

'Tomorrow we can go to the park,' I said. 'I can time you.'

At four the next afternoon, Jim and I had already been in the park for a couple of hours, with him practising his sprints, and me timing him. The sun was still high, but clouds were massing on the horizon. It was still, and apart from us there was only one other group of boys kicking a football on the other side of the oval.

'We should get going,' I said.

'One more lap,' Jim panted, his forehead covered with beads of perspiration.

'It's getting on,' I said, 'Mum's expecting us.'

By now it was four-thirty and the shadow of a summer storm started to creep over the oval. A breeze stirred the leaves in the eucalypts, muting the noise from the boys kicking the football for a moment.

'Just one,' Jim insisted.

'Promise? On the count of three then,' I said.

He sprinted across the track, legs pumping.

'Good time!' I said.

'Can we do it again tomorrow?' Jim said.

'Why not? What are holidays for?' I said, but my sarcasm was lost on him.

Australia Day, 26 January 1968 – the day of the zone titles, eight weeks before the Australian Championships. Jim was sitting at the table in his shorts, tracksuit top and runners, slowly spooning porridge as I stumbled into the kitchen. My eyes felt crusted. I sat opposite him with my back to the door. The sun streamed into the kitchen as I grabbed a piece of toast from the plate in front of me. I saw Jim roll his jaw, staring at the bowl of fruit on the table.

'What's wrong?' I asked.

'I should have done more track work,' he murmured.

'You did everything right,' I said. 'You couldn't have done more. Come on, Jim—'

'I'm not ready,' he said, refusing to look at me.

Just then Dad came through the kitchen door and lifted an apple from the fruit bowl, rubbed it against his thigh and strode to the wire door. 'C'mon, let's go,' he said.

Outside, it was a quiet Monday morning – no cars on the road, two little boys playing on the nature strip.

Dad reversed down the drive, Jim in the front seat, me in the back, turned into Watt Road and drove out onto the Midland Highway. That short drive seemed to take forever. Jim didn't speak, shifting restlessly in his seat as we drove past parched paddocks marked by rusty wire fences, dry water holes and weather-beaten houses with faded iron roofs. We turned onto the Goulburn Valley Highway, drove past the old milk bar with its broken side window and corroded down pipes and pulled up at Shepparton oval. The white lines on the oval had been freshened up, and coloured flags had been placed at the finish line.

We walked around the oval to the cluster of competitors.

'Good morning,' Mr Lawrence said cheerfully.

'Have we kept you?' Dad asked.

'Just got here.' He turned to Jim. 'G'day Jim,' he said. 'Warm-ups, son.'

Dad and I watched Jim follow Mr Lawrence and start to do short skips and sprints followed by stretches and jumpstarts.

When the race was called, Mr Lawrence walked him to the starting line. I saw Jim take off his tracksuit top, jump up and down on the spot then bounce from one foot to the other to loosen up.

'Crawley's the man to beat,' Mr Lawrence said as he walked towards us.

The gun cracked. The first one hundred yards Jim moved fast and was leading at the top of the straight. Then he seemed to stumble. Crawley passed him, then Norman. Somehow Jim managed to hold onto third place.

A group of people ran towards Crawley, slapping him on the back, punching the air and shouting. Jim stood alone at the finish line about ten yards from them with his hands on his knees, dragging breath into his lungs. A hot wind swirled dust into the air as Mr Lawrence, Dad and I jumped the fence and hurried towards him. Jim raised his head, his hollow cheeks rising and falling with each breath.

'Put this on,' Dad said, handing Jim his tracksuit.

'I don't know what happened, my legs were like lead,' Jim said.

'Forget it. We've got eight weeks to the Australian Championships,' Mr Lawrence said. 'You'll be back in form by then.'

Jim groaned.

CHAPTER 12

THE FOLLOWING SATURDAY I WAS sitting on the platform at Spencer Street station with Jim, Dad and Mr Lawrence. I knew Jim liked me to go with him, so even though it was my last year of school, I surrendered my day with Albert Camus to go to Melbourne to watch Jim compete. It was six in the evening and we were heading home.

Around us others milled, also waiting for the train back to Shepparton. Red rattlers whistled through the station not more than ten feet from where we sat, the grating of their iron wheels sending a shudder through me, their carriages leaving behind a gusty penetrating wind.

'Feel like a pie?' Jim stood before me, his shoulders blocking the late afternoon light.

'Nah, I'm not hungry yet. You've earned it, I haven't.'

'Train to Euroa now boarding,' shouted the stationmaster.

I watched as people clustered around the doors, jostling to grab a seat. It was like musical chairs. Within minutes, the train had gone, leaving us and a smitten young couple on the seat next to us at the station. Feeling bored, I meandered to the end of the platform and looked out over Spencer Street. In the dusk people went about their business. An elderly man stopped abruptly in the middle of the street to examine his shopping bag then walked on, others trudged up and down with blank faces.

The high-pitched sound of the stationmaster's whistle pierced my ears. I spun around and walked back towards the others. The young couple were still sitting on the bench near Dad, a few people were flicking through magazines at the newsagent and there was a huddle of people around the kiosk. When I looked for Jim he was still at the kiosk, where he'd been for at least ten minutes.

I watched as Jim stood patiently while the attendant avoided him and served everyone else, even those who were standing behind him.

'What's taking so long?' I asked, as I walked towards him.

'I think I'm next,' Jim said.

'You'll wait your bloody turn,' the man behind the counter said with a sneer of contempt. 'Be thankful I serve your type at all.'

His words seemed to echo through the station.

'My brother was next,' I said, trembling with anger.

'Huh,' he said, glancing at the woman next to me who was pretending not to notice a thing.

'But, he was here first,' I protested. I wanted to shake the woman almost as much as the man. Why wasn't she saying something?

No one else said a word. Some stood watching, others turned away, pretending they couldn't hear.

In Mooroopna everyone knew each other. I had come to tolerate, but not accept, their bigotry. But here, in Melbourne, no one knew us and I was shocked to see such prejudice. I don't know why but I hadn't considered that Melbourne, a large metropolis containing so many different people, would be racist, no better than small-town Mooroopna.

'What's going on here?' Dad was striding across the platform towards us. He stopped between me and Jim, his bulk pushing not only us aside, but a couple of customers as well. I noticed the woman edge away, eyes down.

The man behind the counter glanced at Dad, avoiding the angry glitter in his eyes. After a long moment he spoke, his voice meek but still gruff: 'I think this kid was next.'

'You're damn right, he was,' Dad said in a loud voice, swearing for once in public. He stood with arms folded firmly across his chest, as the man behind the counter looked down at Jim and said with a grunt, 'Whaddaya want?'

Arsehole, I thought to myself.

From the corner of my eye I saw Jim look at me. He paused, and I could see his mind ticking over, then, he turned back to the kiosk man and said, 'Pie and sauce, thanks,' each syllable clear and distinct.

None of us spoke on the train back to Shepparton. Dad was brooding and staring out the window, pretending he could see into the darkness beyond his own reflection in the glass. I sat silently next to the window, electricity running through my veins. I imagined myself knocking newspapers, lollies and cigarettes to the ground, overturning everything. I knew from the way Dad pressed his temple that he was probably thinking much the same thing. It was how he always got when the Cats were losing and he looked as if he were about to burst out of his skin and win the game himself. Next to me Jim massaged a shoulder.

The silence grew, and eventually Dad rallied and began to ask me about my studies – he genuinely seemed to know nothing about my life, judging from his questions. I had long ago steeled myself against my father's lack of interest in me – I knew that his investment in Jim was crucial to his view of the world and of himself, whereas I was a given. Perhaps I knew even then that Jim was a project and I was a son – Dad didn't have to prove a thing to me, and perhaps I didn't have to prove anything to him. I didn't know then how much it hurt, nor did I allow myself to feel that pain for a very long time.

Another long silence ensued, until Mr Lawrence broke it. 'You'll do well next week, Jim. I'm feeling pretty confident.'

Jim turned to him.

'Crawley's the man to beat,' Mr Lawrence said, 'and you're the man to do it.' He grinned, and Jim gave him a brief smile.

That week Jim trained harder than usual. Each morning before school he stood on the back verandah waiting for Mr Lawrence to pick him up for training. 'Harder. Harder,' I heard Mr Lawrence shout as Jim sprinted up and down the path at the back of the house. Then I would hear the car back down the drive as they drove to the park where Jim would do his warm-up laps, stretches, exercises and sprints. As I was leaving the house to go to school, Jim would only just be traipsing in, peeling his drenched singlet from his back and jumping under the shower.

Sunday 24 March 1968 – the Australian Track and Field Championships in Sydney. Jim flung back the hotel sheet and jumped out of bed. I rolled over and pulled the unfamiliar blankets to my shoulder. Light showed through a crack at the edge of the blind.

'What time is it?' I croaked, pulling the pillow over my head.

'Six-fifteen,' Jim said. He disappeared into the bathroom and I heard the sound of running water and Jim gargling. I dragged myself out of bed and pulled on my jeans and shirt.

Just then someone knocked on the door.

'Up yet?' I heard Mum say, as I went to open it. 'Come on, let's go down to breakfast.'

'Jim's still in the shower.'

'Well, don't be long,' Mum said. 'Dad's already down there waiting.'

Downstairs in the dining room we found cereal, jugs of milk and fruit juice, sliced bread, butter, and jam in tiny packets, and a bain marie full of scrambled eggs, sausages, bacon, mushrooms and tomatoes.

'We don't have much time,' Dad said, as we sat down. 'Mr Lawrence will be here soon.'

We ate hurriedly, Mum forcing food into Jim –a bowl of cereal, four sausages, five eggs and countless rashers of bacon. 'Robert, give him some of yours,' she said, taking two of the three rashers off my plate.

Before I had a chance to complain, Dad chimed in, 'The boy has to eat. Go and grab yourself some more.' I rolled my eyes and acquiesced, used to it by now.

'Excited, Jim?' I said when I returned.

'A bit nervous.'

'Let's go,' Dad said.

'But Dad, I haven't finished my breakfast.'

Dad looked at our plates. 'Get on with it then. We've got no time to waste.'

Mr Lawrence was waiting for us in the foyer, and outside it was a quiet Sunday morning – few cars on the road, two women with prams on the footpath talking animatedly.

Mr Lawrence drove us to Moore Park, with Jim in the front seat so they could talk. Dad sat behind him with Mum tucked in the middle. Dad spent the entire trip peering over Jim's shoulder, looking from him to Mr Lawrence, pushing Mum virtually into my lap. Mum didn't speak. I looked out the window at the houses, some weatherboard, others brick veneer, all on matchbox blocks. This was the first time our family had travelled interstate together, and it had been a long and tiring train trip. Mr Lawrence had decided to drive up so we'd have a car when we arrived.

When we approached the oval I could see the grass had been cut short and the white lines on the brown running track hugging the boundary had been freshly painted. We parked the car and walked along the boundary to the stand.

'The change rooms are over here,' Mr Lawrence said.

Mum, Dad and I walked up the steps of the stadium. It was half full. There must have been four hundred people sitting on their seats, eating, talking. We stopped about halfway up and Dad stood looking out over the oval. By the time we had settled ourselves, Jim and Mr Lawrence reappeared on the oval, walking briskly towards the warm-up track. Jim, now in his red tracksuit, went through his routine of short sprints, skips, run-throughs and stretches.

'Men's two hundred and twenty yards,' came over the PA system.

Mr Lawrence walked Jim to the starting line, waited while he stripped off his tracksuit, then stepped away as Jim began to jump up and down on the spot.

'That's Pender already in the blocks,' Dad said, looking through his binoculars even though the starting line was less than two hundred yards away.

Crawley, Jim and the other competitors settled into their starting positions. The gun cracked and Crawley was first out of the blocks, his long rhythmic strides keeping the other competitors at bay. As they turned into the straight Jim picked up pace, his face straining and the muscles in his quads working. Fifty yards before the finish, Jim was a stride behind Crawley, followed by Pender. Suddenly, in the last few yards, Jim accelerated and drew even with Crawley as they raced across the finish line.

'Who won?' Mum shouted, turning to Dad whose eyes were glued to the binoculars.

Dad shook his head uncertainly as the words, 'The referee has called for a photo,' came over the loudspeaker. Everybody in the stadium went quiet. Jim stood near the finish line with his hands on his knees, trying to catch his breath. I turned to Mum and for a second forgot to breathe. Dad never took his eyes off the officials' box.

Then over the loudspeaker I heard, 'Jim Pickering 22.7 seconds, Allan Crawley 22.8, Mel Pender 23.4 seconds.'

I turned to Dad who was punching the air and shouting, 'He won! He won!'

Mr Lawrence ran towards Jim and slapped him on the back, Dad, Mum and I were hurrying down the steps and nearly sprinting over the freshly painted track towards Jim. As we approached, Jim looked up and smiled, his chest still pumping.

'Oh Jim,' Mum said, tears filling her eyes.

'Well done, son.' Dad patted him on the back.

'Yeah, good on you, Jim,' I added awkwardly.

'We've got a few hours until the semi-final,' Mr Lawrence said. 'We need to work on those hamstrings.'

Mum, Dad and I went back to our seats in the stand, which was almost full now, with people standing, shouting and cheering as the athletes battled to gain a place in the final. Others sipped tea or coffee from their thermoses while waiting for the next heat. I left my parents and wandered aimlessly around the track until I heard the call for the men's two-hundred-yard semi-final over the loudspeaker. We watched the race anxiously but Jim won with a greater margin this time. It was another hour before the final and none of us found it easy to sit still.

When the final was eventually called, Jim came out of the tunnel first, accompanied by Mr Lawrence.

'He's drawn lane two,' Dad said looking through the binoculars.

I watched Jim warming up and stretching.

'Final call,' came over the loudspeaker.

Jim took off his tracksuit and stepped towards the starting line with the other competitors, breathing deeply to fill his lungs with oxygen.

The gun cracked, Norman sprang out of the blocks, Lewis had his head down, but within seconds, Jim was in full stride. As they turned into the straight Lewis, Norman and Jim were neck and neck, but thirty yards before the finish Jim's strides grew longer and he shot to the front. I heard Mum start yelling and the stadium roar as the runners crossed the finish line.

'Jim Pickering 20.4, Greg Lewis 20.9 and Peter Norman 21.5.'

'Edinburgh, here we come!' Dad said.

That night we stayed in Sydney to celebrate. Jim loved Chinese food so Dad took the five of us out for dinner at Jimmy Lee's restaurant. A group of people walking past our table noticed Jim and one said, 'Well done. We saw the race.' Another said, 'You're a champion, mate.'

Jim, a little embarrassed, politely thanked them but Dad couldn't help a small boast: 'That's my son.' The older man in the group looked at Dad and there was a short uneasy silence, then he turned to Jim and said, 'Keep up the good work.'

As they walked away the waiter brought a bottle of champagne and filled each person's glass, even though Jim and I were still underage.

'Well done,' Dad said, raising his glass.

'Hear, hear,' Mr Lawrence continued. 'You'll do well in Edinburgh, Jim.'

Jim took a sip, pulled a face and put his glass down quickly. I liked the taste – it was sweet and fruity – and after I'd finished mine, I surreptitiously swapped my glass with Jim's and finished his, too. The adults were so absorbed in reliving every moment of the day they didn't notice.

The following night we were sitting on the train from Sydney back to Benalla, where we'd left the car. Outside it was dark and the rattle of the wheels on the steel tracks was hypnotic. Jim was sitting opposite me, his head lolling against the window as he dozed. Mum was next to him, flicking through a magazine that she must have read cover to cover more than three times now, and beside me, Dad was reading the *Shepparton News*, leafing through the pages confidently, occasionally snapping the paper upright with a quick flick of his wrists then settling for a moment as his eyes skimmed the print. He must have brought the paper with him to read in his spare time – he was never a great reader – then he tensed, and I turned towards him. He was reading intently.

'Look at this,' he said, pointing to an article on page three. I looked over his shoulder and saw in bold print, 'GIRL ASSAULTED'. Mum dropped the magazine to her lap and sat waiting for Dad to read.

'Mooroopna: Fifteen-year-old Meredith Langdon was bashed yesterday on the way home from school. The girl, an Aboriginal, was snatched from the street, assaulted and left for dead.

'Police believe the three attackers dragged the girl into a car and drove her to the Goulburn River. There they assaulted her, leaving her battered and unconscious. She is in a critical but stable condition in the Goulburn Valley Base Hospital.'

'Oh dear God,' Mum said, colour draining from her face. 'That poor girl.'

Jim looked at me, his dark eyes troubled.

'Bastards,' I said, knowing that was what Jim was thinking. For once, neither Mum nor Dad said anything about my swearing.

'Meredith Langdon,' Dad said, exhaling slowly. 'That's Lily and Fred's girl – remember? Their son Wayne played for the All Blacks. They lived on the Flats, and Fred worked for Harry off and on, when he wasn't painting. Poor things.'

I recalled a tall lanky boy, round-faced, fast, who played at centre halfback, and his sister, thin and quiet, with a wild mass of hair pulled back into a ponytail. I also remembered Dad's many conversations with Harry about taking on more Aboriginal workers. Harry employed Aboriginal men on his building sites but he never met them after work to socialise.

'You boys need to get some sleep,' Mum said, her throat lumpy. 'It's been a big day.' I saw her give Dad a speaking look.

Jim's face was tight with rage. Perhaps old wounds were opening as he sat contemplating Meredith Langdon and what had happened to her.

I closed my eyes and listened to the complex rhythms of the wheels on the rails, but my thoughts kept returning to Meredith Langdon. Even the wheels seemed to repeat her name: *Meredith Langdon Meredith Langdon Meredith Langdon* . . . I used to see her occasionally meandering along O'Brien Street after school, crossing the river to Watt Road: her long thin legs bare and her hair escaping from its elastic band. That vision of her being snatched from the street, dragged into a car, bashed and left for dead, resounded in me again and again. Now, as I sat thinking, watching the moon cast a thin shroud of light through a mask of endless clouds, I began to think of those three men, and whether I knew them. I was sickened to think I might.

'Next stop Benalla,' the conductor announced. I looked at my watch to see it was seven in the morning. I had slept for six hours. Through crusty eyes I saw Mum leaning back on the seat, her magazine forgotten in her lap, Dad reaching for the suitcases on the rack above the seats, and Jim looking out the window. The stale smell of sleep filled the carriage. The arm rests were pockmarked with cigarette burns, the floor covered in unidentifiable stains. My first thought had been of Meredith Langdon. The embers of my childhood came flooding back – the fights with Craig and his mates, people turning their back on us in the park, the school council's attempts to stop Jim from enrolling at Shepparton High and Mrs Shields' endless snubs and insults. I had forgotten how hard those early years had been for me; they must have been far worse for Jim.

Back then, Jim and I knew not to wander down to the Flats to play with the Aboriginal children. They were different from us, Dad said. It wasn't safe, although he never explained why. He kept Jim so busy with football and then running that he didn't have time for much else. But I couldn't help wondering if Jim disobeyed Dad now and then – it would explain his long absences – but if he did, neither he nor any of the Aboriginal kids ever betrayed each other by so much as a glance. Sometimes he would say things quietly, as if in explanation, or perhaps to remind himself: 'They're Yorta Yorta,' he'd say. And round the time of the referendum he told me that Henry Penrith, the athlete, was Yorta Yorta and Woiworrung, and was trying to tell the government what Aboriginal people needed. I didn't take enough notice of how aware Jim was of the Aboriginal communities around us or even realise that he must have crossed the river to know as much as he did about the people and how they lived.

THE DAY AFTER JIM'S WIN, we were back at school. Everyone was discussing the attack and proposing suspects. 'Who cares?' Bob Birch muttered as we were heading back into class. 'She's only a bloody Abo.'

'Yeah,' echoed Ken, 'bloody Abo,' but to my surprise Craig elbowed them roughly out of the way and pushed past them. I was glad Jim was in a different class.

Dad got home later than usual that night, and I heard him talking to Mum in their room, his voice bitter. I couldn't make out everything they said, but I gathered Dad had been round to visit the Langdons, and I heard Mum cry out at something he said. I tiptoed down the hall and paused outside their door.

'No,' I heard Dad say wearily, 'they refuse. Fred doesn't trust the police. Reckons they've interfered with girls in the past, and worse.'

'Oh, that poor girl,' Mum said, her voice breaking. 'Those animals.'

'If I thought any of my team were involved, so help me . . .' I heard the sound of a fist thumping something.

'Perhaps it's for the best,' Mum said. 'It's a horrible ordeal for a girl, and she's been through enough already, poor thing.'

'It makes me sick to the stomach,' Dad said, and I heard the bed springs creak. Turning silently, I scooted up the hall in my socks and flung myself down at my desk.

'What's going on?' Jim said.

'Nothing,' I hissed. 'Ask me later,' and I buried myself in my books. Dad and Mum came out of their room and headed for the kitchen, still talking quietly, and when I heard the door shut firmly behind them I turned back to Jim.

'I'm not sure, but I think Meredith Langdon might have been – you know – raped.'

'What!' Jim looked as if he'd been punched.

'I might be wrong, but I think Dad went round to see her family. He's furious, and Mum's really upset.'

'Why . . .'

'I mean furious with whoever did it. Dad said something about them refusing to do something because they didn't trust the police. Maybe she's refusing to press charges . . .'

Jim snorted. 'That'd be right.'

'Why? What do you mean?'

'The cops wouldn't do a thing. Her old man's right – what's the point?' He held my gaze until I looked away, feeling ashamed and confused.

Meredith never came back to school. Her recovery was slow and painful, according to Mum, who visited the family now and then. The police made no progress, and after a while kids turned to other topics of conversation.

My matriculation studies came easily (except for maths) and, my main interest that term was playing Hamlet. The Langdon case receded further behind rehearsals and my increasingly serious feelings for Lin; just once the thought crossed my mind that Lin could have been the victim instead of Meredith, but it was too painful to contemplate, so I pushed the whole thing from my mind. These things happened, but not to girls like Lin, or so I believed then.

Under the sharp watchful eye of Miss Bristol, I spent many hours with Lin pacing out scenes, reciting lines, a change of intonation here, a groan or sigh there.

'Try to hear the natural speech rhythms in the lines,' Miss Bristol would call, her arm floating before her as if she were conducting an orchestra. Each night, over the next three months, I rehearsed my lines, until each syllable was perfect. I cut corners with my studies to practise.

'You've done enough rehearsing!' Dad would say. 'Acting is not a profession.' But no matter what he said or thought, this was my chance to take centre stage and I was going to grab it.

As opening night loomed, teachers assembled sets and students put the finishing touches to props. Mum, Lin's aunty Lorraine and Miss Bristol made our costumes, and we had our final fittings. I so wanted to please Miss Bristol; there seemed to be a lot at stake.

A week before opening night things got hectic. I cut class to study my lines, though I knew each and every one by heart. After school I would scrape together some homework before another five or six hours of rehearsals with the whole cast. It began to feel as though the separate moments, the broken fragments of memory and line, would finally coalesce into something much more than we'd ever imagined.

On the morning of my big night I woke with sweating palms and lay in bed rehearsing my lines. By afternoon my shoulders felt like lead. Mum insisted we leave home at five.

'Why so early?' Dad said, teasing her.

'Better than hanging around,' Mum said in a shaky voice.

'Relax, he'll be fine.'

'I can't.'

I was trembling but eager, adrenaline pumping through my veins.

That night the school hall was packed – every seat taken; students lined the walls, many sitting in the aisles, others standing at the back of the hall. Castle battlements had been painted on the backdrop, where King Hamlet's ghost would appear, and a small graveyard had been painted in one corner.

When the curtains rose I stepped into Hamlet's skin, and inhabited his tortured mind for the next two hours. Now there was no such thing as rhythm and intonation, there was no possibility of forgetting a line – they were all mine, and the meaning sprang from me effortlessly. The devious machinations of the world – its trickery, its deceit, its refusal to yield answers – seemed ready to crack open before me.

We were performing an abridged version of the play, but by the end of it I was exhausted, until the crowd burst into applause. I walked back on stage holding Lin's hand in mine as we bowed, extending my arm to the audience. *Sir Lawrence Olivier eat your heart out*, I thought to myself. The wall of noise from the audience was deafening. I felt an overwhelming sense of pride – three standing ovations!

After the performance, I sat in the change rooms with other members of the cast. I was on top of the world, feeling both content and invincible. Then Mum, Dad and Jim came backstage.

'Well done,' Mum said with a huge smile on her face as she walked through the door. 'I'm so proud of you.' She hugged me and kissed my cheek.

'Fantastic,' Jim said. 'Amazing. I had no idea . . .'

I looked at Dad. He smiled, but there was a hesitancy, and by the time the 'Well done!' had left his lips I knew I'd lost him.

That night I lay in bed, tossing and turning, binding myself in my bedclothes. My cheeks were burning. I felt hollow, dispirited. I knew that Dad was unimpressed even though I could not say how I knew. I just *knew*. Once again, I hadn't lived up to his expectations, whatever the hell they were. I wanted to get up, go into their bedroom and scream at him. But I didn't, I just lay there with my throat throbbing, thinking, 'I hate you.' I had wanted Dad to burst through the door and cry, 'That's my son.'

Finally I gave up on trying to sleep, got up and walked to the window. Dad's 'Well done' played over and over in my mind. I remembered his excitement at Jim's time trials. In a moment of clarity I thought that perhaps theatre just wasn't his thing, and it had nothing to do with whether or not I lived up to his expectations. Unlike football, athletics and the Cats, theatre left him cold.

I stood there silently at the window and exhaled slowly. My throat seemed to loosen a little as I stared at the blue-grey night. Dad was just Dad. The slowness of his smile, so like my own, was not from distaste or a lack of interest, it was awkwardness, uncertainty in an unfamiliar world. He couldn't barrack in a theatre. He couldn't raise hell at half time if the kid didn't play right. I rested my head against the cold pane and thought, *So this is what they mean by growing up.*

The following morning, I was back at school, bleary eyed and weak limbed. It was a warm day and instead of playing football with Jim and the other kids in class I was sitting in the quadrangle reading *Brave New World*. Miss Bristol came over to me. 'Great job,' she said. 'You should be proud of yourself.'

'Thank you.'

She smiled warmly at me and in an uncharacteristically familiar gesture she ruffled my hair. 'You did a really fine job,' she said again, 'you should be proud.' I smiled to myself through the glint of sunlight on my eyelashes as she walked away. But there was sadness there too. Not just because of Dad's indifference to my acting, but because in a few short months the cocoon would be broken and I would suddenly be cast into another world, bigger and stranger than anything I had known thus far.

I noticed in that year, perhaps more than ever before, how different Jim and I were: Jim was obsessed by his diet and training and driven by his determination to make a name in the athletics world; I was fixated on my studies. I barely saw him and, when I did, we were teenagers in men's bodies, sitting on the edge of a bench or a desk, talking or silent, but always unable to articulate the things that had grown between us.

Jim was preoccupied with training for the Commonwealth Games, and seemed more and more silent and turned in on himself. When he got back from winning gold at the Australian Championships, he wrote '16 July 1970 Edinburgh' in big black letters on a strip of paper and stuck it to his Jesse Owens poster. To him, John Maynard Keynes and *Brave New World* were background noise; he preferred to train after school rather than study, even though he was bright enough to pass without much effort.

We completed the syllabus a few weeks before the exams and I spent my study leave in the school library wading through past exam papers, writing essays, haunted by words, numbers and dates. Every moment of my waking hours was spent on preparing for those final exams. When the results came, followed by the university offer, I knew I had achieved that one silent goal I had held against my chest all those years: to leave.

Lin was my only regret: she had chosen to study nursing at the Mooroopna Hospital, and nothing I could say would persuade her to transfer to Melbourne. Cost and family ties made it impossible. For once her bright eyes were solemn, and her wide mouth trembled as she raked her hands through her hair. We both cried, and made wild promises, but perhaps she knew it was over, although I still hoped we could hold onto each other despite the distance opening up between our new lives. That wide generous mouth and strong slender body had been both the symbol and source of such love and such pleasure that I couldn't imagine life without her. I closed my eyes for a long moment and held the picture of her in my mind, hoping to inscribe it deep in my memory.

At Melbourne University I studied law. Demonstrations against the Vietnam War, student drama and the challenges of my first-year law subjects absorbed all the time I had when I wasn't pining for Lin. If I thought about Meredith Langdon, it was only in passing, to wonder if she'd recovered, and whether or not anyone had yet been charged with her assault. It seemed to be old news. I saw little of Jim, although Mum kept me up to date with his news. He'd passed his matric, but I knew it was a mere hiccup in his training schedule.

In October, after nearly a year of grieving for Lin, I met Jenny who, at that time, had joined the debating society. We spent many hours, lustful and serene, at the Botanic Gardens or playing pool at Johnny's Green Room, or drinking too much coffee and red wine and going to as much theatre as we could.

Both of us became increasingly immersed in student politics. Political activity on campus had been brewing in the sixties, with Aboriginal protest movements, women's liberation groups and protests against the Vietnam War boiling over in the early seventies. Dr Jim Cairns, a Labor parliamentarian, asked people to occupy the streets of Melbourne in silent protest against Australia's involvement in the Vietnam War. He hoped to bring the city to a standstill to influence public debate and national policy. Tony Blundell, a new friend, set up a stand outside the student union, handed out brochures, anti-war posters and badges and spruiked the cause to anyone who would listen. At his suggestion, Jenny and I set up what we jokingly referred to as a branch office, a stall outside the uni caf, to disseminate similar anti-war paraphernalia.

Tony organised an open-air panel discussion on the south lawn of the university between James Jupp, an academic in political sciences who was well known for his left-wing views; Hugo Wolfsohn, who delighted in debunking all ideologies; and Frank Knopfelmacher, who supported the war. Tony chaired the debate.

It was a warm autumn day; Jenny and I sat with a thousand other students at the back of the crowded lawn. Students shouted abuse; some complained that Tony didn't give equal time; others heckled the speaker, drowning out their words; and still more stood at the back of the crowd with banners saying, 'Peace now' and 'Make love not war'.

Friday 8 May 1970 – the day of the Vietnam Moratorium. About one hundred thousand people filled the streets of Melbourne. Some marched from the Treasury Gardens along Spring Street to the steps of Parliament House. Tony, Jenny and I, with thousands of others, walked along Bourke Street in the fresh autumn air. People stood on balconies and at windows of city buildings looking down, waving and shouting support. Jenny held a banner that said, 'Give peace a chance'. Monash University had a sign with 'I wish one day there was a war and no one turned up', and the women's liberationists' placard said, 'If you were being raped would you ask for negotiations or immediate withdrawal?' There were three men dressed in brown storm-trooper uniforms with Nazi armbands, standing on the footpath with a poster that said, 'Support our troops in Vietnam'. They heckled the crowd, shouting obscenities. The police stood close by to ensure no violence broke out.

At 3.15 pm we arrived at the steps of Parliament House. Over the loudspeaker we were asked to sit and observe a minute's silence. Before the minute was up the crowd broke into the chant, 'All we are saying, is give peace a chance'. It was like being at a football grand final at the end of 'God Save the Queen'. Then Jim Cairns, who was standing with Sam Goldbloom and others on the roof of a kombi van, stepped to the microphone, a loudspeaker on each side, and raised his hands in victory. 'A great day for democracy . . .' he started. I sat on the cold hard bitumen, saw banners flapping in the sharp wind above the heads of the crowd and, despite the weather, felt a warm flush of excitement.

The next day Jenny and I were in the cafe with Tony discussing the moratorium. Tony sat opposite us, sipping coffee and talking, his voice drowned out by the autumn rain banging against the window, the hustle and bustle of other students and the intermittent cry of the attendant behind the counter calling out orders. 'You guys should join the Congress for International Co-operation and Disarmament,' Tony said. 'I've been a member for ages.' He butted his cigarette in the dirty glass ashtray. Jenny knew the work the Congress did promoting peace from her time with the debating society and had already canvassed the idea of us joining months earlier.

I looked at Jenny as if to say, 'Why not?'

'Great idea!' she said.

That afternoon Tony took us to a dusty basement in Little Lonsdale Street to meet the coordinator and some of the volunteers. We walked down steps, along a bare brick wall to a large open-plan office with people sitting at battered old desks. At the top of the wall were narrow glass windows that looked onto the street. Gary, the coordinator, sat in a glass-partitioned office at the back.

'Hi,' Tony said as we walked through the door.

'What's doing?' Gary asked.

'Meet some friends of mine, Robert and Jenny,' he said. 'They want to help.'

'Pleased to have you on board,' Gary said. 'We need all the help we can get.'

Behind Gary, taped to the exposed brick wall, was a big poster of the faces of four children. Each face was painted a different colour – red, black, white and yellow – but underneath the paint their skin was the same colour. At the bottom was printed, 'Underneath, we are all the same'.

'You can lick envelopes, answer phone calls and distribute anti-war information – for a start at least,' Gary said.

'When can we begin?' Jenny asked.

'Once you've completed our induction program we'll put you to work, don't worry. We'll give you a desk and you'll mainly be helping draft dodgers find safe houses and conscripts find sympathetic doctors to help them fail their medical.'

Lying in bed that night, the poster of the four faces remained with me, despite all the things I'd seen and the people I'd met. The sad eyes, the bewildered expressions.

I turned up for work three days later at ten o'clock, ready to roll up my sleeves. It was another cool May morning, but the sky was blue and cloudless. I was introduced to John, a uni student from Monash and the volunteer with whom I would share a cubicle, whose black afro reminded me of Jimi Hendrix. We passed the afternoon and many more like it at a bench licking envelopes and drinking stale instant coffee.

One Friday night nearly two weeks later, I brought Jenny home for dinner and that was when my relationship with my father changed. We sat down for dinner – Jim off at some training camp, Titan under the table as usual – and I bragged about Jenny's debating skills. Then Jenny talked to Dad about the Vietnam War and everything changed. The bond between them was almost instantaneous, something I had never managed in almost two decades.

Mum had made up the spare room for Jenny – there was no question of our sleeping together – and when Jenny excused herself and went off to bed, I lingered to see if Dad's new openness would persist. For a long moment he sat in silence, and I feared that we were back to our old awkward ways, but after a time he said quietly, 'Speaking of injustice, that poor girl is still in rehab and the cops haven't done a bloody thing about finding who did it to her. She may never be right, poor kid.'

I was surprised to hear him swear. 'The girl who was raped?'

'Yes, Meredith Langdon.'

An image of that skinny black girl with the wild hair flashed into my mind. 'Do the police have any leads?'

'Leads!? They might if they could be bothered looking. There's all kinds of rumours flying around town, but nothing ever comes of them, and Meredith isn't talking. Too traumatised I bet. It makes me sick to my stomach.'

This was Dad in vigilante mode, ready to ride out and save another Aboriginal kid, this time, I hoped, without bringing her home. Perhaps because I'd moved away, or perhaps because I was older, I saw for the first time that Dad meant well, had probably always meant well, even if he went at problems head-on.

I couldn't resent the bond between Dad and Jenny. It was as if my father had emerged for the first time from a fog: I saw him clearly and perhaps he saw me in a different light through Jenny. All of the love and affection I had craved began to flow in a current of understanding after that. My father began to confide in me, even when Jenny wasn't there. He spoke to me as one would to another adult, about his hopes and dreams when he was growing up, about the early days with Mum, and on my birthday in June he pulled me into a rough and affectionate embrace from which we both found it hard to let go.

I began to go back to Mooroopna more often. Jim was always there, an increasingly silent presence, and to my shame I paid him very little attention. I told myself that we were moving in different directions, and, just as I had always done, I ignored any fleeting signs of misery or anger, putting them down to the rigours of training. While I felt at home in Melbourne now, I still yearned to be with my father. He may have treated me like an adult but I realised that, more and more, I became a child when I was with him, hankering after him, hanging on his every word. I let Jenny do the challenging, and if the need arose I always sided with my father. Jenny didn't complain. She was too astute not to see what was going on, and she knew it was a closeness I craved more than anything. She was confident enough not to feel threatened.

I was with Jenny in my room preparing for an exam when I got a call from Dad telling me to book a flight to Edinburgh in July. Jim had been selected to run in the two hundred and twenty yards at the Commonwealth Games.

Saturday 24 July 1970 – the day of Jim's big race. I'd arrived at Edinburgh airport the day before and gone straight to our hotel, where I caught up on some sleep and waited for the others to come back. I wished I could have taken more time from my studies, but as it was I was stretching things to the limit to see Jim run. Still, it would have been great to see something of Scotland, and even England. I told myself drowsily that if I graduated in law, there'd be nothing to stop me travelling whenever I liked. I must have fallen into a deep sleep, because the next thing I knew it was morning, and Mum was shaking me awake.

After a hurried breakfast, we all caught a taxi to Meadowbank Stadium. The race was scheduled for three but Mum and Dad wanted to find their seats and soak up the atmosphere. That taxi ride seemed to take an eternity. I wound down the window and breathed in the damp warm air. The sky was overcast and the whole world was washed by summer rain.

The taxi stopped opposite a large block of grimy stone apartments outside the stadium. This was Jim's world, Dad's world: together they shared a common language. Theirs was a world of stopwatches, diet and exercise. They talked to each other in a kind of shorthand I had long since given up trying to follow. And there were smiles about personal bests, lengthy conversations about track conditions and detailed analyses of competitors.

We stood in a queue waiting to go through the turnstiles, clutching our tickets. I was missing Jenny, and didn't pay as much attention to the day as I should have, but when I walked up the stairs of the open-air stand there must have been fifteen thousand people, all roaring, cheering and shouting. Some were standing to watch the long jump, but one woman sat on the edge of her seat, silent tears streaming down her face, her whole body frozen. I walked along the concrete path searching for our seats.

The green oval had been freshly mown, the lines freshly painted. One end of the oval had a scoreboard displaying names, times and results. An eight-lane track encircled the oval and on the opposite side was a roofed stand. In the middle of the front row were eight empty seats with red cushions for the Queen and her entourage.

I found my seat and edged along the row.

'Aah,' Mum said with a sigh, 'here at last. I was beginning to think we wouldn't make it.'

We settled down to watch the events that preceded Jim's big race, and eventually Dad panned the oval with his binoculars and said, 'There's Jim and Doug – won't be long now.'

I looked towards the warm-up track and saw Jim in his tracksuit doing his usual warm-ups – skipping, short sprints, run-throughs and stretches.

'Men's two hundred and twenty yards,' came over the PA system.

After a few moments Mr Lawrence said something to Jim, who took off his tracksuit and walked towards the starting line. I watched him bend down to touch his toes, then bounce from one foot to the other as he waited.

'Hurry up,' I heard Dad murmur under his breath. 'Roberts is already in the blocks.'

Jim and the other competitors settled into their starting positions. The gun cracked and Jim was first out of the blocks, his long gait keeping the others at bay. As they turned into the straight, a runner in green and white picked up pace, his powerful legs driving him forward. Forty yards before the finish, he and Jim were neck and neck, followed by a runner in red. Then in the last four yards Jim thrust himself forward and broke the tape.

'Gold!' Dad shouted as he jumped up and down, punching the air. He turned and dragged Mum and me into a bear hug.

CHAPTER 14

WITHIN DAYS OF THE END-OF-YEAR exams, students began leaving campus to return home. Sitting on my bed with my bag packed, I looked out the window at the blazing morning sky. Mooroopna seemed a pleasure now, rather than the death sentence I had perceived it to be just a year before. I thought about what the summer might hold. Jim was at a special training camp, Jenny was with her parents, and Tony Blundell, my best friend at uni, had gone to see his grandparents in Sydney. I considered the long summer with just Dad and me, and Mum of course, and I couldn't wait. Dad had lined up a part-time job for me so I could make a bit of money for next year, but I'd still have time to relax and hang out at home.

I closed the bag, ran downstairs to my old VW and tossed the bag into the boot. The tank was full, the air was fresh, and I breathed deeply as I drove. This felt like freedom.

When I got home to Elizabeth Street, I was struck by nostalgia for the place. Nothing had changed – the frayed rug on the wooden floor with its tarnished fringes curled at the edges; the stained doily on the cabinet that Dad and Uncle Ian had built; the lace curtains half drawn and the tall floral lamp standing in the corner of the room. I stood there, feeling a rush of love for the place and breathing in the warm smell of home.

Dad greeted me as I came through the door, his handshake firm, clapping me on the back with gusto. I couldn't help but smile.

'Cuppa tea?' he asked. 'Your mother's off shopping.'

'Thanks, that'd be great.'

Dad pottered around in the kitchen boiling the jug and getting out the tea things. He seemed preoccupied.

'What's up?' I asked finally.

'Craig and his mates have been arrested for the attack on Meredith Langdon. Meredith refused to speak to the police – too traumatised, poor kid – but a witness finally came forward who saw them driving away from the scene of the crime. Fruit picker. Been off working interstate and knew nothing about it.'

'Craig Woodhead?'

'Craig Woodhead, Ken Armstrong and Bob Birch. Bloody animals.'

Wordlessly, I sat down. Craig, a rapist? He was violent, but to have raped and nearly killed someone? I was stunned. Dad pushed an open packet of biscuits in my direction. 'Have one of these. Tea won't be long. I thought there might be something on the news.' He turned on the radio just as the ABC news music was finishing. We waited while the announcer spoke about Pope Paul VI's tour of Australia, and finally the announcer turned to local news. 'Three Mooroopna youths have been charged with assault causing grievous bodily harm over an attack on a fifteen-year-old Aboriginal girl in March last year. The victim was found unconscious beside the Goulburn River with serious injuries to her head and body. Her alleged attackers are due to appear in the Shepparton Magistrates Court at a date to be fixed.'

'Those bastards,' I said. 'They bullied Jim for years, graduated to arson, now they've nearly killed someone.'

'And you don't know the half of it,' Dad muttered, but would say no more. I knew why they had chosen Meredith Langdon. She was black, so to them she was a nothing, a nobody. They had meant to hurt her, meant to rape her, perhaps even meant to kill her. The way Craig and his dad spoke about Aboriginal people they may as well have been vermin; to the Woodheads they were sub-human. The only time I'd ever seen Craig really scared or apparently repentant about anything, was when he'd been caught, or when someone bigger and tougher than he was, challenged him. It seemed as if not even his powerful father could rescue him now.

'Grievous bodily harm,' Dad hissed, his eyes ablaze. 'I'd give them grievous bodily harm if I could get them somewhere quiet.'

I realised that one of the reasons I was happy living in Melbourne was that Mooroopna, with its racism and segregation, seemed light years away. In Melbourne I could forget.

'Since they arrested those maggots the town's talked about nothing else,' Dad said. 'But it won't bring about change. Nobody really cares. Even the police took their sweet time. And one woman blamed Meredith – said girls should know better than to walk around by themselves!'

'What about the families? Mr Woodhead and—'

'You don't want to know. They're animals. Just because she's Aboriginal . . .'

He looked away from me. Meredith Langdon's attack had touched a raw nerve. Despite his rage, there was an undercurrent of uncertainty in his voice I hadn't heard before. Could he be questioning himself? I tried to think of something to say.

'Jim—' he said finally, his voice cracking. He coughed and started again, 'Jim used to sit on the end of his bed in the dark.' He glanced at me, and I wondered if he was going to blame me for something. 'Or he'd spend hours staring out the window.' Dad shut his eyes for a moment, opened them again and grunted.

Why mention Jim, I thought to myself.

'We always gave them a leg up,' Dad said after a long moment. 'Didn't we?'

Then, he fell silent.

That summer Dad and I spent a lot of time together. 'I have a project for us,' he confided in me, nodding his head towards the garden, gesturing for me to follow. Dad had decided to build a new back fence to stop the morning glory, which grew wild up the embankment, from creeping into the garden and suffocating his tomatoes. He intended to nail wire spikes along the top of the fence to prevent possums raiding his fruit trees and vegetable garden, and leaving their droppings on the concrete pavers. To Dad, that fence protected the order of his manicured garden from the chaos of the thick scrub edging the Goulburn River. The bush was out of control, or so he said. Dad had rigid boundaries and didn't recognise how much the fence said about his inner life. It gave him a sense of order. Dad was determined to conquer the wild, and, if he could, to harness it. He never understood the subtle rhythms of the bush, the balance that allowed it to survive in a harsh climate and generally poor soils. He failed to appreciate that what he labelled chaotic was the natural order of things.

By now, I understood that Dad's grimaces as we dug holes for the posts were expressions of satisfaction, not frustration. 'This is tricky,' he'd say reassuringly, as he took my hand and steadied it to show me how to chisel out a rebate for the rail. I realised that his smiles at my failed attempts to nail wire mesh to the palings were affectionate, and not a sign of mockery. As we worked we were comfortable with each other's silences, but when we talked it was with an easy intimacy. He listened to my suggestions, agreed or disagreed, but always treated me respectfully and I felt we were closer now than we had ever been.

One morning Dad and I were in the back garden nailing trellis to the fence when I broached the subject of Jim. 'How's he getting on at training camp? Have you had any news?'

'Nah . . . nothing yet . . . but he'll be okay,' he said. 'It's not easy training for gold – there's a lot of pressure.' He seemed to want to shrug off Jim's strange silence, but I had the feeling he was baffled. Jim's attitude towards him had changed and he didn't know why.

When Jim came home at last, I saw that he was curt with Mum and Dad, although he seemed a little more at ease with me. One warm Sunday morning in late January Jim and I were sitting, talking, in the hammock slung between the shed and one of the big trees in the backyard.

'Remember when we were kids and Dad pitched a tent and let us sleep out here?' I asked.

'That was a long time ago.'

'And the night the wind was up and the branch of a tree scraped across the roof?'

'You're talking ancient history.'

During that conversation Jim seemed withdrawn and preoccupied.

'Is something wrong?' I asked.

'Not really, it's just that I've got a lot riding on this,' he said. He avoided eye contact but I saw that his face was full of anger.

'What do you mean?'

'It's big. It's gold.'

Suddenly I recalled Dad's words to Jim years earlier: 'You need to be better to be equal.' Was that what he meant by a lot riding on it?

As if he'd read my thoughts he said, 'I've devoted my entire life to this, I want to win.'

But I could see he was holding back. There was something he wasn't telling me.

Mr Lawrence had spent a lot of time with Jim, refining his technique, working on his attitude, overseeing his training, and discussing race strategy. Jim had become obsessed. All he could talk about was the gold medal, but he seemed bitter. He was determined to win, but his voice was angry and resentful when he spoke about running, and he seemed preoccupied most of the time. Something significant had changed. Back then I thought that was just how athletes were when they were training for gold. I assumed he was worried, rehearsing each step of the race over and over in his mind. It was all-consuming. But now I realise his running, his need to win gold, meant something much more, and there may have been something else causing him pain that he hadn't mentioned.

One Saturday, Jim and Mr Lawrence had just returned from Melbourne after a three-day training camp. That night at dinner Jim seemed distant. It took all Dad's doggedness to get him to speak about his training regime and his times. In the past Jim had enthusiastically told Dad all about his performances, but now things were different. He said the bare minimum and it was clear something wasn't right. And that's how he was all summer.

Even the way he spoke to Mum was different. Instead of lengthy conversations about how he was getting on, standing up to the pressure of everyone's expectations, Jim cut Mum short. Mum pulled back, unwilling to confront the issue. Maybe she too put it down to pre-race anxiety.

It seemed to take months before Craig and Ken and Bob appeared in court. Meredith and her family had left Mooroopna to stay with relatives in Melbourne by the time they were released on a bond. Dad was incensed. 'It's as if *they're* the criminals, not those bloody mongrels!'

'They just want to keep her safe,' Mum said. 'You can understand—'

Jim, who'd been sitting in the kitchen, shoved back his chair and walked to the sink to get a drink.

'You can understand why they'd want to protect her,' Mum finished quietly, taking Jim's glass and filling it for him. When she handed it to him I saw her wrap her hands around his and hold him for a few moments as if to steady him.

'I know; I do; but it's just wrong . . .' Dad said.

'It's all wrong,' Mum said, and began scrubbing potatoes with unnecessary vigour.

The *Shepparton Advertiser* reported on the trial, making much of the youths' 'previous good character', which was attested to by representatives from both school and church. There was no mention of sexual assault, but the girl had been beaten so severely that the judge in his summing up expressed disgust at the abhorrent crime and gave all three of them a roasting. He announced that he had two courses open to him, either imprisonment, or a bond, but that neither was the ideal punishment. However, giving due consideration to the fact that this was a first offence, and that the youths had been of previous good character – I nearly choked when I heard that – and had their lives ahead of them, he ordered each to pay a hefty bond and to be of good behaviour for three years.

That night at dinner, Dad slammed the paper down on the table as he finished reading and began to pace back and forth, muttering to himself. Mum looked stricken. All those years of bullying and now this. Jim was staring at the table, his face taut and wretched.

'There's no justice in this stinking town,' Dad said, 'not if your skin is black.'

'Jack . . .' Mum glanced anxiously at Jim, who hadn't moved.

'Don't "Jack" me. I've had it. I'm off!' He stormed out of the house, slamming the door viciously behind him. It was as if the sentence were a personal affront to him. I glanced at Jim, but he wouldn't meet my eyes. His jaw was locked and he was breathing hard through his nose.

'Eat your dinner, boys,' Mum said, as if we were still at school. 'Don't mind Dad. He'll calm down. He's probably gone for a walk to cool off.'

The rest of the meal was silent. Jim took his plate to the sink with half his meal uneaten and scraped it into the compost bucket, then headed to his room.

When Dad came home he looked utterly spent. Mum glanced up from her knitting, got up and began to fill the kettle. 'Sit down, Jack, before you fall down. Where have you been?'

'The pub.'

'I see.'

Mum had never made a fuss about Dad and Harry drinking, so I was surprised by her tone.

'So who did you meet?'

'Nobody. Ernie Woodhead was shooting his mouth off right, and Brian Birch and Colin Armstrong were down there with him, raising a glass, the mongrels. Like father like son.'

'Jack!' But Dad would not be silenced.

'You'd think they'd be ashamed. You'd think if they had any decency they'd leave town, but oh no, not them. They were buying rounds, sucking up to their mates. I heard Ernie Woodhead say something about "boys will be boys", and Brian Birch complained about how Bob couldn't hold his liquor! As if getting drunk was some sort of excuse for what they did, the animals.'

I turned just as Jim reached the kitchen door, but it was too late to try to stop Dad. He was furious.

'I tackled them then, I couldn't help it, and you know what Ken Armstrong said?'

We shook our heads, mute.

'He said, "I dunno what all the fuss is about. It's only a bloody gin." So I hit him, or I would've except Harry had come in and grabbed my arm . . .'

'Thank goodness for Harry,' Mum said. 'Now that's enough, Jack. This isn't helping anyone.'

But it wasn't enough for Dad. He turned to Jim, who was standing in the doorway, his face unreadable.

'What have I always told you, eh Jim? If you're black, you've got to be twice as good in this stinking town, and even then they treat you like shit.'

CHAPTER 15

SUNDAY 4 SEPTEMBER 1972 – the day for which Jim had been training for as long as I can remember, the most important day of Dad's life and the day of the Olympic two hundred metres. I had arrived at Munich's airport late the night before Jim's race and next morning we went straight to Olympiastadion, my head still groggy from jetlag. In the heavy traffic we travelled bumper to bumper, and the trip seemed to take way too long for the distance we had to travel. The race was due to start at three and Dad was glancing at his watch as the driver wove through the traffic. Mum and Dad had been in Berlin for a week watching Jim's preparation and sightseeing between times – the English Garden, the Deutsches Museum, Nymphenburg Palace. Titan, who was getting old and stiff, had been entrusted to Harry. Dad had worried about leaving him, because the two of them had rarely been apart. I was in the midst of studying for my exams, so I had very little time to spare for sightseeing, but there was no way I was going to miss Jim's big race.

For a while now, when people saw him at a competition, I could tell by the way they whispered to each other that news of his success had spread through the entire athletic community. Recently, when Jim walked into a stadium, he seemed resolute, even angry, and there was none of the quiet friendliness that had marked his early years.

Jim had climbed a mountain using raw talent and dogged determination, and I hoped, today, he would reach the summit. I had seen first-hand how deep was his need to prove himself the equal of those around him.

Dad, too, had invested much more than time and energy in this race – his heart and soul, his pride and his sense of self-worth all hinged on Jim's winning gold.

'Wir sind hier,' the driver said, snapping me out of my thoughts.

The taxi stopped outside the stadium, and I gazed up at the concrete pillars from which hung the swooping, tent-like roof of the stadium. As I walked up the stairs, the roar of seventy-five thousand cheering spectators hit me: the sound was deafening. People were standing, shouting, watching the relay; one man sat with his head in his hands, his face frozen. Another woman, two rows behind him, jumped up and down on the spot waving her arms and shouting. We walked down the concrete steps looking for our seats.

The plush green oval reminded me of Meadowbank Stadium in Edinburgh – freshly cut lawn, and crisp white lines marking the eight lanes of the red-brown track.

Dad pulled out his binoculars and scanned the aisles. Mum was getting us all coffee, dismissing the hot dogs and smelly sauerkraut.

'Where's Mum? The athletes will be coming out soon,' Dad said, peering past me, dropping his binoculars to his chin for a moment.

'She'll be here.'

Ten minutes later, Mum edged down the aisle balancing three cups of coffee and settled gratefully into her seat as I took two from her and handed one to Dad.

'Just in time,' he said. 'What kept you? The athletes are coming out onto the track.'

'I know, I know, but there was a queue.'

'He's looking good,' Dad said, turning back to face the track. 'He looks light, fresh.'

'Men's two hundred metre final,' echoed over the PA system.

I watched Mr Lawrence and Jim walk towards the starting line. Jim took off his tracksuit and began to shake his arms, bouncing from one foot to the other as he always did and jumping up and down to limber up. Then he bent down to touch his toes and stepped towards the starting line. He was on the inside lane, his favourite position, with Larry Black from the States next to him, then Pietro Mennea, Valeriy Borzov, another American, and a couple of Germans from both the East and the West.

The whistle sounded and as the competitors took their place at the starting line I heard Dad murmur, 'Borzov is the man to beat.'

The choreography of the race began, as together they bent, right knees to the ground, left legs outstretched behind them, their hands spaced on the track in front. Then, they lifted their heads, looked down the lanes and waited for the sound of the gun.

Dad was on the edge of his seat, his binoculars jammed in the sockets of his eyes and fixed on Jim. It was as if his whole life hinged on this moment. I looked around me and saw seventy-five thousand people sitting on the edge of their seats, waiting in silence for the starter's pistol. I could almost smell the adrenaline in the air.

Jim, Black and Borzov settled into their starting positions. The gun cracked. Black was first out, his legs pumping, his movements polished and smooth. Valeriy Borzov, in second place, seemed to be on autopilot. Pietro Mennea was a close third, followed by Jim. With each step I could see Borzov and Mennea slipping behind and as they turned into the straight Jim was on Black's heels. At the fifty-metre mark Black seemed to stumble and Jim went from a cruise to full throttle, moving further and further ahead with each stride. Five metres before the finish line Jim lunged forward to come first, followed by Borzov, then Black and Mennea. Twenty seconds and it was all over.

'He won! He won!' Dad screamed, jumping up and down punching the air.

Mum raised both hands to her face and I saw tears in her eyes.

I was so proud of Jim – my brother the Olympic gold medallist. I was thrilled with his success, confident that now he could enjoy life a bit, and be happy.

Jim stood with his hands on his knees beyond the finish line, trying to catch his breath. The other competitors walked towards him, slapped him on the back and folded to the ground. Jim raised his head and looked towards the scoreboard.

'Gold! Gold! You little beauty! Gold!' Dad said, breathless, jubilant and incredulous. He thrust the binoculars at me and said, 'Here, have a quick look then pass them to your mother.'

People were shouting and screaming, but as I focussed on Jim I saw that he looked at them as though he couldn't see them, almost as though the stands were empty. I didn't know what he was thinking but one thing I did know was that something was wrong. Something was missing. It seemed as if Jim's eyes were turned inward, dark and still and blank. It was not that he was overwhelmed by the moment; if anything, it was the opposite. He looked underwhelmed, and terribly tired. *A strange response, I thought to myself, for someone who has just won an Olympic gold medal.*

Dad, however, was over the moon, veins popping from his neck like pipes, his wide, restless eyes surveying the crowd, lapping up the excitement, his face red with joy.

Over the loud speaker I heard a voice echo, 'Australia wins gold.'

This changes everything, I thought to myself. I imagined Jim sitting on the back of an open red sports car being driven along the main street, passed Benny's shop, with all the school kids lining the street, screaming and shouting. I thought of Ernie Woodhead, Steve Chapple and Mrs Shields standing with old Jim Halloran outside the newsagent, looking utterly perplexed.

Jim had just put Mooroopna on the map, something that they had failed to do. I could imagine the resentment simmering in them. The way they'd begrudgingly force a smile, the way nothing would change for them.

Next day, eleven men from the Israeli team were taken hostage and everything changed.

Mum and Dad made the most of their time in Europe, taking a whistle-stop tour of as many countries as they could fit in to their few weeks away. Once they returned, I gave them a day or two to recover from their jetlag then called them.

'How was your trip home?'

'Fine, fine. It's good to be home and to see poor old Titan. Mum and I are as pleased as punch – we couldn't be happier.'

'Did you stop over at Singapore on the way home?'

'Mum's still a bit overwhelmed,' he said, not listening to my questions at all. 'Tonight we're celebrating. Mr Lawrence, Harry and a few of the guys from the club are coming over to break open the champagne, or more likely the beer.'

Dad was still full of excitement. His pitch was electric and I understood why, although for me the deaths of the Israelis cast a pall over the Olympics.

'What a bloody fantastic effort! All those cold mornings that I dragged him out of bed, those late nights at the track and those Saturday and Sunday meets – it wasn't easy.'

'Yes, Dad. You did well.' He missed the gentle sarcasm. I thought about the way Jim had looked when he won the gold medal and wondered if Jim shared Dad's enthusiasm. It was clear that his reserve was much more than pre-race anxiety. His radio and television interviews were withdrawn and flat. I wondered if he and Dad were still distant with each other, or if they'd been reconciled over Jim's triumph.

'Is Jim back yet?'

'In three days.'

'Are you going to the airport?'

'Of course.'

'And Mum?'

'I'm sure she'll want to come.'

'When you spoke to him, how did he sound?'

There was a short silence and then Dad said tentatively, 'I didn't speak with him, Mum did.'

Something had happened to Dad between the time he left Munich and now. He was excited but he sounded hesitant.

'What did Jim say to Mum?' I prodded.

'They didn't speak for long because he was busy.' Dad was barely able to get the words out.

'How did he sound? Was he upset about the massacre?'

'Mum said he was quiet. She said she thought he was still coming to terms with everything.'

Dad seemed to vacillate between the joy of Jim winning a gold medal and his anxiety about Jim's return. The deaths of the Israelis seemed secondary somehow, and although he acknowledged how terrible it was, he never really seemed to feel it, whereas Mum always looked stricken if one of us mentioned anything to do with the massacre.

There was something inside Jim that Dad never understood. Focussed on gold, Dad didn't notice Jim's blank stare when he stood on the podium to receive his gold medal; in some ways he had been oblivious when Jim sat on the end of his bed as a child, looking blankly out the window. Now, Jim had become alien and I had the feeling Dad was waiting for me to align myself with him. But this seemed deeper than a simple misunderstanding and I held back. Something had forced itself into their relationship and Dad was carrying a lot of hurt and anger – I could hear it in his voice.

'How are you going to celebrate when Jim comes home?'

'Not sure. Jim told Mum he doesn't want to do anything.'

That wasn't like Jim. He had always said when he won gold he was going to party. In the past he had wanted to please, especially Mum and Dad. He must have known how much it meant to Dad to celebrate the win in Mooroopna, the place where Dad had fought his own fights as well as Jim's, and his son's refusal to share his triumph seemed somehow contemptuous.

At Dad's suggestion I returned home a week later. Jim had arrived three days earlier and conversations between them were strained. Each time Mum or Dad tried to speak with Jim he was short, unwilling to share Dad's excitement and enthusiasm about the win.

Dinner that night was uncomfortable, small talk sounded forced, and Mum and Dad seemed to be walking on eggshells.

The next morning I found Mum in her bedroom changing the sheets and turning the mattress.

'Things have been a bit difficult round here, I gather?' I lifted the mattress for her and we turned it over with a wallop.

'It's Jim – he's upset, won't talk.'

She hesitated, then, choosing her words carefully, she said, 'Why don't you take him for a walk and try to talk to him, one on one. I'm sure the massacre affected him, but I think there's something else . . .'

'I tried but he refused. He's been stuck in our room since he came home.' I saw her rub her thumb against her index finger as she did when thinking. There was something unresolved in her mind. I had the sense she was trying to convince herself of something.

'Why is he so upset?'

'I thought when he won gold everything would be okay. That he'd forget about the past and move on.' She sounded baffled, torn between feelings of shame, resentment and sympathy. What did Mum mean when she said, 'forget about the past'? Was it the pressure Dad had put on Jim to win gold? The strict training regime he had imposed on Jim? Or his insistence on early nights and his refusal to allow Jim to spend evenings with the few friends he'd made in Melbourne? Is that what Mum was referring to? I was unsure. I looked at her closely to see if she was holding back but her face was closed.

'That's it; we're finished in here,' she said brightly. But she paused in the bedroom doorway as we left, her head bowed.

That afternoon, Dad was sitting in the lounge watching TV.

'How're you going?'

He leaned forward in his chair and turned towards me. The bitterness in his face was plain. 'You do everything you can to give someone a better life and that's the thanks you get.'

I sat down and asked, 'What do you think's upsetting him?'

Dad rubbed the side of his face. 'He came from nothing. I gave him a gold medal. Set him up for life.'

It was useless to try to talk to Dad when he was like that, so I sat quietly. Jim had lost his birth parents and Mum and Dad had given him everything. I thought back to when he'd first came to live with us, the way Mum and Dad had embraced him, looked after him. I recalled the trouble Dad had gone to enrol him in the right school, the hard work and the long hours Dad had put into Jim's training to help him win gold.

But then I remembered the frightened look on his face when he first came to live with us and the sudden stiffening of his shoulders when Mrs Axen introduced him to the class on his first day of primary school. I recalled his wet eyelashes when Craig, Ken and Bob bullied him in the quadrangle at school. Then I remembered the way Jim looked at Mum when Dad shouted at him that first time, 'She's your mother, for Christ's sake. You're not on the bloody reserve now.' I remembered the look on his face when Dad said, 'You will speak English in this house, do you understand? Don't you ever let me hear you speaking that gibberish.' For all Dad's kindness to Jim, he could still be cruel.

Once, when Jim had tried to tell Mum a story of his own when we were lying in bed, Dad had come in and cut across him. 'You're not with blacks anymore, Jim. Forget the dreamtime stories. How the sun was made is not important. What about Famous Five? Or Noddy?' Mum had smiled sympathetically, but Jim had turned his head away as though betrayed.

Next morning, I went outside to throw the scraps onto the compost heap. It was a cool spring day, the sky filled with clouds that sent shadows drifting across the grass. Since I had been living in Melbourne, Jim and I had drifted apart, my life at university and Jim's training had come between us. But as young boys growing up in the same house we had shared a brotherly bond and I decided to talk to Jim in the hope that he would reconcile with Dad, who was off somewhere with Harry.

Back inside I tapped timidly on the door.

'What?'

'It's me,' I said as I opened the door.

He was sitting on the bed with his back against the wall, reading. Titan was curled up beside him, and the room was thick with the smell of the old dog. He was too stiff and slow to go with Dad, but Jim was a good second-best.

Jim looked at me, resting a hand on Titan's back. He said nothing, and I had the feeling he regarded me now with suspicion. The atmosphere was tense.

'How's tricks?' I asked.

'Who's asking?'

'Stop that. We all care about you, you know that.'

'Do I?' His anger rose quickly, hot, stinging.

'What is it with you? Mum and Dad don't understand, I don't understand. They did everything for you. Why are you being like this?'

'I'm sick of playing happy families.'

I could hear the pain in his voice, but I had no idea what he meant. 'What are you talking about?'

He looked at me in surprise. 'Ask them,' he said in a strange tone.

I heard a tremble in his voice and he looked away.

'What's going on?' I persisted. 'Look what you're doing to Mum and Dad. Get over yourself.'

He just stared at me, and I realised I was getting nowhere. Jim wouldn't tell me what was wrong. If he knew something and hadn't told me . . . I found myself thinking childishly that he wasn't being fair keeping secrets. I remembered those times in our childhood when he'd disappear for hours on his own. It was as if he'd left us while his body was still here in the room. The silence lengthened. Disappointed and upset that Jim could no longer confide in me, I left the room.

That afternoon I returned to Melbourne and went straight to the library to write my essay. I spent the next three days revising with Jenny until I was exhausted. It had been a long few days of caffeine-fuelled study, and that night, not able to sleep, I got up and walked sullenly to the window. Standing in my pyjamas, I pulled open the heavy drapes and peered into the night.

Next morning I called home.

Mum answered and I could tell by her voice that something was wrong.

'What's happened?' I asked.

'Jim's gone – he and your father had a big blue and Jim stormed out of the house.'

'Are you okay?'

'Not really, but I'll be all right. It's your father I'm worried about.'

'Put him on.'

I waited in silence for Dad to pick up the phone.

'Mum said you had a blue with Jim and he left.'

'Ungrateful bastard,' Dad spat.

'What was it about?' I asked.

'How could he?' His voice was breaking.

'What are you going to do?'

'Nothing, what can I . . .?'

There were several layers in Dad's voice: the dominant one was agitation, but below that was betrayal and emptiness. We talked for a bit and then I put down the phone, oblivious to the sun streaming in the window. Thinking about my last conversation with Jim, I realised I'd held back because I didn't want to have a full-on argument with him, but now, doubt crept in. Why was Mum so torn? Why was Dad so bitter and angry? What were they hiding? And Jim's rage was palpable, even though he refused to talk. 'Ask them,' he had said. What was it that I had to ask Mum and Dad? I thought about Jim's eyes, so dark and still and blank after he won the gold medal. This was no misunderstanding, no minor tiff.

Sitting in chambers twenty-five years later, my desk covered in briefs, I tried to calm myself. It was warm outside, and the sun streaming in had shifted me back to that conversation with Dad when Jim left, after they argued. Back then, Dad hadn't told me the truth; he'd deceived me by keeping silent. Now, I sipped my tea and, perhaps for the first time, felt the need to be honest with myself. Jim had lost his family and his identity. Growing up, I had chosen not to see his plight despite it being right there in front of me. But I had been blinded by my need for Dad's approval. 'Look how these people live,' Dad had said once. Sure, he was talking about the people out at Rumbalara and their horrible little concrete cottages, which he'd fought against so fiercely, but I felt now that something of the kind had been his justification for taking Jim. And why the pressure to perform? To win? Was he making up for his failure to save the All Blacks from being kicked out of the league? I wished I knew more about his role back then, but Mum was tight-lipped and there were no more newspaper cuttings to give me a clue. Certainly, he had brought the same fierce determination to training the Cats as he'd brought to training Jim.

My mood had shifted from guilt to anger. I'd assumed Dad could do no wrong, but what was he trying to prove? And why did everyone else have to help him do it? Now, I felt incensed about my complicity in Jim's suffering. Dad would not admit it, but he must have believed blacks were not as capable of looking after their children as whites. Back then, it never occurred to him or to any of his contemporaries to support the families living in squalor rather than taking their children from them. My inclination had been to agree with Dad, but now I was sickened by our failure to support black families in need. To this day we preferred to label them as negligent and incapable of caring for children, rather than offering support and assistance.

As a teenager, I'd been so busy nursing my childish resentments, I had been blind to all those scraps of knowledge – Jim's stoic misery, his mysterious absences, when I assumed he was off running – not wanting to understand, choosing instead to adopt Dad's views and ignore Jim's silent protests.

As a young man, I had seen Jim as selfish and inconsiderate, but now, all these years later, I realised my criticism of my brother had been misdirected. It was Mum and Dad who were responsible, who had deceived me as well as Jim; we had both swallowed that deception.

Jim and I had shared our childhood, and much had passed between us. Knowing that he was stolen I felt much closer to him – I wanted him to know that I knew the truth about his having been taken, that I understood, that I wanted to reconnect with him. To lose that would be an even greater loss than our estrangement. But I had my reservations about our meeting. Was there any possibility that this could end well? Was he angry with me for not supporting him? Did he, in some perverse way, blame me for what had happened? I hoped he would tell me more about himself and his life, to help me understand what it means to be Aboriginal, because, although I had an Aboriginal brother, I realised I was shamefully ignorant.

GOOD AS GOLD

CHAPTER 16

THE MORNING WAS ALREADY HOT when I arrived at
Jim's house near the Barmah State Forest. I'd taken Friday off,
so I'd have time to visit Mum as well as Jim. Luckily, the forecast
was for a pleasant day. In the still air, the eucalyptus leaves hung
motionless and the sky was an intense blue. I sat in the car looking
at the simple weatherboard house with its neat fence and hardy
garden. The palms of my hands were already sweating, and it wasn't
simply the heat. My clothes felt heavy and uncomfortable, but I
was grateful that the day was relatively mild. Up here, February
days could be fierce.

I got out of the car and walked up the path to the verandah,
where a big old daphne was flourishing in an old fuel drum. At the
sound of the bell a shadow emerged at the end of the hall beyond
the dull glass in the door, and when it didn't move I rang the bell a
second time and waited. Then at last I heard footsteps, each stride
down the hall echoing in my chest.

The door opened and Jim regarded me silently, his face
impassive. His eyes drifted past me to the Mercedes. Jim had
always been hard to read and he seldom gave anything away. As
usual I couldn't guess at his thoughts. He didn't move from the
door, standing behind the fly wire, settling comfortably against the
wooden frame. I counted the wait in breaths. He was looking out

beyond me, hands in his pockets, his eyes squinting against the light. It didn't take me long to lose count or patience. 'Can we talk?'

There was the distant yap of a dog, which sounded as though it was coming from behind the house down by the river or from the thick scrub next to it. Jim turned and started to walk down the passage.

I opened the wire door and followed him down the hall. On a small side table pushed against the wall halfway down the passage was a photo of Jim and Mary and two kids that looked to be not quite teenagers. The air smelled of nicotine.

As I entered, Mary was already rising out of her chair to greet me. Her hair seemed shorter and her eyes darker than I remembered. Her face was lined but the corners of her lips curved up, giving the impression she was smiling. There was something about her that seemed familiar, but I thought it must just have been my memories of the funeral. The thought crossed my mind again that she would have been a beautiful young woman. There was a calmness about her; she gave the impression she had never been angry, and I imagined she was good for Jim.

The light in the kitchen was dull and when Mary raised the blind above the sink I could see the verandah posts and the dense blue sky.

'Remember me?' she said as she turned towards me.

I could feel Jim staring at me as I sat down.

'From the funeral,' I said turning to face her and trying to ignore Jim.

'There's a pot of tea on the bench – if you'd like a cup.'

I nodded and feigned a smile and Jim fingered the paper on the table in front of him, rolling a corner and then flattening it as though it was this pursuit he had been at before I disturbed him on a Saturday morning at ten.

The three of us sat or stood in silence, and I was reminded of someone saying that English speakers find a long pause in conversation much harder to endure than people from many other cultures. I tried not to shift in my chair, or cough, but I was well outside my comfort zone. Mary smiled.

Eventually she moved around to the teapot and poured a cup for me, and herself, looking out of the window reflectively, taking her time. Finally she said, 'I'll leave you two to talk.'

There was nothing sulky or hostile in her departure. She merely turned and left, as though she had intended to do so all along.

Sunlight now filled the kitchen. Outside, I could see the leaves of a jacaranda hanging motionless.

I looked at Jim and tried to gauge his mood as he lifted a lump of tobacco from the packet on the table and carefully placed it on a paper, concentrated on rolling it and ran his tongue along it to seal the cigarette. Then he reached over and lifted a lighter from the bench. Each movement was controlled and methodical, a routine practised a thousand times over, with no artifice or airs, just the deft movement of fingers in space. He butted the rollie in the ashtray after only two inhalations, pressing the remainder hard into the glass and twisting his wrist much longer than he needed to.

'I've learnt a lot since Mooroopna,' I offered.

'Is that right?' His voice sounded gruff.

'I know,' I said, quietly.

'You know what?'

'When I went through Dad's papers I found a tin with your documents – it had the Court Order.'

I watched him stand up, walk to the fridge and reach for a six-pack of beer, the four bottles clinking companionably as they moved. He sat down and knocked the cap off against the edge of the table. It was an oafish action. He took a long swig and wiped his mouth with the back of his hand. He was putting on a show. His expression didn't change, his eyes were fixed on the bottle and, as the alcohol washed through him, I knew something had shifted inside. The silence between us lengthened.

I scanned the room. The walls were white, the floor covered in vinyl, the whole room simple and neat. Outside, the fierce light pressed down on the dry grass and a few tough plants. My eyes were drawn to two streaks of colour – red and yellow – which I realised formed the bedraggled remnants of an Aboriginal flag hanging across the branches that extended over the back verandah. Beneath it sat a woman, dozing in the sun. Every so often the flag above her burst open and then fell limp again.

'That's my mother,' Jim said, following my line of sight. My stomach clenched, and I remembered the night Jim came to live with us. That first wild night, when his eyes had darted around the room, his teeth chattering involuntarily as he bit his lip to stop himself crying. I recalled the long nights listening to him lying in bed sobbing after Dad told him baldly, 'Your mother has died.' Soon after that Jim was at school being jeered at and goaded by Craig and his mates and being called a 'coon'. I pieced together a picture of his childhood. More often than not I walked past our bedroom door in those early years to see Jim sitting on the side of the bed, ashen faced, looking blankly out the window.

But what about his mother? What had she suffered through all those long empty years? I didn't like to stare, but I'd seen a thick-set woman with long slender legs. Her face bore an uncanny resemblance to Jim's, with the same high cheekbones and large dark eyes. There were wrinkles around her eyes and deep lines beside her mouth. She sat erect, as if defiant, her chin high, her hands resting on the arms of the chair.

I imagined her shock and grief when she first discovered Jim was missing, the fruitless searches over days and weeks, in the hope of finding him. Grief and suffering were etched in her face. The pain had never left her, even now when her son had come home to her.

I wondered how she would feel if she knew who I was. Or perhaps she did. Perhaps Jim or Mary had told her. I swallowed, feeling suddenly ashamed. After a life of lies and indifference, maybe she'd want to swap roles – to have the upper hand. Maybe she'd want to hurt me, just as she had been hurt. I tried to imagine how I would feel in her position. But it was impossible. It made me realise, though, that it was my own guilty conscience that was producing these fantasies.

Suddenly Jim burped, sharp and deep, and looked at me. 'Have a beer.'

I did not let reason dissuade me, but reached over and twisted a bottle from the pack.

'Where's the opener?'

Jim nodded towards the drawer under the sink.

I walked over and found the bottle opener, my back to Jim, my face filmed in sunlight. It wasn't manicured out there in the garden but it was handsome, washed in khaki, grey-green, wheat-coloured light. I had missed it when I first moved to the city, that raw beauty.

I had not noticed the silence we had slipped into, but it was darker than the uncomfortable territory we had occupied before. Jim sat completely still, no fidgeting or twitching, no careless movement of a finger along the side of the stubby: it was the rigor mortis of fury. I thought of the hush before a storm.

But what spilled from Jim was not the lashing rage I had expected. There was none of the drunken slurring I had seen at my father's funeral. Here was Jim, articulate, clear, but bloody minded. This was the man I had seen interviewed a hundred times on television; this was the man whose determination and hard work had led him all the way to gold. It was, as it had been all those times before, both terrifying and exhilarating at the same time.

'Your parents lied to me,' he began.

'They lied to me, too,' I said, in that old reflex of self-justification.

'Hardly the same thing,' Jim said, and I fell silent with shame. 'They told me my mother was dead. *And* my father. They stole my parents, my family, my people, my country.' He ticked them off on his fingers. 'They took my stories, my history, my language, my past, and they took all those years when I was growing up.' He looked me in the eye and said, 'What gave them the right?'

I had no answer.

'So, did they want me that much that they had to steal me? Because when they got me they started to turn me into a white fella, because I wasn't good enough the way I was. I was black. I was an Abo.' He spat the word at me. 'I had to win a gold medal to prove I was as good as you, and those animals—' He swallowed hard and fell silent for a moment. Then he said, 'Dad always told me I had to be good as gold – nothing else would do. But what he meant was that I was nothing without that gold medal. I wasn't enough by myself; I would never be enough, until I proved myself better and faster and stronger.

'When we were kids, I thought Jack knew everything. I fell for it all, hook, line and sinker. He got me up before sunrise each morning and worked me till I could hardly stand. He told me I could really be somebody. But it didn't matter how often I won, I still wasn't white. I still wasn't good enough. That gold medal wasn't worth it; none of it was worth it. I paid too much.'

I nodded mutely. 'When did you learn the truth?'

'When we left the oval after the Australian Championships. As I was walking to the change rooms a journo from *Truth* came up to me and said, "Your mum and dad want to meet you – they're in the stand." I thought he was talking about Jack and Betty. But he said, "No. Your real parents – your Aboriginal parents." He sprang it on me just like that.' He swallowed, as if his throat were constricted. 'The first thing I thought was, *Bullshit! He's looking for a story.* But I could tell from the way he spoke that he knew much more about me than I did.' He paused and ran one hand through his hair as if he was suddenly weary. 'My knee-jerk reaction was, "I don't want to hear this," so I said, "No," and pushed past him.'

He focussed on the ashtray, unable to look at me, and I felt tears start to prick behind my eyes. How he must have regretted that decision. Not knowing what to say, I said nothing.

'That night I sat at the end of my bed in the dark and looked out the window. I knew Jack was keen for me to win gold and I knew it was because he believed that it would raise black people in the eyes of the community. But there was something else to it, something deeper – madder – about his obsession with me.

'At first I thought it was a cultural difference – how was I to know? But something strange had happened at the Australian Championships. I'd won my first heat and was waiting for the second when Jack came up to me and said, "Prove yourself." Just that. It was brutal. I felt that I had to win to be good enough for him. Because I'm black, you know.'

I didn't need to nod.

'But when the journo told me about my black family everything changed focus and I could see things clearly for the first time. For Jack, winning was much more than proving that blacks are worthy. The law may have allowed black kids to be taken from their families but I knew Jack felt bad about it and I knew Harry would have given him grief on those summer nights when they were sitting on the verandah with their legs on the rail and their beers in their hands. To him, I had to win to justify what he had done to me and to my parents.'

It all made sense, and I felt my jaw tighten. Jim's mother sat metres away from us, resting in the early afternoon sun. How could my parents have done such a thing?

'I wasn't ready to deal with it. I just put it out of my head and trained even harder. There were times after that when I'd think, "I've got to find out now," and then I'd leave it and before I knew it, another month had passed. Somehow, it was never the right time.

Maybe I was scared. I'd grown up in a white family in a white town, where Aboriginal was a dirty word to some people. At the back of my mind were Jack and Betty. How would they react? I didn't want them to think I was rejecting them. Despite what they'd done, they were the only family I knew. I was scared that I might lose them and gain no one in return. That's frightening, particularly for a boy, or a young man. But I was certain the day would come when I would do something about it.'

I could hardly bring myself to look at Jim, the memories were so clear on his face that they almost overwhelmed him. Outside, I could hear the thrum of cicadas.

'Then, after Munich, I decided to find out once and for all.'

I understood now – I'd seen those eyes after he'd won gold, seen the pain in him, although at the time I'd understood nothing.

'I didn't want to upset anyone, but I wanted to know. So I started asking around. I thought my parents wouldn't be far away because they had already tried to contact me. It wasn't easy. I went to the journo from *Truth* but he'd resigned and gone overseas to work, somewhere in Europe, and no one seemed to know exactly where he was. Nobody else knew anything about me – I was the story that was never told.

'Next, I went to Births, Deaths and Marriages to see what I could discover, and then I spread the word in the communities around Mooroopna and Shepparton. Mostly, they tried to help but one bloke turned his back on me. "You think you're white, don't you? Look at you."' His shoulders slumped with sadness at the memory, as though it exhausted him. It must have taken him by surprise at the time. He hadn't expected to be rejected by the very world he longed to join, after a childhood of not belonging in the white world. Jim must have realised then that he was caught between two worlds: a white world that thought he was inferior and a black world that believed he thought he was superior. It was a terrible irony.

A huge pressure of disgust built inside me. I wanted to tell Jim our parents were wrong but I couldn't find the words to start. As I looked at his grey-flecked hair I searched my memory for remnants of the past. I wished I had taken a moment to talk to Jim, to ask him what he was thinking when he was sitting on the end of his bed.

'After that, I went through church archives and then to the department. That pissed me off. It took months and when they finally released some documents they had been blacked out. Anything to do with Mum and Dad's history and medical records was illegible. The fucking red tape! Someone waves a pen in parliament and suddenly I'm not allowed to know who my parents are.'

Jim's search for his biological parents was like walking through a maze of mirrors, each mirror strategically placed to mislead and redirect him – and every other Indigenous person in his position. Files were marked 'confidential' or 'never to be released' and government bureaucrats told him lies so he would lose confidence and give up before he found anything. I was still naïve enough to be shocked that the bureaucracy deliberately created obstacles to prevent him finding out about his parents.

When I looked up, Jim was gazing at me. He glanced down at his hands, already anticipating the next phase of the story, and I was relieved to see his features soften a little.

'I got lucky. One night I was drinking at the George Hotel in St Kilda and stumbled across a bloke from the department. I arranged to go to his office in Spring Street the next day and he gave me a big brown envelope with my father's file. This time nothing had been blacked out. The bloke was retiring, so he wasn't worried about breaching confidentiality or losing his job. One letter in the file complained that Mum had been told by the police I would be kept safe until my father returned from seasonal work. Another letter pleaded that she was a good mother – she had registered my birth, she'd made sure I'd been baptised and had all my vaccinations.'

As Jim spoke, his lips tightened and I could see the fury in his eyes. I recalled the bureaucratic lie in Dad's papers – *'Because of the mother's neglect, the County Court of Victoria has dispensed with the mother's consent to adoption and hereby places James Albert Clarke in the foster care of Jack and Betty Pickering.'* I swallowed hard and took a deep breath, but I couldn't get the words out.

'From the files, I worked out that Dad had been in the army at Puckapunyal. He'd been wounded during the war, but after he was demobbed there was nothing for him – no support, no help, no acknowledgement of his sacrifices or his contribution. My mother told me he went off fruit picking – what else could he do? He died a year after I won that gold medal.' He stopped and swallowed hard. 'That's what you get for serving your country.'

I stared at the face staring back at me. His hands were shaking; he looked angry, bitter, but mostly he looked hurt. It seemed absurd to me that the department had refused to help him locate his dead father. This was not the fifties. We weren't living under a Communist dictatorship. This was a first-world democracy. It was . . . well, it was madness.

'I gave the file to the Aboriginal childcare agency and they helped me fill in some gaps, trace my mother and help me make contact.' He paused for so long I thought his story might end there, but then he continued. 'I'll never forget that first meeting with Mum. Driving to Warrnambool with the social worker. I was shit scared she wouldn't accept me. But when I got out of the car, there must have been twenty people there – uncles, aunties, cousins, even a younger half-brother. They hadn't seen me since I was seven. They were pulling me in all directions and my mother wouldn't let go, just kept cuddling me and crying. It was a bit scary.

Beads of perspiration had formed on his upper lip despite the ceiling fan circulating the air. Jim leant forward, his voice rising in anger once more. 'After that first meeting, it was a fucking hard grind – it's not easy getting to know your family, trying to make up for lost time, trying to fill in the gaps and find out about the people who've died before you could get home, like your own father.' I felt a scalding shame at the thought of all he'd lost, and at my own blindness and indifference.

'And what's really difficult is trying to let go of the hurt and the blame. Sometimes, I get cranky and think to myself, "Where were you when I needed you?" Or "Why did you let it happen? Why didn't you come for me?" I never understood how a parent wouldn't want to know what had happened to their child. Then I feel guilty because she did everything she could, and I know there's nothing more she could have done about it and it was the hardest time of her life.'

Jim fell silent. I sat opposite him holding my beer, trembling with suppressed emotion. I had never felt such anger before, or such shame; I wanted to grab my dead father by the scruff of the neck and punch him.

'I don't remember much about what my real father was like – I can't remember how he walked, or if he was funny or if he barracked for a football team,' Jim was saying. 'Jack coached the Cats to three premierships and was there when I won my first medal. So where do my loyalties lie? I've got this family who brought me up, stood by me through thick and thin, but then I've got this other family who are my real family, my blood, but weren't there for me – couldn't be there. They have the same colour skin, but I had nothing in common with them – nothing at all. I don't have blood ties with my foster family but I didn't have shared experiences or . . . or closeness with my real family.'

Jim looked at me sombrely. I couldn't speak, and as I slowly shook my head, my heart was sore for all my brother had endured, and was still enduring. There was a slight breeze from the open door now, and the air was cool against my face. Jim's rage had faded – he seemed calm but sad. The wall of hostility between us seemed to have disappeared, but my shame at the thought of how my father had treated Jim had not.

Without thinking I said quietly, 'I'm sorry.'

He nodded. 'Yeah,' he said. It wasn't dismissive, just a recognition that that was only part of the story.

After a minute he got up, walked to the door and looked outside.

'Come on,' Jim said. His voice was matter of fact as he reached for the keys on the table and opened the door.

'Where are we going?' I asked, getting up to follow him.

'You'll see,' he said.

CHAPTER 17

IT WAS ABOUT ONE IN the afternoon when we climbed into Jim's ute and bounced and rattled over the gravel, hitting potholes and flushing flocks of galahs off the side of the Moira Lakes Road. The air in the ute was stifling, so I wound down the window.

At the corner of Moira Lakes Road and Murray Street, Jim pulled up near the Barmah Hotel. The yellow brick building, covered with large signs advertising beer, looked as though it had just been built, its walls clean and fresh. For a second I thought Jim planned to drown his sorrows, then immediately felt ashamed of the thought.

'Hungry?' he said.

'Yep. It's been a long time since breakfast.'

We got out of the car and strolled towards the hotel. Jim's dust-coloured jacket and khaki pants seemed to fade into the tones of the landscape. He was gazing up at the gums, which were starting to stir in a faint breeze. Looking at him now, he seemed at ease, almost serene.

We found a table, ordered – a steak for Jim, lamb shanks for me, tap water for the table – and Jim took up where he'd left off.

'Jack believed blacks are inferior,' he said, giving me a straight look. I found I had nothing to say in my father's defence, despite all the work he'd done to try to help Aboriginal people. He was an assimilationist, I realised now, and I doubt he would have found anything amiss with the label.

'He tried to make me white,' Jim continued. 'I confronted him about it. I didn't mean to say anything more than that, because I knew he wanted the best for me, but he was out to prove something to the world. And I told him so. I loved running but it wasn't about winning gold – it was about winning Jack's approval.'

As Jim spoke, it occurred to me, perhaps for the first time, that we had both been competing for Dad. Growing up, I knew Dad loved me, even though he had no interest in Shakespeare, Sartre and all the other things I was passionate about. But Jim and Dad seemed to share everything. They spent almost every available hour training or going to meets or talking strategy. Sadly, each of us had been searching – aching – for what the other had. I wanted Dad's attention and understanding and Jim wanted Dad's unconditional love.

'But he couldn't accept it.' Jim stopped and sawed at his steak until he could collect himself. 'He looked me in the eye and said, "After everything I've done for you." He just didn't get it. It hurt. So I tried to hurt him. I told him I knew he'd lied about my parents. We had a big blue and I left. I knew he'd never understand.'

'But what about Mum?'

'She'd lied, too. At least, she hadn't told the truth.'

We ate for a while in silence. There was nothing else to say in defence of my parents: they had both lied, crushing Jim's spirit as casually as they'd crush a beetle.

'So where did you go? After the fight I mean?'

'I went to Melbourne. Mary has family there, and I knew they'd put me up.'

I realised yet again how little I'd known of my brother's life. He must have known Mary and her family for years. I wished I could ask him about it, but it seemed like prying somehow.

'Yeah, they're some of the Cummeragunja mob. Anyway, I turned up on their doorstep and they took me in. No questions.

And Mary's dad started to talk to me. Just quietly. Asking me what I remembered about my parents, my family, where I came from. And bit by bit he talked to me about my dad's people. He told me I had to face my past. That's why I went to the funeral; I needed to deal with the past, and with Jack. It was hard, but I did it. I got drunk because it was the only way I could face it. I'm not proud of it. It's not who I am anymore. Thanks to Mary and her dad I stopped drinking years ago.'

I wondered about Jim's father-in-law – he seemed to mean a great deal, but I didn't want to interrupt him to ask.

'Jack died without admitting he was wrong. He never told me he loved me or that I was worthy. I grew up feeling empty.' He sliced up the last of his steak and continued. 'Mary's dad helped me see Jack's limitations. And as hard as those conversations were and as difficult as it was to go to the funeral, I feel better – not good, but better – than I did.'

'And now?'

'Things are different for me now. Now, I feel connected, part of a community. Mary's dad and I talked a lot about letting go and moving on – he said this stuff weighs you down, and he's right. He'd take me out fishing on the Murray – Dhungala he calls it, he's Yorta Yorta, like my dad.'

'Your dad was Yorta Yorta?'

'Half Yorta Yorta, half white. He was stolen, like me, but Mary's people knew his people.'

Generational abuse, I thought, *generational loss.*

'I've been able to find a better place for myself, thanks to Mary and her dad.'

'Tell me about him.'

'I don't know if you ever met him. We were just kids back then, and nobody mixed much. It's strange to think Fred and Lily knew Betty and Jack. Weird.' He paused, and I racked my brains to think how our parents could have known Mary's parents. The names sounded vaguely familiar, but nothing came to me.

'That Cummeragunja mob were all pretty amazing – the James family, Pastor Doug Nicholls, Bill Onus, Bill Cooper . . .'

'Bill Cooper?'

'Yeah, he was one of the founders of the Australian Aborigines' League. Tried to petition the King so Indigenous people could be represented in parliament, but they weren't having any of that. He even took a petition to the German Consulate after Kristallnacht to protest against the Nazis persecuting the Jews. Don't think anyone else even noticed.'

'I had no idea . . .'

'Nah, very few people do. The Cummeragunja school was getting better results than lots of white schools back then, thanks to Shadrach James, but despite that they tried to kick him out because of his activism.'

'And Mary's dad?'

'He grew up around those old blokes. He was only young at the time of the walk-off, but he still remembers them. They shaped him. He's a painter, but he's worked all his life for our people. Never stopped. A proud Yorta Yorta man, but quiet. Strong and quiet. I learned a lot from him.'

I didn't know what to say. His voice was warm when he spoke about his father-in-law, and his face had relaxed into softer lines.

'I still have a way to go. Jack thought a gold medal would earn me respect, but I want to be respected for who I am, rather than because I have a medal or a house or a car.'

I thought about my slick Mercedes parked outside his house and felt a twinge of embarrassment. He was right. What did all that matter.

In the toilet we lined up at the urinal, and I suddenly remembered the two of us pissing in the river, and smiled. But it was not the time – or the place – for cosy reminiscences. Back in the car, Jim crossed the Murray and turned left into what looked like a long driveway. The land along the Barmah Road was flat and well treed, and opposite the entrance to the driveway the Barmah Forest stretched into the distance. The afternoon sun washed over the land, bleaching the grass and glittering on the eucalyptus leaves. The breeze had dropped and everything was still once more, our dust cloud hanging in the air behind us.

With the bright sun on the windscreen I thought about when Jim first came to live with us. We had shared a lot. Nearly fifty years, I thought. Fifty years is a bloody long time. I looked at Jim. He held the wheel casually, with his right elbow on the windowsill. I could see he was in a better place now.

'Where are we headed?'

'Cummeragunja, the place where my dad was born – and Mary's dad.'

He drove through a small settlement, turned left towards the river and pulled up in a clearing. I could see the river beyond, fringed with the pale trunks of river red gums. 'Have you heard about the walk-off?' he asked.

'I don't think so,' I said cautiously.

He smiled and shook his head. 'It was the first Aboriginal strike, in 1939. There was a manager – McQuiggan, a cruel bastard – who treated the people so badly they started to complain in writing. Starvation, intimidation – he used to carry a rifle around with him – victimisation, poor and crowded housing, hopeless sanitation. But no one would listen. So eventually they walked off their land. You can imagine how hard that was for them. Most of them never returned. And a lot of them went to Mooroopna. Mary's people did. Those kids in school with me could have been my cousins, but because Dad and been stolen, and Mum was Gunditjmara, nobody knew about me and I didn't know about them. They were Yorta Yorta.'

We stepped out of the car and walked towards the river. The ground was dry and powdery underfoot, the grasses drying off in the heat. Jim scanned the river, and I watched a cormorant with its wings spread out drying in the sun.

'My father's people roamed this forest,' he said. I could hear the pride in his voice, but his words made me feel uncomfortable. They created a distance between us that I didn't like. I felt childishly hurt. It seemed he had closed the gate on those days when we sat on the end of the jetty fishing, playing backyard cricket before dinner and snakes and ladders on the lounge-room floor. It was stupid to feel that way, I knew, when his whole history had been denied to him, but I wanted him to acknowledge that we had a past, too.

I knew that I was feeling only a fraction of what he had felt his whole life: the denial of what was real for him; all the small but consistent refusals to accept his world. It was a flicker of light against the wall of the cave, but it was something I had not understood until now. This country that he strode through now so confidently held none of that pain. He had learned to understand this country, was connected to it in a way that transcended the petty divisions and bitterness of that other world, the one I knew. Although part of me still wanted to assure him that Dad had done some good in the world, I sensed it would have diminished what Jim had lost, so I said nothing.

'Mary's dad showed me an old stone axe in a hollow log not far from here,' he said. In his voice was a wistfulness mingled with surprise, as though he too could not grasp the contrast between his people's ancient and unbroken connection to the land, and the loss he'd endured.

When we came to the river, Jim eased himself down beside a big tree and leaned back on it, gazing out across the water. I found a clear patch nearby and sat down – I'd worry about my jeans later.

Looking at him I saw some of the warmth I remembered from our childhood. He seemed tender and kind – there was a calmness about him. I knew he belonged here. To him, this land meant much more than winning a gold medal. It made his struggles with white culture fade into insignificance. He was happy.

Jim hadn't grown up in the forest, with its sacred sites, initiations and rituals, but his ancestors had, and so had Mary's.

'What about your mum?' I said.

'What about her?'

'You said she was Gund—'

'Gunditjmara, yeah. From down Warrnambool way. Her country is coastal country, those western plains, Tower Hill . . .'

'Aha. Warrnambool. So how did they meet?'

'In Melbourne. Mum had grown up at Framlingham, where a lot of Gunditjmara people went, but the government wanted them out. First they kicked out any so-called half-castes, then they changed their mind and let the families reunite. Mum had been sent to Melbourne to work as a domestic, and ended up working at the Repat in Heidelberg. Dad was sent there after he was wounded in New Guinea.'

'And the rest is history,' I said, hoping for a smile, but of course it hadn't been like that. Jim had been stolen.

The silence was broken only by the cry of a water bird somewhere out of sight.

'Do you remember your parents? Your home?' I had always wondered what thoughts tumbled through his mind all those years ago when he sat on the end of his bed gazing out the window after school, or stood alone on the bank of the Goulburn on weekends throwing stones into the water, or disappeared for hours at a time during school holidays, walking or running beside the river or along the road out to Rumbalara. Did he mourn the loss of that rich life with his family, playing, exploring, fishing? He must have yearned for his mother – could he still remember her face, her eyes, the sound of her voice, her touch? In spite of what Mum and Dad had done for him, he must have felt so alone.

'I remember Mum better than Dad, because he was away working so much. My uncle . . . I remember him . . . he's still alive. And I remember home. It was different. Different country, different place, different home. But I loved it.' Jim lifted his head and looked at me, his eyes clear and dark. The air was filled with a brooding silence. I sat, feeling a throbbing inside my head and a weight in my chest. I sensed his strength, his determination to survive, and beside him I felt soft and weak.

'I brought you here because I want to show you who I am,' he said. 'I don't want to upset you but I do want to talk to you. I can't take you to my mother's country, but this is just as important, even though it's not where I started life.' He clambered to his feet and headed back along the track to the car. 'Come on.'

'That house is where my dad was born,' he said, as he pulled up in the shade of a solitary tree opposite a small weatherboard house with a broken cane lounge on the verandah. 'I can't show you my home, but when I went back there, to my people, the trees I climbed as a young boy were still there, the country looked the same . . . though everything seemed to have shrunk.' He smiled. 'I remembered the birdcalls, I remembered fishing with my uncle, and going out shooting rabbits. That land was my childhood, just as this land was my dad's and Mary's dad's; both places are sacred to me and my ancestors.'

'A lot has changed,' I said, feeling how utterly inadequate that was as a response.

'I was seven when I was taken away from my country, but I still have a connection to it – it's my culture, my heritage and my history.' He emphasised each of these with a tightening of his fist. 'But how could I learn the traditions and beliefs of my ancestors when I wasn't there for them to teach me? I was brought up in a white house with white values, and those two cultures couldn't be more different. What happened to me destroyed everything I—' he stumbled, and the words that followed had a formality to them that masked a deeper truth. '. . . everything I believe is important. What happens to our traditions? How can a culture survive if each generation has to start afresh?'

I felt a knot of indignation tighten in my stomach. I knew the way we treated Jim and his people was shocking. I knew that to us, land is a resource – we own it – but to his people it owns them. For the first time I felt what it meant to have stolen that from them. We herded his people into missions and reserves, stole their children and tried to breed them out of existence. To be part of a people that committed such atrocities was shameful. Jim looked at me, waiting for me to acknowledge what he'd said. Not sure I could trust myself to say anything profound, I held back, but I nodded, too stricken to speak. It was clear nothing else mattered to him, certainly not his gold medal, and certainly not his white family. No one had said to him, 'You are important, your identity means something, your family is invaluable, your traditions and heritage are an intrinsic part of who you are.'

'We are a living culture,' he said.

'I understand . . . at least I think I do.'

'It's simple. A Catholic can go to church on Sunday, say grace at meals and observe Lent. A Jew can go to synagogue on Saturday, and a Muslim can pray to Allah, and they can all still be members of the wider community. My people are no different. We have our rituals and celebrations and we do the usual things that other Australians do. We are not barbaric or primitive because we perform rituals that go back thousands of years. Every culture does that – it's normal – it's just that ours are probably the oldest unbroken traditions on Earth. We understand we need to accept your laws, adopt your language, your way of thought and your way of reasoning if we want to be part of the modern world, but we shouldn't have to lose everything. And you, your people, need to listen.'

Again I felt the sting of 'your people', and the boy in me mourned for the distance that had opened between us.

Suspended between my feelings of guilt and sorrow I knew I had to speak. But what could I possibly say? 'Jim, I . . . I'm sorry. I'm sorry for not being a better brother, and for being so blind all these years. And for not trying to find you, or find out the truth.' I sighed. 'I'm sorry about my parents. And I'm sorry my people did what we've done, and keep doing it.'

There was a long silence, with only the whirr of insects and the click of the cooling engine. I thought of my mother's face when she saw Jim, and all those years of loving him as a son, and felt torn.

'They did try you know . . . Mum especially, and Dad . . .'

Jim sighed in frustration. 'I know. But . . .' He stopped, thinking about what to say. 'I was a black person in a white world. I was lucky in some ways, I know. But it came at a price. I lost my sense of self – that's what happens when people tell you you're something that you're not. And then you find out you are stolen so you get angry, and feel helpless, and deceived and don't know who to trust. So you start to drink or take drugs. You turn into a victim and think the whole world owes you a living. If it hadn't been for Mary and her dad . . .'

Jim looked over at me. 'Dad never asked me what I wanted, he always thought he knew best. Three meals a day are important. A white education is useful too. But there are some things that matter more.'

Could I understand Jim's anger? Of course. I was angry with my parents for lying to us, and it was far less important to me. That lie didn't break my heart.

'Since I left, I've thought a lot about those times at school – the goading and the bullying from those mongrels – "ya black bastard", "coon", "dirty Abo", and even "you don't belong here"!' He laughed bitterly, the memories still sharp despite the passing of so many decades. 'And it wasn't just the kids. I can't tell you the number of times other people pretended not to hear when a shopkeeper said, "You'll be bloody patient" or "You'll be lucky if I serve your type at all". I'm not talking about forty years ago, either. I'm talking about the last decade. Just months ago I was in Melbourne.'

I turned my head sharply to look at him.

'Yeah, I know. I go there. I might not work in the big smoke like some people,' he smiled, 'but I've got an actor mate who does shows down there, and I've been doing some work with the Koorie Heritage Trust. I'll tell you about it later. Anyway, it took us forty minutes and five tries to get a taxi. They drove off on us. Can you believe it? They saw us, black fellas, and just took off, even though we'd booked them.'

'Didn't you call to complain?'

'Oh yeah. Made a big fuss. Even made it to the papers and they said they would reprimand the drivers, blah blah blah. Nothing's changed.' He looked weary. 'Let me tell you something that will shock you.'

'What's that?'

'There are more children being taken from their homes today than at any time during the last century.'

I remembered hearing that elder on the radio say the same thing, and once again I was speechless. Surely it couldn't be right. 'Wait. What?'

Jim nodded and gave me a sad smile.

'But, how can it be that we hear so much about the stolen generation but so little about this? I thought those days were behind us.'

'Aboriginal women live in constant fear that a social worker will knock on the door, tell them their kids are being abused, or maltreated or neglected and remove them.'

'That's outrageous – it can't be right.'

'Look, Mary has a close friend – they grew up together at Rumbalara. Since her husband died, Joan hasn't had enough money to buy new school shoes, or uniforms, even the school bus fares are beyond her. She lives in fear. And what drives you crazy is that the white woman across the road, who's in exactly the same trouble, doesn't have to worry about government officials turning up on her doorstep.'

'That's wrong.'

'Just look at where the funding goes. Instead of setting up a lunch program, or a second-hand uniform shop at the school for low-income families, the government employs a truancy officer for Indigenous communities.'

'But why . . .?'

He started the engine. 'Now you're asking the right questions. Let's go. It's getting late.'

As we drove back to Jim's place, I thought about the land we were travelling through and what had transpired there. I thought about Jim's dislocation from his family, his old people, and his heritage, but most of all I thought about Dad's inability to see Jim as equal, which had destroyed their bond and caused him to shun Dad for the rest of his life. Jim and I had been able to breach the wall of hostility between us, at least I hoped we had. We'd made a start, anyway, I was pretty sure of that. Surely Mum or Dad could have done the same. They could have tried.

As I got into my car Jim said to me, 'D'you want to meet me in town on Thursday?'

'Melbourne, you mean? Sure, why?'

'I could show you round the Koori Heritage Trust. We haven't moved in any of the artefacts yet, but the building looks amazing. I think you should see it.'

'Thanks, I'd like that.' I fished out my wallet and handed him a card, feeling embarrassed that it was necessary. 'Either of those numbers will work, and I'll be at Mum's tonight and tomorrow . . .'

He nodded, thrust the card into his back pocket and said, 'Tell her I said hello. See you, Rob.' He walked back to the house, turned at the door and waved, his head up, his shoulders back – the man who had won gold. Then he disappeared inside.

I was getting into my car when I saw Mary come to the front door and hurry down the path towards me. I got out and waited for her.

'I just wanted to say goodbye,' she said, 'and thank you for coming. It means a lot to him.'

'Thanks,' I said, 'it means a lot to me, too.'

'Your parents meant well,' she said, 'they were better than most.'

I shrugged.

'Your dad was good to my brother.'

'Your brother . . .?'

'Wayne. And he did what he could for me when . . .'

I must have looked as nonplussed as I felt.

'You don't know who I am, do you.'

'I'm sorry, I—'

'I'm Meri – Meredith Langdon.'

CHAPTER 18

I COULDN'T FACE TALKING TO Mum – or anyone – after that, so when I left Jim and Meri's place I drove to Echuca, too stunned to think clearly. I crossed the Murray, remembering its broad expanse at Cummeragunja, and drove until I found a small park. I pulled into the kerb, locked the car and found a seat under a tree, staring blankly at the park in the late afternoon sunlight. I needed to think, needed to absorb all I had learned.

I felt emptied out with shock. *Meri*, not Mary. Meredith Langdon. The woman who had suffered so terribly as a girl at the hands of the very same people who had tormented Jim as a child, and yet somehow she had survived and moved beyond it – above it in fact. She and her father had rescued Jim from the despair he'd fallen into, and together they'd built a life together, away from the town that had done them so much harm, but still within their own country. I was stunned by their strength.

The sun settled behind the trees to the west as I sat there, thinking about our lives when we were growing up in Mooroopna. I couldn't know for sure, but now I thought Jim must have formed bonds with the other Aboriginal kids in town. How else would he have known Meri? Dad and Mum had known her parents, and Meri's brother, but I don't remember ever meeting them. Those times when Jim had disappeared for hours and come home saying he'd been running – perhaps he'd been out at Rumbalara with his own people. And if his dad hadn't been stolen, had grown up amongst other Yorta Yorta people, perhaps they would have recognised Jim and been able to place him, tell him his parents were very much alive and spare him years of suffering. Jim might even have known his father.

The thought that he'd missed out on meeting his father filled me with sorrow, and I found that I was crying quietly, for Jim, for his mum, who had lived through those long years without him, for his dad, who died never knowing him, and for Meri Langdon.

Next morning I woke to the sound of Mum in the kitchen. 'Your mother is always up at the crack of dawn,' Dad had often boasted. She was sitting at the table in her dressing gown reading the paper, with a cup of tea at her elbow. 'Good morning,' she smiled, putting down her cup and pointing at a glass opposite. 'I've made you some orange juice.'

'Thanks.'

'How did you sleep?'

'Well. I was exhausted.'

'You had a long drive.'

I nodded. It was a deeper exhaustion, but now was not the time to explain. I'd thought about telling Mum that Jim had married Meri Langdon, but it didn't feel right. It wasn't my story to tell.

'So now, tell me how you got on with Jim,' she said.

I'd dawdled on the way to Mooroopna, wanting to give myself time to think about all Jim had told me. When I got to Mum's, the whole place was in darkness, and I crept into my old bedroom feeling like a teenager who'd stayed out too late. As I lay in bed too agitated to sleep, I thought of Meri, and all she had suffered. Was it my place to tell Mum who she was? I decided it wasn't.

'He took me to the house where his father was born,' I replied, sipping the juice.

I saw Mum wince as she folded the newspaper on the table. There was a quiet, awkward moment, and then she said, 'How was he?'

'Jim?' He's much better – Meri's father has been a great help I think.'

'Fred was always a good man.'

'Fred? You mean you know about Meri . . . I mean, you know who she is? How . . .?'

'I didn't recognise her straight away – she's changed a lot, and . . . and I wasn't myself that day, but after the funeral it niggled at me – where had I seen her before. And then one morning I just woke up with the answer. She's Meredith Langdon.'

'Why didn't you tell me?'

'I didn't think it was my business. I thought Jim would tell us if he wanted us to know.'

I could hardly condemn her for that, since I'd had much the same thought.

'So, what did you talk about?'

I hesitated. 'Growing up, what he's learned since he left home . . . the fight with Dad.'

Mum's face crumpled and she suddenly looked old and tired. 'I hated it,' she said bitterly. 'I blamed myself.'

'Why? It wasn't your fault.' It worried me that Mum had to face this emotional upheaval so soon after Dad's death.

'It had been brewing a long time. Your father always wanted Jim to win a gold medal. He wanted him to be better than everyone else because he thought Jim would be accepted then. But I was concerned about him respecting himself, and his Aboriginal heritage.'

'Did you ever say anything to Dad?'

'Of course. But you know your father, he was always so stubborn; he knew better than everybody else and it always turned into an argument. So in the end I gave up.'

Mum shrugged then said, 'When Jim was younger – you'll probably remember this – I would sit on the end of his bed and read you both a story, then Jim would tell me a story from the Dreamtime. I always listened, but if your father came into the room he'd roll his eyes and storm out, and once it ended in an almighty blue. I got sick of the arguments and so I stopped reading to you or telling you stories because I could see how much it upset your father if Jim told his own stories. It threatened him. He was always afraid he'd lose Jim, and in the end he did, through his own stubbornness. And my failure to protect that boy is something I'm going to have to live with for the rest of my life.'

'Why?'

'Because it's too late to do anything about it now.'

'Is it? You could try and talk to Jim.'

'I don't even know if he would talk to me. For all I know, he probably thinks I agreed with Dad.'

'What do you mean?'

'You know, that he needed the gold medal to prove he was somebody.'

'Didn't you?'

'Of course not.'

I got up to make myself some toast. 'I'm meeting Jim in Melbourne next Thursday. He's going to show me the Koorie Heritage Trust's new building'

'Oh?'

'I can sound him out about maybe meeting with you for a talk, if you'd like.'

'I'd like that a lot, Rob.'

Next morning, a quiet Sunday like countless Sundays I'd spent at home, Mum and I were planning our day over breakfast. I didn't have to leave until late afternoon or early evening, which gave us enough time to visit friends or go for a drive, or do a bit of gardening. Whatever Mum wanted to do was fine by me.

'Let's clean up the garden,' she said. 'I let it go while Dad was sick, and it needs some attention. I'd like to spread a bit more mulch, too, to stop everything drying out so quickly.'

'Have you ever thought of replacing that back fence?' I said.

'No. Why? You and Dad built that.'

'Yes, I know, but it blocks all the morning light from the garden, and you could probably see the river if it wasn't for the fence.'

'Hmm. Let me think about it.'

While we ate our toast, we chatted about what we'd do, then Mum got up to switch on the radio for the news. I half-listened to news of the Telstra share price, Jeff Kennett sounding off, Pauline Hanson and One Nation seemingly bent on a path of self-destruction, waterfront reform, the Howard government's welfare reform, the republic, and then in local news, something about a fire at the Koorie Heritage Trust building in Lonsdale Street. 'Fifteen fire crews took almost an hour to control the blaze, which broke out at 7.00 o'clock this morning. The arson squad is investigating.'

I looked at Mum. 'Oh no. Jim was going to show me round. He'll be devastated.'

'Poor things,' said Mum. 'Should you ring?'

I hesitated for only a moment. 'I will.' I grabbed my phone and called.

'Yes?' It was Jim.

'Jim, it's me, Rob. I've just heard about the fire at the Koorie Heritage Trust. It was on the news.'

'Yeah, I had a call earlier. They're saying it was deliberately lit.' He sounded utterly dispirited.

'Jim, if there's anything I can do, let me know. Happy to do it pro bono. Anything.'

'Thanks, Rob. Can't think straight yet. I'm still going down on Thursday to have a look, if you want to come along.'

'Sure, I'd like that. Thanks Jim.'

'At least the building was empty. If we'd lost our artefacts and our books and records . . .'

'Grateful for small mercies, eh?'

'Yeah,' he said, 'I guess so.'

I told Georgia, my secretary, to keep all of Thursday afternoon free, in case Jim needed time to talk or to go through the burnt-out building. We'd agreed to meet in Lonsdale Street outside the site at noon. The smell of ashes filled my nose as I stood in the shade waiting for Jim. Scaffolding obscured the façade, but even from outside I could see that the arsonist had been thorough. The building was gutted.

Jim came striding along the street and I stepped out of the shade to meet him. His face was impassive as he eyed the burnt-out shell.

'We were three weeks away from opening,' he said. 'After more than two years of hard work, all gone in one night because of one racist dickhead or one disgruntled worker.' His voice was bitter.

'So they're pretty sure it was arson?'

'Yep, it was torched, we just don't know who did it or why.'

'Do the police have any leads?'

'Not that they're sharing with us.'

We walked up and down the footpath and peered in through the windows, but the place was a ruin, open to the sky and reeking of burnt timber and metal. After a while I stopped Jim and said, 'Come on, let me buy you lunch and we can talk. This is doing you no good.' He nodded and we headed towards a quiet restaurant where I used to meet clients sometimes. I was keen to arrange a meeting between Jim and Meri and Mum as soon as I could. They needed to make their peace.

We ordered a couple of steaks, and I thought about how best to broach the subject of a meeting, but before I could speak Jim said, 'What was that line about problems from the play you did? When we were kids.'

'Hamlet?'

'Yeah.'

I thought for a minute. '"When sorrows come, they come not single spies. But in battalions!" Is that what you mean?'

'Yeah.' He turned his glass of water carefully on the table.

I was surprised he'd remembered any of the lines I used to spout as I walked around the house trying to memorise my part all those years ago. That he'd remembered those particular lines seemed ominous. 'Why? What's happened?'

'It'll be on the news soon enough, I guess . . .' he hesitated. 'Meri's niece has died . . . in jail.'

'I'm sorry, Jim. That's awful. Poor Meri . . .'

'Sometimes it all seems hopeless – we're never going to get past it.'

'But it's not just on you. It's on all of us.'

'They locked her up for not paying her fines.' His voice trembled. 'I keep imagining how she must have felt, alone, everyone in uniform, guns on their hips, standing over her.'

'If only she'd told somebody, maybe . . .'

Jim hesitated. I could feel him weighing his words, delicately balancing what he felt with what I would understand. 'It's not that simple. Who could she tell – a black woman in a white jail? The police don't understand us, they've got no idea.'

I thought I had learned so much, thought I had begun to feel closer to this man and understand Aboriginal culture, but I was still stuck in a narrow 'white' way of thinking. The truth was I trusted the police, and the courts, to do right by me. I'd come a long way, I realised, since my student days, when nobody trusted the cops. In a naïve way, I even trusted the government. But I could see that for Jim and Meri, and most Aboriginal people, it wasn't like that.

'But they should have known leaving her alone in a cell might lead to self harm—'

'Hang on a sec,' Jim interrupted. I heard the frustration in his tone and a welling dissatisfaction that he usually kept hidden. 'That kind of thinking won't bring change. We've seen that over the last twelve years. It's *twelve years* since the royal commission into deaths in custody, and nothing's changed. Nothing.'

'But there's the Koori Court, that must have made a difference, surely.'

'Yes, of course, and it's good that Koori elders can be part of the process, and that offenders can understand what's going on and have the support of their families, but . . .'

'But?'

'But not everyone gets to use it, and the jails haven't changed in decades. There's a cultural gulf between your people and my people that's been there since invasion.'

I felt the sting of 'your people'.

'Black people are always judged by white standards, because whites have all the power. They tell us how to live, make us feel as though we're not good enough – it's assimilate or die.'

I felt the deep pain and bitterness behind his words and knew that they were true. How could anyone survive unscathed after so many generations of abuse? I thought of the sentence handed down to Craig Woodhead, Ken Armstrong and Bob Birch, for nearly destroying Meri: a three-year good behaviour bond.

Jim took a deep, shaky breath. 'She was twenty-one. A silly girl who got too many parking fines and didn't know what to do about them. That's all. So they locked her up, and now she's dead.'

A month later I was sitting in Mum's lounge room waiting for Jim and Meri to arrive. Jim had reluctantly agreed to discuss with Meri the possibility of visiting his old home after I'd broached the subject on the day after the fire. Meri must have persuaded him somehow, because when he phoned, he sounded calmer and warmer. Yet again I was awed by Meri's strength and kindness.

Our conversation over lunch on the day of the fire still troubled me. As he'd talked, I'd felt my world view – everything I knew without questioning how I knew it – begin to split apart under the strain of confronting a profoundly different world view. It seemed that whenever I felt I had begun to understand a little of my brother's world, another deeper level opened up before me, and I was once more as baffled and uncertain as I had been that day beside the river.

Mum had been baking for days to prepare for the visit. I could tell she was nervous, fussing over what to wear as if she were meeting royalty rather than her estranged son and his wife.

They arrived right on time, and I went out to meet them as they pulled up. Meri looked calm, but Jim seemed anxious, although it was difficult to read him at the best of times.

'Come in,' I said. 'Mum's waiting. She's cooked enough cake to feed an army.'

Meri smiled and followed me into the house, with Jim walking behind, his eyes darting here and there, noting the changes since he was last here so long ago.

As we came into the lounge room, Mum struggled to her feet and held out her arms. Meri went to her and kissed her on the cheek, and Jim bent awkwardly and kissed her, too, while she patted his back nervously.

'Sit down, sit down,' she said. 'I'll get Rob to put on the kettle so we can have a nice cup of tea, eh?'

I took my cue and headed for the kitchen, but before the kettle boiled, Meri and Jim and Mum had followed and settled themselves around the kitchen table.

'No waiting on ceremony,' Mum said. 'We're going to have our tea out here. It'll be like old times . . .' her voice petered out awkwardly.

I handed around the tea, plonked the milk and sugar on the table and began to slice the sponge. Mum whisked the tea towels off the other dishes and hung them over the back of her chair. As we passed around the milk jug, Meri smiled at me, and a look passed between us. I wasn't sure what it meant, but I took a breath and said, 'Look, let's not tiptoe around all afternoon. We all need to talk and clear the air. Jim? Mum?'

Jim nodded, and Mum said quietly, 'Well, I'd just like to say first that I'm so happy you two found each other. I always liked your parents, Meredith – Meri – they were good people.'

Meri smiled quietly and nodded, but Mum hadn't finished.

'Jim, I'm sorry for everything we did, or I did, to hurt you. I realise now that we did you a great deal of harm. We didn't mean to, but that's no excuse. Dad thought he knew best. He meant well. He thought you – all blacks – were capable of anything, if you had some help.'

Jim gave a huff of bitter acknowledgement.

'I told him we shouldn't have pushed you into going for gold. He thought it would be the making of you, and all it did was strip you of your self-esteem. We often argued about it. I didn't want you kids to know – I thought we had to present a united front. Seems silly now. He couldn't see that he was telling you – not in so many words, but still – that without him, without white people and a gold medal, you were nothing.'

'What did he say to that?' I butted in.

'He said I didn't know what I was talking about.'

Meri was watching Jim intently. His face looked both pained and proud.

Mum sipped her tea. 'Rather than you being accepted into a white world, I wanted you to have self-respect. I thought if people respect themselves they don't drink and they don't take drugs and they are well placed to work hard and improve their lot.'

Perhaps for the first time I understood my mother, and saw beyond the monstrous lie she'd failed to challenge. She got it; making Jim follow Dad's dream, denying him his own dreams, his parents, his family and his heritage was like saying you're not good enough. It was paternalism and it stripped Jim of his dignity and self-esteem.

Jim seemed to have relaxed a little. Hearing how Mum felt seemed to help, and yet there was still the fact of that first dreadful lie.

'I've never forgotten that last terrible fight,' Mum continued. 'You and Dad were shouting at each other. The dreadful truth had come out. For Dad, it was you learning the truth about your parents still being alive; for me it was you realising the appalling lie we'd told you. I remember you said, "You had no right to keep me from my parents and my family," and you were absolutely right.' Mum's whole body had tensed at the recollection of the fight and she shut her eyes as if she could wish the memory away.

Jim nodded and took up the story, knowing it needed to be said, that the air finally had to be cleared. 'You spent my lifetime telling me my parents were dead – you *stole* me. I said it then and nothing's changed. I lost all respect for Jack then – I knew he would never understand – it was hopeless.' Jim looked down at his hands.

'I remember him hissing at me, "That medal is the best thing that ever happened to you." And I said, "You mean, it's the best thing that ever happened to *you*!"'

Mum nodded sadly. 'He was furious you'd said that. I knew then that that was the end of it. He couldn't accept it. Couldn't face—' she paused and I finished the sentence for her.

'—the truth.' No one spoke.

Finally, Jim shrugged. 'I guess he tried. He said something like, "*We're* your family. Look what we've given you. Don't turn your back on it. You've won a gold medal – look forward for god's sake." He didn't have a clue.'

'No,' said Mum, 'you're right.'

'The last thing I heard him say was, "So this is the way you repay us, eh?"' His voice cracked.

There was a long silence. Meri's eyes were full of pain as she looked from Mum to Jim.

'Dad was scared, Jim,' Mum finally said.

'Of what?' Dad had never been scared of anything.

'Of losing you.'

Jim considered the comment. He could see there was truth to it, but fear was no excuse.

'We argued again that night,' Mum said quietly, as though she'd been waiting to say it for years. 'I told him to find you and tell you ... tell you we were wrong to take you,' she bowed her head for a moment, then looked Jim in the eye, 'and very wrong to tell you your parents were dead.'

'What did he say?' I asked.

'He said, "Forget it. It's all over."'

No one spoke. After years of lies and secrets the truth was out. I felt a chill at the thought that for decades I'd believed Jim was ungrateful and selfish and that Dad was the injured party.

Mum spoke again, her voice filled with an old grief. 'He did love you, Jim. Right to the end.' And that was another truth.

There was a long silence, during which Meri reached over and squeezed Jim's hand.

'I'm glad we've spoken,' Mum said, looking at Jim.

'Yeah. I've wanted to clear the air for a while,' Jim said gruffly. Meri smiled.

'I hope you'll come and visit me sometime,' Mum said, looking at Meri. 'And bring the children?'

'They'd like that,' Meri said. 'You can never have too many grandmas.'

I wondered if the day would come when we would meet Jim's mother, but I didn't have the courage, or the temerity, to ask.

CHAPTER 19

IT TOOK A YEAR FOR the Koorie Heritage Trust to open in temporary premises. Jim and Meri invited Mum and me to the ceremony in Manchester House in Flinders Lane, where Sir William Deane opened the premises. 'Everything about this centre is calculated to foster the mutual tolerance and respect which is a vital component of true reconciliation,' he said in his speech, and I wished Dad could have been there to hear it, and to see how attentive Jim was to Mum. He had nothing to fear from Jim turning back to his people: his heart was big enough for both his families.

We strolled around the permanent exhibition with its stories, exhibits, maps and transcripts detailing the lives and cultures of our first Australians. Jim and Meri's kids were there, too – Jackie, a nurse, and Josh, a PE teacher. Mum spent more time with them than she did looking at the exhibits.

'The Trust has thousands of artefacts,' Jackie told Mum, 'some from before the invasion, some from living artists. You should see the paintings, they're awesome.' I watched Mum absorb 'invasion' without flinching – she was full of surprises.

We walked past exhibitions of boomerangs, spear throwers, shell necklaces, woven bags and baskets, fish hooks, stone tools, musical instruments, feather skirts and possum-skin cloaks, all beautifully made.

Jim came up to me when I was looking at an eel trap, strongly woven out of plant fibre.

'That's Gunditjmara work,' he said. My mother's people made traps like that. They'd build stone weirs to funnel the eels towards the traps, then they'd smoke them so they could trade them or store them.'

I must have registered surprise because he said, 'They were a settled community, living in stone houses and farming. But that doesn't fit the story of the primitive savage, so most people don't know about it. And white fellas destroyed the houses . . .' he shook his head. 'Still, there's enough left to know.'

'Have you been there?'

'Yeah. Remember I said I went back to meet my mum and all the family? Well, my uncle took me around then. It's pretty amazing. A lot of people are working towards having it put on the National Heritage List.'

'I didn't know,' I said. 'We never learnt a thing about any of this at school, did we.'

He raised one eyebrow quizzically then, after a long pause said, 'I'm glad you came. I'm glad the kids met you and Betty.'

'Me too,' I said, ignoring the little pang I felt at him calling Mum Betty. 'It's been amazing. I can't wait to see it all when you get a permanent home for all this.'

Jim sighed, and I knew there was a lot of work and money and time needed before that could happen.

'If I can help,' I said, 'I'd like to.'

'Thanks, Rob. I'm sure there'll be lots to do.'

I glanced at my watch. 'Mum, I'm sorry, we've got to go.'

She looked at me in surprise. 'Where has the time gone?' She smiled at Jackie. 'It's been a lovely day.' Then she turned to Jim. Any hostility between them had faded away. 'Thank you,' she said, and pressed his arm warmly.

Jim kissed Mum on the cheek and shook my hand, and Meri and the kids hugged us before we stepped out into the night.

It was only a block to Flinders Street station, so we decided to walk and catch a train to Spencer Street. Mum could have managed the trip home alone, but she was old now, and I didn't want to risk it. I'd left my car in Mooroopna and we'd travelled down together on the train. It gave us time to talk, it was more relaxing than the car, and I could do a bit of work. With Dad gone, I treasured the time I had left with Mum, and had taken a few days off work to spend with her, make sure the house was in good order and she didn't need anything.

It was a calm warm evening. We walked along Swanston Street to the station, and caught a train the one stop to Spencer Street, which Steve Bracks had recently called an 'embarrassment' when he announced its refurbishment. The train to Seymour was leaving in ten minutes, so we'd timed it well.

As we got on I noticed three Aboriginal men sitting near the back of the carriage, wearing stained jeans and baggy T-shirts. I headed for two empty seats towards the front of the carriage, but Mum touched my arm and said curtly, 'Over there,' pointing to two seats towards the back of the carriage almost opposite the men.

I followed her apprehensively, but didn't say a word. One of the men was chewing a wad of gum, rolling it around his tongue while he talked to the other men. Another sat on the aisle, the sleeves of his shirt tight around his forearms, stomach lean and biceps bulging. The third was bulkier.

As we sat down, the lean man turned his head, casually looked at us and returned to the conversation. They were talking quietly amongst themselves, and although I couldn't hear clearly, it sounded as if they were discussing the cricket.

Mum was annoyed, I could tell by the set of her jaw, and I felt a quiver of shame. When I next glanced at one of the men and caught his eye, he smiled and the gulf between us seemed to disappear. It was astonishing to me that I had felt that way, after just stepping out of the Koorie Heritage Trust and spending time with my Aboriginal brother and his family. What had I assumed would happen? I'd thought they would be drunk, or loud and disruptive. In truth, the opposite was the case. Despite everything I'd experienced with Jim, everything he had shown me about his home, his birthplace, and his family, I had somehow failed to hear what he had been trying to say. I promised myself that in future I would counter these foolish fears – no, these prejudices – with rational thoughts.

During a pause in their conversation, Mum turned to the men and said, 'We've just come from the opening of the new Koori Heritage Trust. It was lovely. I'd really recommend a visit.'

The man on the aisle smiled and said quietly, 'We've been too busy to do much in Melbourne, but thanks, we'll check it out.' He was open and friendly and I had the feeling he wanted to talk.

'I'm Betty by the way, and this is my son, Robert,' Mum said, her voice still a little clipped with me.

'I'm Corey and this is Nathan,' he said, gesturing to the man chewing gum.

Nathan glanced at Mum and smiled, then nodded at me. He seemed the silent type, a little shy of strangers, I thought.

The man at the window lifted his head and said, 'I'm Peter, pleased to meet you.'

'Are you coming or going?' Mum asked.

'We live in Shepparton. We've been down for a conference on community work,' Corey said.

'Really?' Mum's eyes brightened.

'We do voluntary work with Rumbalara – it's a co-operative. It's run by Indigenous people to support Indigenous families.' Corey's voice was warm.

'Ah,' Mum said, 'I know Rumbalara. Out on the Toolamba Road. We live in Mooroopna, she added, 'or I do.'

'Yep, that's the one,' Corey said. 'The main office is in Shepparton.'

'So what kind of work do you do?'

Corey glanced at the other two, and Peter sat up a little straighter and said, 'We do house repairs and maintenance, sometimes take the kids to and from school, and help the kids with their homework while the parents are working.'

'Play football, netball . . .' Nathan added.

'The idea is to support the family,' Corey said, 'stop the authorities taking their children because they say they're being neglected.'

'Sounds like a good program,' Mum said without hesitation. Nobody could have guessed that she had raised one of those stolen children.

I looked at Corey and his friends with new respect. Here were men prepared to stand up for what they believed, willing to work to improve the lot of Indigenous people, men with generous spirits looking for practical solutions. I remembered Jim's story about the woman who lived in fear of her children being taken because of poverty, and leaned forward, keen to know more.

'A lot of Aboriginal mothers don't want anybody to know they are doing it tough because they're scared they'll get a black mark against their name and unannounced visits from the Department of Community Services, who might take their kids,' Peter said.

'If the house isn't clean and there's no food on the table and the children aren't at school, they can take them,' Corey continued.

'Surely Child Protection take white kids in those same circumstances, don't they? Shouldn't this apply to all children?' I said, choosing my words carefully, anxious not to offend.

'That's not quite right,' Nathan said. 'Child Protection only take white kids if they are being physically or sexually abused, malnourished or they're seriously ill and their parents are not doing anything about it. And nine times out of ten, it's not the kids that are taken away, it's one or both of the parents, and the kids are settled with another family member wherever possible.' Nathan spoke with quiet insistence. He looked me right in the eye and I could see him trying to work out what I believed – was I prejudiced or simply offering an alternate view?

I felt a lump in my throat.

'Blacks and whites are treated differently – don't you think?' Corey said.

'Yes, I agree,' Mum said. 'Why is it that Rumbalara need to get volunteers to do this work? Isn't it better to help parents look after their kids than take them away? I bet it's cheaper!'

Nobody spoke for a few moments, as though each was waiting for the other to answer.

'I heard recently that there are more children being taken now than ever before . . .'

Mum raised an eyebrow, guessing the source of the information, and I felt cowardly for not acknowledging Jim.

Peter nodded and said, 'It's easier to deal with something you think has stopped happening – people believe what they want to believe. If it's still happening, then we have to figure out why, and that's not easy.'

I couldn't speak. It seemed the system that was supposed to be protecting these children was actively harming them instead. Why were black homes in such disarray that the children would be vulnerable? Were white kids removed for the same reasons? And if not, why were black kids?

Nathan seemed to read my thoughts. 'This is inter-generational trauma – damaged families produce damaged kids. And because of the stolen gen, no one can trust the government. So you don't ask for help when things go wrong because you worry they'll take your kids too, and the cycle gets passed down from great-grandparents to grandparents to parents. And if you're struggling, but you're too afraid to ask for help, things just get worse.'

I looked out the window at the grey light filtering through clouds. How had we got to this point so quickly? We'd just met these men. Houses, power lines, trees rushed by, and everywhere I looked I seemed to see signs of need: broken fences, rubbish strewn along the tracks, a burnt-out car. My mood, which had been light and optimistic after the opening at the Koorie Heritage Trust, darkened.

'In the past they took children because they were black,' Corey was saying in a dry, flat voice. 'Now they take them because they don't approve of the way they're being brought up.'

Mum nodded. 'It's easy for us to think that our way is the right way. Or the only way.' She caught my eye and I knew what she was thinking, but neither of us was brave enough to confess our own part in this sorry history.

'They judge us by white standards, by what they think's important. They don't think about what we might want, or what we have to offer our kids.'

Suddenly, the trained slowed. I looked out of the window and was surprised to see we were at Craigieburn already. The three men stood up. 'We're gonna see if we can find something to eat,' Corey said. 'We didn't have time in the city.' He reached over and shook my hand with a strong grip. 'Nice to meet you.'

'Keep up the good work,' I heard Mum say to Corey as I shook hands with Nathan and Peter.

'You're doing important work,' I murmured. 'Good on you.'

I was surprised at how disappointed I felt at the conversation ending so soon, and yet it was also a relief to sit back and try to think of nothing for a while.

Mum was quiet for the rest of the journey – she seemed preoccupied with her own thoughts.

At Seymour I bought us some sandwiches from the café bar, but I didn't see the three men.

Staring out the window at the passing world, I felt a little less comfortable about my place in it. It's not easy to look at yourself in the mirror and admit you are wrong. Watching the paddocks with their ripening crops or sheep, I thought about Jim. Who said our way of life is better than the way Aboriginal people choose to live their life? The idea seemed overwhelming and I felt the ground shift beneath my feet. I wondered how I would feel if I had to live a life that wasn't mine, to accept unfamiliar values and beliefs, to have everything and everyone I had ever known taken from me. I doubt I would have coped as well as Jim. I wondered about the black children being taken today – were they too suffering in the same way that Jim had? Why would we expect their experience to be any different from Jim's?

'Remember Mrs Peterson?' Mum interrupted my thoughts.

'Of course, you went to school with her.'

'Yes, we knew each other since kindergarten.' She smiled fondly. 'Remember, her daughter Issie?'

'Sure, she came to stay with us when Mr Peterson died.'

'Well, she's a social worker now – she works with Aboriginal families on a program run by Aboriginal people. Some time ago she asked me if I wanted to do some voluntary work. But because of Dad's poor health I said no. I'm going to call her next week and say I can do it now.'

'Good idea.' I hesitated, not wanting to blunt Mum's enthusiasm. 'Are you . . . are you *qualified* to do something like this?' I asked.

'Of course not,' Mum said. 'I'd be a volunteer. I'm too old to do much, but I'd be learning from *them*, Robert, not the other way round.'

'But wouldn't you just be another white woman meddling in Aboriginal affairs?' It was blunt, but to be honest I was a little peeved by how readily my mother was shrugging off her own part in a system that had caused so much harm.

Mum considered my comment. 'No,' she said at last, 'I think I can use it to learn about a people I've lived beside my whole life but never really known.' There was a profound sadness as she spoke and I could feel Jim's presence strongly. 'And perhaps I can start to make amends, in a small way.' She gave me a slow, grief-filled smile, her eyes wet, and I thought about the boy who I had so loved, and the man – one and the same – who I had never known or understood. I felt a rush of pride for my mother and her courage and what she had taught me.

The train pulled into Mooroopna Station and we disembarked and walked slowly along the path in the warm night air towards the car park. Listening to the calm commitment of those three young men, their dogged determination to make a difference, their pride in their work and their community gave me hope. I felt ashamed of my unconscious racism, but strangely, I also felt a lightness, an optimism. Part of it was also seeing the pride people took in their culture at the Koorie Heritage Trust. And the renewed connection with Jim. It made me realise that almost everything I had heard and continued to hear about Aboriginal people was bad news, and that I carried a burden of guilt and anxiety that distorted my attitudes and beliefs. I hoped, as some of that started to drop away, that I would see more clearly, and understand more fully, my brother, his family, and his people.

Next morning at breakfast I said to Mum, 'Have you given any more thought to replacing that paling fence at the back with something that'll let you see the bush and maybe the river?'

Mum sipped her tea and said, 'I have, and if *you* don't mind it coming down, then neither do I. What did you have in mind?'

'I was thinking about the wire fencing they sometimes use around pools. There's a place in Shepparton that'd do it. If you like the idea, I can get a quote.'

'Righteo,' she said. 'And save the timber for firewood. It'll keep me warm for a winter or two if I'm careful.'

I hadn't intended to tear down the fence myself, but the quote had been cheaper for a cleared site, and I needed to do something physical to clear my head.

I changed into my old clothes, pulled the trellises off the fence and began to work on the palings, bashing them off with a sledge hammer I found in Dad's shed, dirt on my face, sweat in my eyes. It felt good to be using my muscles after so long. Rocking the sturdy posts vigorously back and forth I cursed Dad's thoroughness. Why had he dug such deep holes and poured so much concrete around them? They were surprisingly heavy when I finally lifted each one out of the ground. For as long as I could remember I had wanted that fence to disappear, but I still felt a twinge of sadness remembering the hours Dad and I had spent building it. Back then it had seemed like a blessing to be able to work alongside Dad, to have a project that was ours alone. But I'd grown beyond that.

As children, Jim and I had roamed along the riverbank, fished, peed and hurled rocks into the river, then stepped out of the Australian bush and into an English garden where everything grew in straight lines and was shaped or pruned or thinned or tied back. I thought about when Jim and I went fishing. We'd sit together waiting for a bite, and in his company I felt a stillness, a fullness that I didn't feel at any other time. For me, and even more so for Jim I suspect, the river had been a place of freedom and peace.

I stepped through the fence line and walked through the bush to a place where I could see the water clearly. Flood debris was caught in the branches, and the bush was as scruffy and untidy as ever. When Jim was by my side, I saw things I never noticed on my own. His sharp eyes found burrows in the long grass, the print of a water rat in a patch of sand, birds' nests high in the trees, and swans or ducks on the water. I'd never really taken the time to know the bush, relying on Jim's knowledge and powers of observation. Without him, it seemed to close against me.

I climbed back up the bank and walked through the fence line. Mum's lemon tree needed a feed, the Hills hoist was listing to one side, and the vegetable patch was bare. I turned around and surveyed the remains of the fence: god, I hated it and all it stood for. Without it, the garden looked lighter and larger, expanding into the bush beyond.

By the time I'd finished demolishing the fence and stacked all the palings and posts behind the shed, shadows were lengthening in the garden. Inside, Mum was in the kitchen preparing tea. She looked up and smiled when I came in, face and hands dirty. Content in my own thoughts I did not have the need to explain them, just kissed her and said, 'Should've done it years ago; that fence hides a hidden treasure.'

I washed the worst of the dirt off my hands and face before heading for the bathroom.

'Dad would never have allowed it,' Mum said calmly.

'I wonder why he had such a set on the bush.'

'You know your father as well as I do – if he had taken down that fence he would have had to mow everything down to the river,' Mum said, raising a sardonic eyebrow.

That was Dad. Everything had to be managed and controlled. Everything had a boundary. When we were growing up we knew our limits and we knew what would happen if we crossed them. He valued discipline and he needed structure.

'He had a tough start in life don't forget,' Mum said, peeling carrots. 'His mother died of tuberculosis when he was six and his father never remarried. He worked long hours in the shop, and Dad and Uncle Ian had to live with their aunty and uncle and their nine children a lot of the time, and when they weren't, they were helping out in the shop. Then there was the war . . .' she sighed. 'He never talked much about that, but I know it affected him. And he carried that army discipline into everything he did – raising you boys, training the Cats, training Jim.'

I propped in the doorway, not wanting to interrupt the flow of reminiscence.

'He meant well,' Mum scooped the peelings into the compost bucket, 'but there was a lot he didn't understand. And he wouldn't listen, not to me and not to Jim.' She wiped her forehead with the back of one hand. 'Sad . . .'

I looked out the kitchen window to the new vista of trees and scrub beyond the back garden. To Jim, the land where he now lived was significant. It was the place of family, history, culture and knowledge, a place of unconditional belonging and acceptance, a place where his father – had he not been stolen – his grandparents and ancestors had held their festivals, initiations and corroborees – the place where the spirits of his and Meri's elders lived. It was the dreamtime of his people.

As a young boy growing up, as a university student fighting for what I thought was right, and as a barrister building a practice, I had been blind to all of this. I'd lived on the surface of things. Listening to Jim, I sensed the possibility of a deeper connection, a deeper knowledge. As I stared out past the fence line, I felt a connection, not just to the brother I had lost and somehow found, but to this land that I had inhabited my whole life and never truly seen or known.

Unfortunately, Dad was never able to open himself up to this new knowledge. He never understood the value of Jim's Aboriginal heritage. Every time Jim looked in the mirror, he was denying a very obvious truth, a fact about himself that no one wanted to face. Dad saw the river as wild, dangerous and overgrown. He saw it, like Aboriginal culture, as something to be cleared away, and if that wasn't possible, he just blocked it out, put a solid brick wall between him and it. Dad never understood that Jim was not necessarily better off with us, that you could not put family, culture, tradition and identity in one side of the scales, and a comfortable life, an education and a gold medal in the other and know which way the scales would tilt. He never understood Jim's heartbreak as a child growing up in a white family, the pent-up grief and rage that had built in him as he grew, and why Jim had stood at the podium with an Olympic gold medal around his neck feeling nothing at all.

CHAPTER 20

PECAN SUMMER, AN OPERA BY Deborah Cheetham about the Cummeragunja walk-off, was premiering in Mooroopna, with Cheetham singing, and there was no way I was going to miss it. I phoned Mum and told her we'd be coming to stay, but that the kids had other commitments. Then I phoned Jim and asked if he and Meri and the kids were going and if we could all go on the same night.

I wasn't sure how we'd all cope with the subject matter, but the last decade had strengthened our bonds, and the arrival of six grandchildren – one each for Ben and Kate, and two each for Jackie and Josh – had helped. Mum, now well into her eighties, spoilt them at every opportunity.

I'd booked tickets, and arranged to meet Jim and his family in the foyer of the big red Westside Performing Arts Centre, out on the Echuca Road. When we arrived, the place was buzzing, and I saw Jim and Meri with Josh and Jackie over against one wall talking to friends. The opera had a big cast – including the Indigenous Dhungala Children's Choir – and a lot of local people were there to support their relatives and friends. For many, the opera was telling their story, or the story of their parents or grandparents.

Mum kept stopping to talk to people she knew, but eventually we reached Jim and Meri, and there were hugs all round.

'Thanks for getting the tickets, Rob; I owe you,' Jim said with a quiet smile.

'No problem,' I said. 'Glad you could come. Kids not interested?'

'Oh, they're interested all right, but they want to take the children. Some of their friends are singing in the choir. They're going to go to the Melbourne performance and take in the sights at the same time. The kids don't get much of a chance to see the city.'

I handed out the tickets and we all filed into the hall, Mum and Meri and Jenny catching up on the grandchildren's news, Jim and I following behind.

'You know Deborah Cheetham's Jimmy Little's niece,' Jim said.

'I didn't, no.'

'She got a good old Shepparton welcome when she went into one of the shops,' Jim said.

'You're joking.'

'Nope. They wouldn't serve her because she's Indigenous.'

I swore under my breath as we found our seats and settled down. 'She should name and shame them,' I said, but Jim just shook his head.

'She's got better things to do with her time. She's been working with Indigenous kids from here and it's made a real difference. Wait till you see.' He turned to Meri who was chatting to a friend in the next row.

I leaned around Jenny and said to Mum, 'You know this is about the Cummeragunja walk-off, don't you, Mum.'

She nodded. 'I was just a girl, but I remember it. There was a lot of awful stuff in the papers about it.'

Just then the lights went down and the orchestra began to play. Rich voices filled the auditorium, and down on the stage a slender woman appeared.

When Deborah Cheetham came on stage I was transfixed. She was playing Ella – head down, shoulders slumped, despair and grief palpable in the air around her. Her daughter Alice had been taken from her, her pleas ignored. She looked helpless, hopeless. I couldn't help thinking about Jim's mother, and wondered if he was having the same thoughts. It was heartbreaking, and for a moment I thought it might be too much for Mum, but she was tough.

Later, Ella stood alone on stage, head raised, voice soaring into the darkness – Alice had returned. They were Deborah Cheetham's words, sung by her to her own people, the Yorta Yorta, to Jim and Meri, and even to me and Mum. I felt in that moment as though finally, in the triumph of that celebration, Jim and his father and all the other children and babies who had been stolen – were still being stolen – had somehow been vindicated.

After the show we found a corner of the foyer to talk. Mum was looking tired and shaken, so I found her a seat and said to Jim, 'We'd better keep this brief. Mum's had it.'

Jim squatted down beside Mum, steadying himself with one hand on the back of the chair, and she turned and rested her hand for a moment on his cheek.

'Oh Jim,' she said, 'when they tore that girl from her mother's arms I thought my heart would break. To think we did that to you.' She fumbled in her bag for her handkerchief.

Jim lowered his head.

'And your poor mother . . .'

'I found her, Betty, and we've had some good years together.'

Mum nodded, but was too overcome to speak, dabbing at her eyes, her head sunk in sorrow.

Meri bent down before her, one hand on Jim's shoulder, the other on Mum's arm. 'Betty, Betty,' she said, 'we can't change the past. What we do about it is what matters. Come on, let's get you out to the car.'

Jenny and Meri walked Mum out to the car, steadying her as we made our way to Homewood Drive, where I'd parked. Once she was settled in the front seat I turned to Jim and Meri.

'Thanks,' I said. 'I appreciate—'

'No worries,' Jim said. 'I'm glad we came. I've never been to the opera. It was better than I thought – much better. Reminds me of what we can do when we get half a chance . . .'

'Weren't the kids great,' Jenny said, and Meri smiled.

'We'd like to invite you to the Trust to see a show, if you're interested. I'll get Jim to call you when I know the details.'

'We'd like that,' Jen said warmly.

The show Meri had mentioned was a fashion parade put on in the new year by a group of Koorie teenagers – *Kooriez in Da Hood*. I strolled into the lounge room to tell Jenny.

'That was Jim on the phone, about that show at the Koorie Heritage Trust.'

Jenny glanced up from her book.

'Apparently the daughter of one of their friends has been chosen to take part in it.'

'So what exactly is it?'

'I'm not entirely sure, but Jim said the kids do workshops – about identity, family history, culture, that kind of thing.'

'And . . .?'

'Well, they learn about traditional Aboriginal designs and how to screen print, then they design and print their own hoodie, and model it. Sounds like a pretty big deal, so I said we'd be there.'

'What about your mum?' Jen asked. 'She'd love it.'

'Jim and Meri are going to bring her down on the train.'

'That's kind,' Jen said. 'They can all stay here if they like. Did you say?'

'Good idea. I'll call him back.'

On the night of the parade we met Jim, Meri and Mum at Southern Cross station and stowed their luggage in the boot, then I dropped them all at the Koorie Heritage Trust and parked the car. Jim and

Meri had opted to stay with friends, but Mum would come to us, and then travel home with them on the train the next day.

When I caught up with them on the ground floor of the Trust, Meri was talking to Jen about the program.

'The idea is to speak to these kids in their own language. They get help from industry specialists to design their hoodies, then they exhibit them at the Trust and the graduates become mentors for future programs. At the end of it all they can sell their designs.'

'Sounds like a great program.'

'Yes, it gives kids at risk an opportunity – it gives them hope.'

I was surprised to hear Mum say, 'Some of the young people are from Shepparton TAFE.'

'Really? How do you know?'

'Remember Issie Peterson? Remember I told you about volunteering? Well, some of the young people she works with are taking part in the show.' She looked as pleased and proud as if they were her own grandchildren.

'Good on them,' Jen said.

'Issie's a great girl,' Mum said, 'like her mother. Quiet, strong . . . no nonsense.'

'Rob,' Jim said, 'now you're here, let's wait outside. The kids are going to arrive in a limo.'

'Don't want to miss the red carpet, eh Mum? Come on.'

At eight, a pink stretch Hummer pulled up in front of the Trust with the contestants. The first person to step onto the red carpet was a tall, thin girl with the words, *Wajarri language: strong Indigenous women laugh, live and love*, painted on her hoodie. Three boys wearing similar blue hoodies followed, each with a unique design. Next came a girl wearing a hoodie with black feet treading across a red ochre landscape.

'Look, there's Brenda,' I heard Jim say, 'our friends' daughter.'

A tall, thin, attractive girl with long wavy black hair, brown eyes and a self-conscious smile stepped out of the Hummer wearing a black fedora, jeans and a white hoodie with a picture of children playing hide and seek on a river bank. It was a tranquil scene, capturing a moment in time before the arrival of Europeans.

Once all the contestants were out of the Hummer, people started to file into the Trust and find their seats. Jim looked relaxed and confident. I saw him, followed by Meri, stop to laugh and joke with some of the people as he moved through the room.

We found our seats and the music kicked up a notch as the contestants, one by one, danced down the spiral staircase. When they got to the stage they danced in unison – hip-hop I think – and as the number came to an end, the three judges walked to the stage. The music and strobe lighting stopped, much to my relief, and the judge from *Sass and Bide* picked up the microphone. There were some introductions, then the judge turned to the contestants.

'The winner will be offered a full-time position at *Sass and Bide* as a designer, working with some of the top names in the industry, and will be contracted to design a range for *Australian Indigenous Fashion Week*,' she said. When the applause died down she added, 'And the runner up will be offered an internship with David Jones.'

All eyes were focussed on the judge's face; some contestants stood frozen, others shifted nervously from side to side. The silence lengthened, then the judge drew a card from her pocket, smiled at the contestants and said, 'The winner is . . . Kat Ashby!'

'Brenda should have won,' Jim said later as we made our way down the aisle.

'Never mind,' I heard Meri say.

'I liked her design the best,' Mum said staunchly.

The crowd was filing out of the building and we waited for Jim at the entrance.

'I'm ready for bed,' Mum said, 'but don't let me stop you young ones.'

There was a snort of laughter from all of us, and I looked at Jim. 'I'll drop you at your friends' if you like. Can we do breakfast?'

'Good idea. Let's meet here at ten o'clock. I want to show you some of the exhibits. And don't worry about a lift – it's the opposite direction from you. We'll be fine – they live right on the tramline.'

Next morning was surprisingly fresh following the warmth of the day before. Mum and I arrived at the Trust just before ten o'clock – Jen sent her apologies, pleading a prior engagement. Two teenagers in baggy jeans and baseball caps were sitting just inside the entrance to the Trust's cafe drinking coffee and listening to Yothu Yindi's 'Tribal Voice' over the sound system. Mum and I found a table and looked out into the foyer where a class of primary-school children were listening to an Indigenous tour guide explaining how a stone had been shaped into an axe.

'There they are,' I said, as Jim and Meri walked through the glass doors. 'Over here,' I called.

Jim leant over, kissed Mum on the cheek and patted me on the back; Meri did the same. 'How are you?' she said to Mum.

'I'm good, thank you,' Mum said, smiling at them.

We ordered coffee and Meri turned back to Mum and said, 'What did you think of the launch?'

'I really enjoyed it. Those young people are so talented,' Mum said.

Just then, a girl in her late teens wearing a black T-shirt with '*Sorry: 13.2.2008*' written on the front walked up to Jim.

'Back again, Jim?' she said with a grin.

'Hi Juliette,' Jim said. 'I want to show my family around.'

'Well, this is a good place to start,' she said, turning towards Mum and gesturing to the café they were in. 'This is the Moogji Lounge. It means special friend. A Koorie elder, Jim Berg, was the driving force behind the Trust. He roped in two silks, Ron Castan and Ron Merkel, to help him set it up back in 1985. Jim and Ron Castan had a unique relationship. 'Jim – Jim Berg I mean –' she smiled at our Jim, was adamant that this café should honour Ron because of his respect for Aboriginal people.'

Mum was clearly impressed by the presentation, as was I. 'Ron was a great support to Jim and the Trust. He wasn't paternalistic, he never presumed to know better and he understood the importance of Aboriginal people having respect for their own culture and white people respecting that culture, too, and he saw the Trust as a way of achieving that.'

Mum shifted in her seat.

'Must be something about Rons,' I quipped, hoping to distract Mum. I'd known both silks slightly, and was a little in awe of them. Both had done good work with Aboriginal people.

'And Jims,' Mum added.

'Thanks, Juliette,' Jim said, then turning to us he added, 'Drink up. I want to show you something.'

Juliette tagged along as we moved into the library and saw wooden fire sticks, a necklace made from gumnuts, and books detailing thousands of years of Aboriginal rock art. There was a Paddy Bedford exhibition in the Darren Pattie-Bux Gallery and a bark canoe dating back hundreds of years. At the bottom of the stairs we saw a kangaroo skin traditionally used as a blanket and a cluster of different-sized coiled woven baskets.

I glanced at Mum. A slight smile played around her mouth and I knew she approved.

As we climbed the spiral stairs, taking our time so Mum could catch her breath, we stopped near a room with glass walls and people sitting opposite each other at desks talking. 'What's in there?' Mum said.

'The family history service.'

'Oh. I see.'

'They reconnect families,' Juliette continued.

Mum gave Jim a beseeching look.

Juliette, oblivious to any tension, chatted on. 'Jim – Jim Berg – often tells the story of a man who had never seen a photo of his mother, his father or even himself as a baby. He was forty-six. Jim asked the man to come back to the Trust the next day and said, 'I'll show you a photo of you when you were a day old in your mother's arms with your dad'. The man cried when he saw the photo. It was a very touching moment. That's what the family history service offers.'

Mum was silent, her face stricken. Suddenly she looked very old and frail. As always, Jim's face was hard to read.

'It's important to know who you are and where you came from,' Juliette said, reading the sign on the door. 'But you guys know that of course. That's why you're here!'

Mum looked away. I turned to Juliette and quietly raised my hand.

'Sorry, sometimes I get carried away,' Juliette said. 'Let me just tell you quickly about our collection,' Juliette said, continuing the tour. 'When the elders come in here and pick up a spear or a club or a shield, they say it becomes part of them. They can feel the strength within the timber. To them, it's more than a piece of wood shaped by our ancestors hundreds of years ago. Some artefacts go back thousands of years. They say when they walk through the collection they can feel the person who actually painted the weapons looking over their shoulder making sure they are telling the right stories—'

Before Juliette had a chance to finish what she was saying someone waved her away and she bade us a hasty goodbye. And then there were just the four of us. After Juliette's buoyant chatter, our group seemed very quiet.

Mum looked weary and Dad's presence was palpable between us. Perhaps his spirit haunted us as much as the spirits of the elders haunted this place. I decided to bite the bullet. 'I wonder what Dad would say if he knew we were here?'

'Your father was a good man, Rob. He meant well, but he's gone now,' Mum replied. 'He would have hated the family history service,' she added as an afterthought.

'It opened the year he died,' Jim said, looking at Mum. 'I wish it had been around when I was searching.'

'Dad told me he'd stumbled across a letter you wrote to the paper asking about your biological parents,' Mum said. 'He couldn't understand how you could turn your back on him. That's the way he saw it, even if it's not what you intended.'

Meri rested a hand on Jim's arm. I could tell Mum and Jim were treading carefully.

'He cared about you, Jim. He worried you would turn your back on him if you went back to your own people. He thought you'd throw away all the opportunities that the gold medal gave you. He couldn't see it any other way. I hope you can forgive him some day.'

'I know he meant well,' Jim said, 'but some harms can't be undone. You can only live through them and try to get past them.' His eyes went to Meri and I saw a look pass between them.

A feeling of deep shame washed over me, for my family and what we'd done to Jim and his family, for Meri and the terrible suffering she'd endured, and for all that white people had done to harm or destroy Aboriginal people, their culture and their country.

Mum looked from Jim to Meri, choosing her words carefully. 'You're right, Jim. What we did can't be undone. We should never have lied to you. We should never have stolen you away from everything you'd known and loved. Nothing, especially not a gold medal, can make up for that.'

I saw that Mum was no longer the dutiful wife, if she ever had been, ready to defend Dad no matter what. I realised now it had never been her true nature. Without Dad she had arrived at a new accommodation – Mum was a woman with her own thoughts and integrity, willing and courageous enough to say what she believed.

Despite all that Jim had endured, there was passion on his face as we walked through the permanent exhibition and he spoke of his heritage. His eyes glowed as he tried to show how much this place meant to him. Here, Jim was at home; here he had been able to reconnect with his family, his culture and his history. The exhibition recounted stories of the dreamtime, and contained artefacts dating back thousands of years; an engraved map of Australia bore the many different Indigenous communities that existed before white invasion. The Trust dignified everything that white Australian history had tried to denigrate, and remembering my father's words and actions here made that denigration more real than ever.

I thought of the rolling woodland of Jim's father's ancestral home, and remembered sitting beside my brother on the banks of the Murray beneath tall red gums at Cummeragunja, listening to him talk about his father, and Meri's father and what he'd learned from him. 'Let go of the resentment,' he had told Jim, 'it weighs you down'. Those words had resonated with Jim, and he'd found the strength to face the future as a proud Aboriginal man.

I watched Jim and Meri walk Mum to the train, one on each side of her. She turned her face up to Jim, smiling, and took his arm, and I understood that, somehow, they had made their peace, without erasing or evading the past; they had moved beyond forgiveness. I wished Dad could have found the same peace. I knew his love for Jim had outlasted his anger and misplaced feelings of betrayal, but still there had been no reconciliation and he had died unforgiven.

As I turned to go back to the office, I noticed the Trust's motto: *Gnokan Danna Murra Kor-Ki – Give me your hand my friend*. It came from a generosity of spirit I knew I could never match, but for my brother's sake, I'd try.

www.ingramcontent.com/pod-product-compliance
Lightning Source LLC
Chambersburg PA
CBHW021426110726
47901CB00008B/2309